Praise for *My Best Friend and My Man*

"*My Best Friend and My Man* glows with sexuality, warmth, and drama! Cydney Rax has done it again!"

—T. Styles, *Essence* bestselling author of *A Hustler's Son* and *Black and Ugly*

"I really enjoyed *My Best Friend and My Man.* There are some parts where Cydney has you laughing out loud and others where you want to reach in and throttle the characters. Cydney has another hit on her hands!"

—Desiree Day, author of *Crazy Love* and *One G-String Short of Crazy*

"Smart, sexy, and wickedly funny! Once again, Cydney Rax displays her keen ability to weave a story of romance and mayhem with characters that you'll both love . . . and love to hate."

—Nancey Flowers, *Essence* bestselling author of *No Strings Attached*

"Cydney Rax is phenomenal with her pen game. *My Best Friend and My Man* pulls you in from the very first page and doesn't let you go until the last word. This blueprint on how to win in the game of love is sure to be a bestseller."

—Joy King, author of *Hooker to Housewife* and *Superstar*

"*My Best Friend and My Man* is truly a satisfying read that pulled me in from page one . . . I couldn't put it down."

—Cheryl Robinson, author of *Sweet Georgia Brown*

"Cydney Rax has consistently provided her fans with literary sundaes, and *My Best Friend and My Man* is no exception . . . a sinfully delicious hot caramel treat!"

—Philana Marie Boles, author of *Blame It on Eve* and *In the Paint*

Praise for *My Husband's Girlfriend*

"The book we can't put down . . . the scandalous new novel . . . you'll find yourself drawn to Rax's juicy tale of out-of-order buppies in love and lust."

—*Essence*

"Provocative."

—*Ebony*

"A twisted tale of infidelity."

—*Today's Black Woman*

"One of the most provocative, entrancing, and insatiable naughty novels of the year has arrived. Cydney Rax is on her way to being a serial bestseller."

—*DisilgoldSoul Magazine*

Praise for *My Daughter's Boyfriend*

"Best guilty-pleasure read."

—*Upscale*

"Emotionally charged . . . scandalous in nature, though tastefully written . . . Rax's novel forces deep reflection."

—*Romantic Times*

"One of the hottest and heaviest secret and lustful relationships to debut in a novel . . . Get ready to hold your breath. *My Daughter's Boyfriend* is a heated and sexy page turner . . . Cydney Rax is a powerful and masterful storyteller."

—Disilgold.com

"A fascinating, witty, and thought-provoking novel full of memorable characters . . . the perfect summer read."

—Zane

My Best Friend and My Man

—a novel—

Cydney Rax

THREE RIVERS PRESS
NEW YORK

For Brandon

This is a work of fiction. Names, characters, places, and incidents either are the product of the author's imagination or are used fictitiously. Any resemblance to actual persons, living or dead, events, or locales is entirely coincidental.

Published in the United States by Three Rivers Press, an imprint of the Crown Publishing Group, a division of Random House, Inc., New York.
www.crownpublishing.com

Three Rivers Press and the Tugboat design are registered trademarks of Random House, Inc.

Library of Congress Cataloging-in-Publication Data

Rax, Cydney.
My best friend and my man : a novel / Cydney Rax. — 1st ed.
p. cm.
1. African American women—Fiction. 2. Mate selection—Fiction.
I. Title.
PS3618.A98M88 2008
813'.6—dc22 2007048324

ISBN 978-0-307-39377-7

Printed in the United States of America

Design by Maria Elias

10 9 8 7 6 5 4 3 2 1

First Edition

Acknowledgments

Can you believe I forgot to acknowledge Brandon in my last book? So sorry . . . I love you very much and am so proud of you. Keep up the good work.

First, to my fantastic editor Lindsey Moore, my awesome agent Claudia Menza, the book designers, the copyeditors, and my incomparable publisher, Three Rivers Press—let's keep doing this. Secondly, mega thanks to my publicist Melanie DeNardo. You are a magical PR person.

I received so much love for *My Husband's Girlfriend.* Thanks to media outlets such as *Ebony* magazine, *Today's Black Woman, Jewel Magazine,* the great Patrik Henry Bass of *Essence* magazine, *Publishers Weekly, Disilgold Soul Literary Review* (thanks, Heather Covington), Black Expressions Book Club (thanks, Carol Mackey), *Booking Matters Magazine,* Tee C. Royal of RAWSISTAZ Book Club, Urban-Reviews.com, *Romantic Times Book Reviews, Upscale* magazine, all the bookstores, and especially the book clubs that selected and read *My Husband's Girlfriend.* Special thanks to Design Divas and SistahFriend Book Club—you ladies are incredible. I cannot thank you enough for all your excellent support and positivity. I appreciate all the libraries around the country (and even overseas) that have included my books as part of their circulation.

To authors: Margaret Johnson-Hodge (thanks for always having my back), Lexi Davis (thanks for helping me with the chat), William Frederick Cooper, Shelley Halima, Shelia Goss, Fred Smith, Alex Hairston, J.D. Mason, Marissa Monteilh, Chelsia McCoy, Philana Marie Boles, T. Styles, Marsha Jenkins-Sanders, Tina Brooks McKinney, R. Moreen Clarke, Desiree Day, Margie Gosa Shivers, Dwan Abrams, Poet Extraordinaire Aberjhani, Joel McIver, Michelle Buckley, Cheryl Robinson, Trisha Thomas, Brenda L. Thomas, Thomas Green, Phil Thomas Duck (I see a pattern here), Eric Pete, Dywane Birch, Shani Greene-Dowdell, Naiomi Pitre, and Darren Coleman.

To my supporters and friends: Wilt Tillman, Glendon (W&G, thanks for your input), BookDivas, Chayo E. R. Briggs (I love you, Papi), Kim Floyd, Darrell B., Mo Bennett, Lillian W., Cynthia Gibbs., Tere R., Mary M., Joan, Cynthia H., Allison B., Pam J. Ward, Claudia, Martha, Jolene, and, last but not least, Dilip (my former boss and energetic, unstoppable PR guy).

To my fam: Mom, sister, D. Thomas, aunts, cousins, uncles, etc. (folks who have been coming out of hiding). Thanks also for buying and spreading the word about my books.

Finally, to the readers, the fans, the supercool MySpace, BlackPlanet, and Yahoo 360 supporters, all the awesome folks who take time to read the books and send an e-mail or sign my guestbook—y'all just don't know. Keep that feedback coming.

I'm at www.myspace.com/cydneyrax or www.cydneyrax.com. I love when you give me a chance and tell me that you get what I write, even if you don't agree with the actions of my characters. May glorious blessings continue to flow in everyone's lives.

— 1 —

Veron

It's Saturday, February 14th, and I'm home alone. It's sad, but I'm perched at the computer desk in my modest but comfortable apartment, debating if I should log on to MySpace to see if I have any new friend requests. I last logged in twenty minutes ago.

I bite my tongue so hard I nearly taste blood when the phone rings. Unexpectedly, it's Ferris Landers.

"What you doing?" he growls in that slow, sexy tone that I love.

"Uh, what's going on with you?" I dodge Ferris, not wanting him to know I'm not doing a doggone thing.

"I know we ain't seen each other in a couple months, and I ain't called in a while, but I was thinking . . . I know you love sushi . . ."

"Yeah," I say, impressed that he remembers, "among other things."

"And does your 'among other things' include second row tickets to see John Legend perform at the Aerial Theater?"

"Oh yeah, it does!" I smile, barely keeping a delighted squeal from reaching Ferris's ears.

"So, if you wanna ride with me, let me know."

Man, if you only knew how much I wanna ride you, I think to myself. Ferris is the first man to introduce me to the wonderful world of doggy style, and I've wanted him to ram my back bumper ever since. I love the feel of his sculpted, hairy chest slumped across my backside, him accurately banging my G-spot like a pro, us moaning and bobbing up and down while waves of pleasure consume us till we're happily exhausted and ready to cuddle for the rest of the night.

"You know, all of that sounds great, Ferris. I'd love to go. When is the concert?" I ask, thinking about what we could be doing after that concert.

"Tonight," he replies in a barely audible voice.

I'm dateless. It's Valentine's Day. But still. Men aren't supposed to ask a girl out with this kind of notice.

"Tonight?" I huff.

"Mmm hmmm." His voice sounds so mushy and gentle my anger doesn't last.

"Ferris," I softly remind him. "I usually prefer to be asked out days in advance—"

"I know, baby girl. I know."

"And normally I *don't* accept last-minute dates," I firmly state, lying my butt off. "But for you I'll make an exception. As it turns out, my schedule has opened up tonight, and I probably can squeeze in some sushi and Legend."

"Whew," he exclaims in an overexaggerated fashion. "I was worried you'd turn me down, so let's go chill out and enjoy each other's company."

My ears warm at just hearing Ferris's commanding voice. I love it when a man takes charge; it makes me feel like he's strong, and I definitely prefer to have a strong man by my side, instead of one who only wants to do what I want to do because he's not smart or confident enough to make his own decisions.

"So what time will you pick me up?" I ask in a sweet voice.

"Uh, can you meet me at Miyako at six?"

"Meet you? As in driving myself to a date?"

"Ye-ah," he says. "So you gonna meet me?"

And for the millionth time, instead of telling a man how I really feel, instead of showing my disappointment, I bite my tongue, and I sullenly reply, "Sure."

Miyako is a popular Japanese restaurant located on Kirby Drive, about five minutes south of downtown Houston. It's not a lavish spot, but the small dining room doesn't make me as mad when I remember that its small booths invite intimacy. I love sitting hip-to-hip with a man who I love, accidentally rubbing elbows or feeling his leg bump into mine and making me shiver. Ahhh, yes.

So I shove my anger aside about what I feel was disrespect. You know, the man wanting me to meet him somewhere instead of making an effort to pick me up. It's almost like some guy agreeing to kiss you on the lips, but only if he's certain that no one else sees us. It just upsets me. But when my mind paints a portrait of Ferris and me huddled together, feeding each other fresh, salty raw fish, and laughing it up while we toast and sip on sake, I let anticipated joy stamp out any negative feelings. Plus, it'll be great to brush up on my doggy style skills.

I'm relieved Ferris arrived at the restaurant before I do. I see him waiting in a U-shaped booth next to the window. He's just like I remember: he loves to sit with his jaw slightly tilted, like he's cooler than cool. He's wearing a dark brown soft leather jacket that looks wide enough for me to squeeze into in case I get chilly later on.

"Hey, baby girl, you look nice tonight," he says, leaving the booth and rising to his feet.

"I do?" I ask, hoping Ferris isn't saying something just to

be saying it. You know how some guys do: they push those buttons and say the right thing so they can gain a woman's favor, but their words may not always be heartfelt.

Ferris nods slowly as he sits back down. He gazes deeply into my eyes, penetrating me, a gesture that always gives me wobbly knees. A surge of warmth rushes through my veins as I sit down, and I know it's okay to truly relax. Enjoy. Get rid of the gritty edge that threatens to overtake my spirit.

"Look, baby girl, if I say you look fierce, you look fierce."

"But you didn't say I look fierce."

He laughs and taps his tiny white porcelain cup against mine, tilts his head, sips sake, and moans as it slides down his throat.

"I see you've ordered drinks for us already."

"I know what you like, baby girl."

All I can do is smile, savor good feelings, and thank God I'm doing something fun for a change.

"Well, Ferris, thanks for being so thoughtful. But I have to ask you—why haven't I heard from you in a while?"

"Because you ain't called."

"Don't even try it," I say, pouting. "I called you quite a few times with no response."

"Well, you must've dialed the wrong number, because I didn't get the calls."

"Did your number change?"

"Nope."

I just stare at him.

"No, seriously, I've been busy working. Working so hard that all I do is fall in bed at night and catch some sleep. So I'm sorry 'bout that."

Nothing I can say to that. I shrug as if to say okay. "Tell me, how were you able to get second row tickets to this Legend concert?"

He coughs and clears his throat. "Just well connected. You know how I do."

"Ah, well, good for you . . . and me."

I nibble on some eel unagi, which tastes both salty and sweet, and I listen while Ferris updates me on the soap opera drama of his manager job at Verizon. I try to sit there and just listen and hang out, but eventually I have to ask. "Ferris, whatever happened to us? It seems like you were feeling me at first, then you kinda disappeared. Usually I don't like to ask men these kinds of questions," I hurry to explain, "because I'm not sure they want to answer them. But I'm trying to do something different," I continue. "So let's talk about what happened."

He pouts and frowns. "I was feeling you, Veron, for real, though. I loved kicking it with you, kissing you, making sweet love to you." I squirm in my seat and try not to grin too idiotlike. "You were everything I wanted—"

"I *were*? I mean, I was?" I say, my eyes glazing at his kind words and the thought of our new possibilities.

"You had it going on, baby girl. You got ass *and* class," he jokes. "But it was me. I wasn't ready for a woman like you."

His kind words were supposed to soothe my heart, my ears, and my anxiety about why Ferris would wait till the last freaking minute to secure a date with a woman he supposedly likes, even though he hasn't called her in months. But although he was saying all the right things, I sensed coldness inside his warmth. It felt as if I was sitting inside a bubble bath of lukewarm water, whose bubbles were turning icy and numbing, rapidly dissolving. And I was aching to trust what I was hearing and feeling what Ferris was telling me.

"Hello, hello," Ferris says, but he's not looking directly in my eyes.

"Mmm hmmm," I pout.

"No, man, I am just hyped we hooked up again, especially tonight. Wooo, boy."

"Oh yeah, why is that?"

"Well, you know, I was just aching to see my girl . . . from the front *and* the back."

I sit up straight in my seat and cross my legs.

"I've missed you, Veron. Some women out here, man, they can't get with the doggy style, acting all Holy Ghosty and stuff, like they too good to turn they asses around."

My cheeks glow, and I giggle in spite of myself.

He smiles, knowing he's won me over. Then he continues offhandedly, almost muttering. "Plus, shoot, even though I have connections I had to pay out the ass to get these good seats. And since Shelly and me got into it last night, ain't no way I'm—" His voice lowers to a murmur. He grabs his cup and swallows more sake, some of which spills clumsily from his mouth, as if he has no muscle control.

"What did you say?" I slide up out the booth and stand up. "Who is Shelly?"

"W-what?"

"What nothing," I say loudly, towering over him. "Who the fuck is Shelly?"

"Sit down, Veron," he says calmly. "You know you don't curse. You're starting to lose cool points with me."

"I don't care about cool points," I lash out, my vision getting blurry.

I'm standing so near this man that I smell the coconut-scented moisturizer spread throughout his thick hair. I'm torn between popping him in his eye and kissing him on his sake-flavored lips.

Ferris attempts to grab my right hand. I jerk away, my face burning.

"Look, baby girl," he mutters.

"Nothing to look at. How could you do this to me, Ferris? Don't you have anything to say for yourself?"

"Why would I have to say anything? What are you talking about?"

His fake innocent look feels like a loud slap. Then I do something I wouldn't have done six months ago. I abandon an entire tray of uneaten California rolls. I leave a good-looking employed man sitting alone in a restaurant. I leave behind the old Veron. I am determined to find a new one.

My heart is searching for answers, for peace, for a man who truly wants the best for me. Why didn't my woman's intuition kick in about the last-minute date thing? Why was I so afraid to tell Ferris no? This incident just reminds me of many encounters I've had with men. It's time to self-reflect and admit the mistakes I've made, and there have been many. But just because I don't always make the best decisions, does that mean I can't still have joy? A perfect day? Someone there to care about me, to understand me, to be solid so I don't have to be constantly worried that I'm not his number one?

This is why I've got to have a serious one-on-one with someone who is successful in the areas of life where I fall short. This is why I must start listening to, observing, and maybe even emulating my best friend/babe magnet Demetria Sparks.

Demetria, who's a little older than me at thirty-something, is the only woman I know who has men competing to take her on dates. Men who smile when they walk close beside her in the shopping mall just because they're associated with her. Guys falling all over themselves to treat her right, to win her over.

Now mind you, Demetria has it going on in the looks department. She is African American mixed with Brazilian, and her exotic features always have men craning their heads to take extra long looks. Her dark brown eyes are about as wide as those of an elegant gazelle. And her eyelashes are so long and fluttering, you can't help but stare and get lost in her allure. So sure she's cute. But these days, with so much affordable cosmetic surgery available, who isn't considered cute? That's not all it is—she's got something else, something that keeps these men crazy about her. I want to know what it is.

Demetria and I met when I was studying for an associate degree at Houston Community College and she was working in the Communications Department as an assistant to the department chair. But then she snagged a better job as an administration manager for the City of Houston. By that time I'd earned my degree and was antsy for something challenging, so she told me about a job opening as an administrative coordinator and arranged for me to be interviewed. I got the job and we've hung out and grown even closer while working for the city.

The more Demetria has excelled in the workplace, the more her confidence has grown. She began meeting all kinds of men, upgrading from the normal scrubs she used to kick it with—and she started hanging around upper-class establishments where the men were restaurant owners instead of struggling waiters, architects instead of construction workers. And I always quietly sat in the background, observing. I was patient at first, thinking her being on a roll with men would last about as long as Paris Hilton's so-called boyfriends. But I'm starting to accept the truth: Demetria Elayne Sparks has everything I need.

— 2 —

Demetria

Veron invites me to tag along with her while she does a little bit of shopping at Bed Bath & Beyond in the Meyerland Plaza Shopping Center. I guess she had a bad date last night, plus she told me she wants to buy two sets of sheets and some big-ass fluffy pillows for her bed. Her big, lonely bed. No, let me stop—that isn't a righteous way to think. Lord knows I could be Veron, couldn't I? But thank the same Lord that I'm not. I don't roll like her, and I guess that's why she needs to pick my brain.

"Anyway, Demetria," Veron says, "seconds after I left Ferris sitting alone in Miyako, he called on my cell. He kept calling me all night, but I didn't answer. I gave him the Busy button at least ten times." Veron smiles. I guess she wants me to pat her on the back and tell her "You go girl" for being strong, but not answering a man's call ain't nothing. In my book, a consistently strong woman has to do much more than ignore a man's pestering calls for one night.

"Okay, so you didn't pick up his calls. But what did you do the rest of the night, Veron?"

She hesitates, then sputters, "I wailed. Hollered. Called on Jesus. That's why I need new pillows."

"Crying about a man won't do any good, Veron."

"Are you saying you've actually cried over—"

I frown and raise my voice, interrupting her. "I'm saying that tears aren't going to move a man. Some men get to sweating under the arms and looking like they're about to vomit when a woman soaks her face with tears. And although some men may want to try and help, have you noticed that's one of the rare times when they really don't know what to do with their hands?" I shake my head in amazement. "So in my opinion, you gotta scrap the tears. Ya feel me?"

"Demetria, you have all these cold, hard rules, but I just can't understand why a man would be attracted to women who have zero emotions, like we're just robots."

"Girl, not crying all the time doesn't mean you're a robot. Not all women roll like Veron Darcey."

Veron runs from me so fast I'm paranoid that my breath stinks worse than sour milk. I pop one long stick of mint flavored gum inside my mouth and figure the girl has major issues. Veron starts sifting through a bin of striped sheets in the linens section, but before she can dig in good, I place my hand over hers.

"Mmm, nope, Veron, don't you even know how to pick out sheets?"

"What's wrong?"

"You need to upgrade from that cardboard feeling one-eighty thread count and get at least four hundred or five hundred."

"They cost a grip, Demetria."

"Quality usually does. And these more expensive sheets will last until your kids are grown," I assure her. If you ever have kids, I think to myself.

"Hmmm, I dunno, girl."

"Look, I'll buy them for you. Well, I'll buy one set. You pay for the other. How's that sound? I just want you to know how it feels to live your best life."

"You sound like Pastor Joel Osteen."

I laugh. "Vee, believe me, Osteen and I don't have a thing in common, except I do care about you; you're my girl and I want to see you happy. I want to see you smile. I don't want to see you have a spaz attack 'cause some NGM acts foul."

"No good man," we say at the same time and high-five each other.

"You crack me up every time you say that," Veron tells me.

"Well, as long as NGMs exist you're going to be hearing me say that," I tell her. "Don't forget the characteristics of an NGM: Men who always blame their problems on 'da White Man' instead of taking responsibility for their own decisions. Men who act like they gots to be the head of the house, yet they don't even have a job, they won't pay any bills, or don't earn head-of-the-household money. Men who put the ring on ya finger but here they are, still slipping out in the streets doing their thing the minute they don't think you're looking. And men who only go out with you because another heffa bailed out," I add, to remind her that she needs to kick sorry-ass Ferris to the curb.

"Yep, girl, you're right," Veron agrees. "Should I get my number changed?"

"Why pay money to change your number just to dodge Ferris? Answer his call once, tell his funky ass hell-to-the-fucking-no, and stop accepting his calls. Mean whatcha say, and move on with 'cha life."

"Mmm hmmm." Veron nods her head affirmatively, but I can tell by the flimsy sound in her voice she's not quite there yet. Sometimes I want to wrap my fingers around her neck and squeeze; I wanna shake her big ole head real hard so common sense can reach her clogged-up brain. But I know my girl needs support right now, not a constant bitchfest, so I soften my tone.

"You'll be alright, sweetie. One day your dream man is gonna ebb and flow with you on the real, and treat you with the mad respect you deserve. You gotta have faith in order for good to line up and happen. Treat Veron like a prize and a real man will treat you like you treat yourself."

Veron raises her hands to the ceiling and shouts, "Amen, Brother Osteen!" I laugh out loud and leave her confused ass alone so she can marinate on what I've schooled her.

You gotta start somewhere, right? I used to be like Vee back in the day. You know how when you're in high school you really think you got it going on? No one can tell you a thing, and you walk up and down the hallways as if you, not the principal, are in charge. Well, growing up and experiencing life will introduce you to the real world, and I'm not talking about an MTV show where scenes are cut and edited. Once you get out here in this big ole indifferent world and go through some real drama, you learn how to survive, when to say no, how to discern what's real, what's fake. And you decide right then and there that you've walked down these tired fake roads too many times to count, so now you're going to exercise your right to walk in a different and better direction. Life's all about setting goals and getting what you want, and if I've learned how to get with the program, girlfriend can learn, too.

After I finally convince Veron to buy a finer grade of silky smooth sheets (one in midnight blue, one in sunshine yellow), we put her stuff in her car and head over to Borders so we can get lattes and I can fill her in on my date last night. The bookstore is half empty, I guess because it's thirty-eight degrees in Houston (freezing for us southerners), and folks wanna stay inside a warm house looking at TV and watching the Texans getting humiliated on the football field.

So we nearly have the cafe area to ourselves. We grab an empty wooden table and sit next to each other where we have a good view of the store's entrance—we need to be able to check out any cuties who happen to come in.

I dig in my purse and pull out the index cards that I always keep around.

"Ahh, haa," Vee laughs. "Give me some blank cards."

"Here," I tell her and give her a black ink pen, too. I hop up and quickly place orders for our coffees. It only takes a few minutes before the drinks are ready, and it feels great to settle in and get comfy.

"So who was your date with?" Veron asks.

"Thaddeus," I say, acting insulted that she would even have to ask . . . even though it's true I could be referring to several men.

"Oh, yeah," she says coolly. "Where was his wife?"

"Excuse me? Marilyn is his *soon-to-be ex*-wife. I've told you that." I frown. "There's a difference. Plus, they don't even live together anymore and haven't shared a bed in a year."

"That's what they all say."

"Hey, sometimes he lets me have his cell phone 24/7. If he's still with her, you think he'd let me hold his phone?"

"I can't tell you what he'd do, Demetria," Veron says in a skeptical voice.

"On top of that, I've seen his divorce papers. The ones he's going to file on her."

"Now *that's* different."

I roll my eyes. "Anyway, Thaddeus picks me up in the Hummer this time," I say, eyeing Veron and daring her to interrupt. "And, of course, I'm looking all fierce. I wore my black leather coat with the mink collar, some thigh-high leather slouch boots I found in Manhattan, and this beautiful knit mini-dress."

"Uh-huh," Veron mutters, glancing at her fingernails as if she's somewhat bored. But I know her ears are burning like fire 'cause she can't wait for me to tell her more.

"So long story short, he made reservations at P.F. Chang's in The Woodlands and we eat a delicious six-course dinner sitting next to a huge bay window with several candles flickering. And during our two-hour dinner he presents me with a beautiful greeting card that expresses how much he loves me, and inside it is a five-hundred-dollar Neiman Marcus gift card."

"Wow," Vee says, impressed.

"Plus, he got me my usual box of chocolate-covered strawberries."

"Ooo," she exclaims.

"Plus a beautiful mixed floral arrangement."

"Dang."

"*And* a new pair of diamond studs."

"Diamond studs?" Veron repeats, as if I'm making up info. "Don't you think that's a bit much?"

"Look, I don't know why he does all that. True, Thad can be way over the top, but he knows I love to be romanced, and I appreciate that he listens to me when I tell him what makes me happy. It's not like I ask him to do all the sweet things he does, but his actions prove I'm important to him."

"I know, but isn't there something inside you that won't let you—"

"If you're asking if I should be noble and tell Thaddeus to take it all back, that my pride shouldn't allow me to accept his gifts, then you must think you're talking to Boo Boo the fool. C'mon now, let's not have a brain fart here. If it were you, I doubt you'd be shoving gifts back in your man's hand!

So why should I? Plus I deserve everything I get, all queens do." We sit in silence for a minute, sipping our coffee.

"I swear to God," Veron finally manages to utter, "Demetria, you are sooo lucky, all I can say."

"Queens aren't lucky. They're *queens*, Vee."

She coughs, then blurts, "Did the queen have sex with her married man?"

"The queen gave the *soon-to-be divorced* man everything he wanted."

"What's that supposed to mean?"

"I licked, sucked, swallowed, pumped, yelled, screamed, talked dirty, did the feathers, the baby oil, dressed up like a proud whore in my see-through baby doll nightgown and matching thong. Girl, you name it, Thad got it."

Veron looks shocked at first, but then covers her mouth and giggles. I lean back in my seat and eye her as if to say, You can't tell me I don't have it going on. And maybe my friend will finally listen to a sister break it all the way down on how to get and keep a real man, instead of settling for half men who lack the potential to be real men.

"Was it any good?"

"Mmm," I sigh blissfully. "As scrumptious as a triple-layered chocolate cake with chocolate icing. Thad sucked on me like I was a strawberry kiwi smoothie; he was squeezing me hard, too, and shaking so violently I thought the building was being demolished. Dude told me he loves me so many times I don't think I could add it up on a calculator."

"Sounds like he's whipped."

I glare at her. "What do you expect?"

"But you didn't tell him that you lo—"

"Telling a man you love him is setting a trap for disaster."

"So are you saying you *have* done that before?"

Frowning, I continue, "If you want to keep a man in his

place, you've got to stop being so fucking emotional, Vee. That pouring-your-heart-out crap scares men. Always play it cool, as if you don't care, and they'll see you as a challenge. You think I got this watch by telling a man I love him?" She gapes at me. "No, nope, no," I continue. "If you want your heart broken, be stupid and rush to tell him you love him, you'll do anything for him. He's the only one for you, all those desperate, pathetic words. Girl, a man won't wife you when you keep acting in a way that he expects. Switch things up now and then and he'll stay intrigued."

"So, Demetria, to clarify, even though this man does all these wonderful things for you, you won't part your lips to let him know you love him? Even if he asks?"

"Nope, I don't do that," I say confidently. "No matter how many times a man pours out his guts and gets emotional, I always manage to maintain my emotional intelligence. I'll be sweet, of course; I'm very affectionate. I'm a wonderful, 'Awww, boo,' type of woman, but I won't make the mistake of telling a man I love him."

"Do they ever ask you why not?"

I laugh, then get serious. "I think men want to ask but lack the balls to come out with it. Or they might pout and make a jokey joke like they're offended that I'm not falling all over them, but technically, no. Few men are brave enough to ask Demetria what's really up."

"Wow, I'm scared of you, too, girlfriend." Veron studies me for a moment and sips her latte. The rich smell of cappuccino fills the room, and I inhale deeply and enjoy the aroma.

Suddenly a medium height black man wearing nerd glasses stumbles into the store. I grab a blank index card and write down 5. I wave the card at Veron and smile. She whips her head around, laughs, and says, "Yep, I feel ya on that one."

"If only this guy knew we're talking about his corny looking ass," I tell Veron.

"Hey, men do this stuff, too."

"My baby isn't rating women," I say. "Thaddeus would never give to other women what he gives to me. No way."

"I heard that," Veron says, "and he gives you so much it's unbelievable at times."

"Well, you can believe it. I'm not making it up. And I love it."

"I ain't mad at you," whispers Veron. "You're so confident that you're his number one. As much as I hate to admit it, I'm jealous."

"I feel ya, boo." I smile sweetly. "Most women are jealous. And I don't blame them. I'm living a life that most chicks only dream about."

"So, Ms. Sparks, what is your secret? It sounds like Thad left his wife for you."

"No, Vee, I'm telling you, I did not hook up with him until I knew he and his wifey were through. Believe me, I know I'm number one in his life, and that's the only way we're gonna roll."

"Well, he treats you like you're Jennifer Lopez or something, and you aren't half as cute as her."

"Fuck you!" I say and roll my eyes. "Jenny wishes she did have this body."

"No, all jokes aside, Demetria, I mean it. You have that wow factor that causes a man to do all these wonderful things. I'm tired of dreaming about what I can have. I'm waiting on the day I can have everything I dream about." Veron sighs and takes a deep, sad breath.

I feel for her, too. It's one thing to dream and dream and dream about the things you want. It's a whole other thing to be able to reach out and physically touch your dream. Like when I was a youngster growing up in Houston with my family. My pops would buy my mom nice gear every once in a while, but she spent so much time thumbing through sales papers and department store catalogs, taking a black marker and making circles around the jewelry, appliances, expensive clothes, and purses that weren't in the budget. I'll never forget the tears streaming from her eyes, because she wished so hard for things that seemed to run away from her.

"Girl, I want to know how to be a man's number one," Veron says with an unflinching gaze. "I want to know what it feels like to be the first woman he calls to go out on a date, instead of the last one. I'm sick and tired of being stuck in that awful 'good friend' zone, you know, when a man views you like a sister or a girl to call when he's lonely, but you're not a woman he wants to kiss and hold and brag about to his friends. I'm tired of doing nice and supportive things for men who will never do the same for me." Her eyes quickly fill with tears.

"Calm down, sis," I say with gentleness.

She thoughtfully chews on her bottom lip, and I take a good look at her. Even though Veron doesn't realize it, the girl is hot. Two different men have passed by our table taking long lustful looks at her and trying to connect with her eyes, but she was too busy to notice, and they gave up and kept walking. Her fault. Her loss.

Veron goes on. "It just seems like even if I do find a man, they start out strong and promising and we may date for a few months. But then what happens? Homeboy mysteriously disappears with a fake lie instead of the hard truth. To make matters worse, I am sacrificing and doing so much: preparing home-cooked meals, washing his funky underwear, paying his bills, giving him cash, going all out for the freaky sex, yet dude still ends up getting restless and leaves for another woman. And usually that second-in-line chick is overweight, built like a New England Patriots linebacker, resembles the Tasmanian devil, is ignorant and ghetto, or she's a straight-up bitch." Veron whispers the *B* word and whips her head around before she turns back to me.

The word gives me an idea. "I'll be right back," I say, hopping up from our table and running up two flights of stairs to the second level.

I head straight for the psychology section and grab the book that's helped me be who I am today. I reach for a copy of *Why Men Love Bitches: From Doormat to Dreamgirl—A Woman's Guide to Holding Her Own in a Relationship.* If anything will do the trick, this will. I've known many women who have read the book and dumped their men because they got that much-needed wake-up call.

And it's time for Ms. Veron Darcey to wake up herself. She's hitting twenty-five this year. She's never even dated anyone really seriously. Now I haven't done much of that either, but our priorities are different: it's not what I've been wanting, but Veron does. Yet most of her relationships last no more than four months—six, if she's lucky. Just when she gets to know a man and falls in love, he ends up fleeing toward the sunset, leaving her dazed-and-confused ass a thousand miles behind. I've seen this happen to my girl so many times it's starting to get hard—on me! Although I try to be real with her, sometimes I can't say everything I want to say. I can't tell my lonely friend how my boy Darren meticulously bathes my feet, then pours honey on top of them and licks and sucks my toes until I start shaking, moaning, and rocking with massive, juicy orgasms. I won't always tell her how Gilbert can't wait to pick me up from Bush Intercontinental Airport at six in the a.m. without complaint. Or how

Thaddeus wants me to go on a Caribbean cruise with him as soon as his divorce is finalized. I don't like to brag, but sometimes I am amazed at how these men run after me, and I want to share but can't.

I shouldn't be the only woman who enjoys getting what she wants from men. And this is why I am going to do something for Veron that could absolutely revamp her life.

I head downstairs. "Okay, girlfriend. You wanna know my secret? You sure you're up for it? 'Cause here it is," I tell her and shove the book in her hand. I sit down and cross my legs.

"Ahhh, I think I've heard of this before." Veron immediately opens the book and starts reading chapter titles: "Why Men Prefer Bitches," "Nagging No More," and "How to Renew the Mental Challenge."

I watch Veron move her lips and flip several pages, hopefully letting some of the words sink in. I feel elated. For her, for me. I want to be able to share everything with my friend; I want to be equals or as close to the same page as possible. Maybe she can teach *me* something for a change. That would definitely be a twist.

"Okay, I'm in," Veron declares. "I want to start reading this book ASAP."

"Great. I'm getting you and me our own copies. I loaned my first copy to a trifling cousin who had the nerve to loan it to someone in Memphis, and I haven't seen it since. Whatev. But I want to re-read it. I bet you will, too. You'll see." I smile and clap my hands. "I'm so pumped for you, Veron. Watch and see, this book is going to totally transform you. But the book is just a start," I continue. "We're going to work on other parts of your life, too."

"Oh, yeah," Veron says, gulping loud and sounding like a little kid. "What else needs to change?"

"First of all, I'm taking you shopping." My eyes light up.

"You don't have to do that, Demetria."

"Oh, I know that, but I want to. You need to give your man the total package, to be someone he can't ignore or resist. And you're going to love it, too."

Veron nods her head slowly, contemplating my advice. She stares at her long, slender fingernails with the chipped red nail polish. She gives me a sheepish look and quietly says, "Demetria, I want to know what it feels like for a man to make love to every part of my body, and I wanna be held in his arms while he kisses me head to toe."

I nod and smile.

"I crave love so badly, and I want to give love, too."

"You will, Vee. But you gotta make sure the measure of love you give out doesn't exceed the love you're getting back. The man should always give more than you. He should always be the one who's more in love with you than you are with him. If nothing else you must remember that, Veron. I mean, every woman who loves a man more than he loves her is a hurt woman, she's frustrated, and she cries so much she can barely function. Did you hear about the time when Diana Ross and Ryan O'Neal were dating? Diana was madly in love with his womanizing ass and wanted to marry him. Ryan O'Neal couldn't care less about her. He dumped her and she's Diana-freaking-Ross."

"Well, Demetria, if she got dumped, what makes you think—"

"No, we're not going to think negatively like that. You are way better than Diana Ross, you hear me? That's the attitude you have to have. Stop comparing yourself to other women. You are ten times better than any woman in this store—except me, of course." She laughs with me and stands up.

I rise to my feet, too, and we hug tightly, then head over to stand in the checkout line.

"Demetria, girl, I thank you from the bottom of my heart. I have nothing to lose, do I?"

"Not a damn thing," I tell Vee. She pulls her orange Sony Ericsson swivel phone from her cell phone pouch.

"Ferris again," she says wistfully, looking torn.

"Don't answer," I snap. "He's history. You want to start new with some fresh meat."

"Yeah, you're right. Ferris isn't worth a nickel," she says and pushes the phone's busy button. "I never want to be treated so low by a man again."

"Good girl. That's what I'm talking about. Keep up your new attitude, and you won't ever be treated low again, by anybody."

— 3 —

VERON

First thing Demetria wants to do with me is change me. Guess I shouldn't be surprised. I know I shouldn't resist—after all, doesn't the Bible say desperate measures require desperate actions? Okay, maybe not, but I know someone famous said that.

So after Demetria and I leave Borders, I let her take me somewhere else—or at least, give me directions there. Although she begs and hounds, I am not comfortable enough to let her drive my new Chevy HHR. And I am capable of saying no, even if it's not something I do all the time.

We end up at Wig World, her second home. A couple of years ago, Demetria decided to sport an expensive, wavy, black, shoulder length hairweave (Jennifer Hudson–style), but she acts as if she was born with that hair. I will say this, though: it's always on point, never looks raggedy, neglected, or clownish. But although she's mad about her weave, she's constantly messing around with various hair-care products, big plastic rollers, and hair decorations, and she says Wig World's stock is way superior to Wal-Mart's.

"You've gotta be joking, Demetria."

"If I were joking you'd hear me laughing my ass off, now wouldn't you, sweetie?"

"Demetria, I'm sorry, but I like my hair the way it is."

"And maybe that's why you're having problems. You need to spice things up. Get yourself a hairstyle that forces men to stop driving their cars, a look that gives them whiplash 'cause they're checking you that hard. You get the picture."

"No man is going to stop what he's doing just to—"

"Girl, are you kidding me? Didn't I tell you what happened to me a long time ago, before I had my first car and I was taking Metro to my job? I was looking fierce waiting at the bus stop on West Tidwell. And this gray-haired dude was driving a white convertible down the street. Girl, dude took one look at me and peeled his eyes off the road and ended up crashing, you hear me? This fool ran dead into the car in front of him that had stopped at the red light. No lie. It was hella funny."

"Okay, yeah, I do remember you telling me that. But Demetria, I don't want men to get in accidents over me."

"Say what? Yes, you do, Vee. You want men to get in all kinds of trouble trying to check you," she insists, giving me a horrified look.

"Okay, fine. But what's wrong with the way I wear my hair?" I ask and pat the neatly cut bangs that lay across my forehead.

"Ponytails are nice—if you're a stallion that's competing in the Kentucky Derby. You're a twenty-something, single, attractive woman who wants to pull the best of the best. Allow the master to give you the hookup. You deserve it, and you're going to fall in love with your new look."

I hush up. For one thing, I know it's too much trouble to try to argue with Demetria. Secondly, I admit it: I love for someone to fuss over me, to exhibit that much passion and concern about something that concerns me. I may not always agree with Demetria's unorthodox viewpoints, but I realize she truly has my back; she's like an older, much savvier sister. She's my role model in some ways. And if I am honest, I would do anything to have some of what she has—men surrounding her and caring for her, and I wouldn't say no to all those gifts Thad got her for Valentine's Day, either. *If I am honest.* So that means I've gotta be committed to doing what she does, even if it makes me feel uncomfortable.

We walk in. "Hey, Ms. Sparks," yells a middle-aged Korean woman who's wearing a blue-jean cap and matching overalls.

"What's happening, everybody? Y'all doing good in the hood?" Demetria yells back, waving at the staring customers.

"That's Koko, the new owner. She's cool as hell," Demetria informs me. "Those previous store managers had to roll out. They'd eyeball every black person the second we walked in the door, acting like we're about to run outta here with weaves on our heads and the price tags still attached. That prejudiced mess burns me up."

"Mmm hmmm," comments a petite, average-looking black woman carrying a baby girl on one hip and holding hands with a squirming toddler boy. "I know what you mean, girl. I can't stand stereotypes like we all chickenheads with gold teeth, you know what I'm saying?"

Demetria scrunches her nose and nods at the woman, and quickly scrambles to the right side of the store. Hundreds of weaves and hairpieces cover the wall from floor to ceiling. I now understand how Demetria feels. It appears that Wig World is a black woman's dream: they stock every hair color, texture, and shape imaginable, plus combs, brushes, flat irons, do-rags, relaxer products, and more. And the price tags show that everything is pretty reasonable.

"Don't have a stroke," Demetria snaps when she notices my wide-eyed cow look.

"No, I ain't scared," I snap back. "Actually, I'm impressed.

Excited. I feel like I'm on *America's Next Top Model,* corny as it sounds."

"Hey, a new hairstyle, foundation, blush, eye shadow, and lip gloss can make a woman feel like she's been born again. And that's our goal. I'm so happy for you I could scream as loud as Patti LaBelle."

"Alright then, back off, Patti," I teasingly command my friend when her hands begin to wrap tightly around me.

After examining six wigs, Demetria suggests I get a three-quarter headband piece that's cut in beautiful layers. The dark brown wig perfectly matches my own straight, thin hair. I feel embarrassed at first when she aggressively pulls the hairpiece on top of my head. Several combs are attached to the synthetic hair, and she has to maneuver the piece on top of mine. She adjusts the piece tightly with a drawstring that she tucks underneath so my real hair doesn't show. Then she brushes my own hair, blending it into the fake hair.

I take a deep, anxious breath. Do I look silly? Is everyone laughing at me? Mentally, I quickly rebound, embracing the feeling of the hair resting on the tip of my shoulders. I've always craved longer hair, but my real hair grows only so far before it decides that it's had enough.

"Girl," Demetria squeals. "You look sooo fine, if I didn't have a man I'd snag your ass for myself."

"Jeez, thanks, I think." I blush.

I swirl around in front of a full-length mirror, checking out my new appearance from every angle.

"Okay, I'm game, Demetria. Let's get this before I change my mind." I laugh and start walking toward the cash register.

"Hey, now, sexy mama."

I turn toward the exuberant male voice and my eyes pop.

"Michael West, where the heck have you been?" I screech, nearly jumping in his arms. Michael is not quite six feet tall, but his bulky body looks powerful enough to make a woman feel safe.

"Apparently, I haven't been where I oughta be! Damn, baby, you working that hair like a mofo."

"It's good to see you, Mike," I say.

Mike and I grab each other around the waist. I enjoy a sincere, tight squeeze that could've lasted longer, but an impatient cough ruins our embrace.

"Oh, snap. Uh, Veron, this here is my girl Francine. Me and Veron go back a ways," he explains to her. This obvious-weave-wearing green-eyed plain-looking tall bony girl hovers over me without smiling or willing to shake my hand. *"Michael,"* she says pointedly. "I'll be right over here." She walks away a few feet but glues her eyes on us.

Oh great, I think. Girlfriend needs to know that Michael West is strictly parked in my "good friend" zone. I could never fall in love with a man whose full-time job is chasing skirts and collecting numbers. I don't want to spend every waking moment worrying that my man is out there hugged up with another woman. And Mike hugs up all kinds of women without regard to age, race, money, size, class, or parenting abilities. My nickname for Michael West is "The Predator."

"Hey man, what are you doing in Wig World?" I ask him, ignoring his woman's hostile stare.

"I'm here to hook my baby up."

"That's nice, Mike. Uh, Michael," I say hurriedly. Michael laughs quietly. "Jeez, Mike, your girl is grabbing on to you like you something special."

"I am something special."

"I wouldn't know that."

"Not that you couldn't have known," he complains. "But you never had eyes for a brotha like me."

"You said it, I consider you a brother, not a lover. No

offense, it's just that, well, I'm glad to see you aren't hurting in the romance department," I sweetly tell him.

I discreetly check out his girl. She's far too skinny to hold on to, and what's with the superflat behind? Exactly what does he see in this chick? It's as if Francine can hear my thoughts, because she flashes me another harsh expression and then resumes looking at bottles of shampoo.

Hmm, I'm assuming she's not Mike's number one. Why else would she be acting like a number two? I do not want to be like her, all paranoid and possessive. A true number one never worries if any other woman is in her man's rotation, because she feels secure. All this is helping: the more I decide what I want in a relationship, the more confident I feel.

I turn to call to Demetria. "Hey, Demetria, look who's honored us with his presence."

Michael stands frozen and speechless as Demetria slowly walks directly to him and clasps both his hands. He advances his lips toward her cheek, but she smiles coyly and moves a step back. Frowning, he reaches for her again. She laughs and shifts her head to the side.

"C'mon," he pleads and grabs Demetria by the shoulders. She blushes, lightly kisses his lips, and raises one of her legs against his.

"Girl, you crazy?" I frantically warn her.

"What you talking about?" she asks.

I point a finger at Francine. She's standing with her back facing us, which is great, but I know that won't last long. Mike walks over to her.

"Whatev." Demetria shrugs and gives me a look as if she can't believe I sliced her action with Michael.

I shake my head at her in amazement.

"We're good friends," she insists, looking at me as if I'm the one with the problem.

"Friends kiss?" I challenge her.

"Sometimes," she says, squirming.

I walk up to her and whisper, "You've let Mike lay his pipe in you?"

"What? I-I don't like to kiss and tell."

"You're a lying wench," I say, laughing. "But that's fine." Demetria thinks she's slick. I notice how she'll give me the juice on some of her romances and flings, while others are under tight lock. But it's not like I have the energy to try to keep an accurate account of her love life.

"He's a cutie with a nice booty," she says quietly in my ear. "So sorry, couldn't resist. He and I have never hooked up, I swear to God," she tells me. But she's staring intently at Michael.

And he's staring right back at her, though he's talking to Francine. "Hey, boo, you found what you want? Take it to the register. Here's some cash. And go wait for me in the car. I gotta handle something." Mike hands Francine a few bills and removes one key from his key ring.

"Just hurry up, Michael." Her heels click loudly against the floor as she storms over to the cash register. Mike looks back at us smiling confidently.

"My boo loves me."

"Uh-huh," Demetria says dryly. She grabs Mike by the hand and looks up in his eyes. "Why you with her?" she asks.

"Uh, what's that supposed to mean?" he says, frowning.

"Don't trip, Michael. I mean, look at her; she's got that anorexic giraffe look, like all she eats is carrots; she has no ass whatsoever, and she's a few inches taller than you. . . . I just imagine you with someone different than that."

"Demetria, knock it off," I cut in. "I don't think Mike is obligated to tell you—"

"Naw, it's cool, Veron," he says. "I ain't got anything to

hide." Suddenly I notice a huskiness in Mike's voice that wasn't there before. "Believe it or not, I see things in Francine that you can't see, Demetria. But still, she ain't got anything on you."

"That's all I wanted to know," Demetria says with poise and releases his hand.

Outwardly there's a frozen smile on my face. But inside I'm a house on fire. It's like Demetria has zero respect for our friend's relationship. Sure, she claims she's never slept with Michael, but I don't believe it, and now she's seducing him right under the nose of his girl. My father always told me if you don't want to be known as promiscuous, stop pulling down your panties.

"Demetria, girl, come on," I say. "You're being inappropriate." I purposefully stare out the store's window at Francine, who's pacing next to Michael's bronze BMW X5.

"Excuse us, Michael," Demetria says, and grabs me by the arm and steers me a few feet away.

"Girl, do not tell me you're defending some chick you just met over me, your so-called best friend? After all I do for you? Is she in here trying to hook you up, change your life? Has she ever loaned you money? Bought you expensive birthday presents? Personally trained you on how to suck dick the way a man needs it to be sucked? Huh, Veron?"

"Okay, don't tell all my business. Lower your voice."

"No, you lower that bad attitude you got. If you wanna be like me, get used to it. Real men aren't blind, Vee. He ain't gonna turn down a kiss or conversation from me, are you, Mike?" she asks, turning to look at him.

There's no way Mike could have heard our conversation, but he rapidly shakes his head no and causes all of us to laugh. I am grateful for the break in the tension. Mike and

Demetria move a little further into the store, and I watch him smile brightly at her and touch her hair.

My cell phone rings again. I pick up the line but don't say anything.

"Hello? You're finally answering my calls?"

"Ferris, you're through. Lose my number."

"But I was wrong, baby girl. I want to make things up with you—"

"Too late for making up, Ferris."

"Say what? You always used to forgive me back in the day."

"Well, it's a new day. Listen carefully, Ferris, because I'm not going to say this twice. Don't you ever call me again, you hear? If you so much as call me or come by my job, I'll stick my foot so far up your ass, my toes will be hanging off your dick."

"Wh—?"

I hang up.

"Dang, this new wig is making a difference already," I say, interrupting Demetria, who's locked in a good-bye embrace with Michael West.

— 4 —

DEMETRIA

"Get ready," I say to Vee. "Because by the time I'm done with you, everything will be brand new."

Vee nods and smiles, and for the first time I feel confident she's ready to let me do what I need to do.

"Hey, baby girl," Mike says. I thought he had left; he must have come back in. "Let me get them digits." He nods at my BlackBerry Pearl phone.

"Of course I'll give you my number . . . but I need someone to pay for this stuff," I say, smiling while I stretch out my fingers to stroke them across his sideburns. The moment I touch him Mike stares deep into my eyes, then reaches for his back pocket and pulls out his wallet.

Vee stares at me.

"What?" I ask her innocently. "School is in session," I explain to her while Mike makes the credit-card transaction.

"Where are you going now, Mike?" I ask him after we're handed our bags and exit the store to stand in front of Wig World.

"What you got in mind?"

"Well, Vee and I are going to hang out a little while longer, but I want you to come with us. Think you can make that happen?"

"Uh, yeah, that's doable. Tell you what, I'll be right back."

He slowly strides pimp-style toward his bronze BMW. I turn my back against Mike and look directly at Veron, intently studying her face as if it's a mirror.

Her eyes enlarge and her mouth pops open.

"What?" I say to her. "Tell me what's happening."

"Girlfriend is *pissed.* He asked for his key back and he's going up to that Yellow Cab that was waiting near them in the parking lot."

"Damn." I laugh happily. "I've got skills."

"Don't be too happy. Mike is so insensitive to dump his girlfriend just to hang out with us and do nothing. I wonder what lie he's making up."

"Don't worry about his lies. His problem. Not ours. We won't kidnap him for too long. I just want him to give us that male perspective about some things. Plus, this isn't about me, this is all for you, so change your self-righteous attitude."

Veron shrugs like she's unconvinced with my explanation.

"Okay, what's going on now?" I say to Veron, whose eyes are still stuck on the action behind me.

"Can't you hear Francine cussing him out? He's handing her a wad of loot and convincing her to get in the cab. I guess he had to pay the piper."

"She'll be all right. If she loves him she'll forgive him."

"You make it sound so easy, Demetria. If that's the case, I should forgive Ferris, but you advised me to kick him to the curb."

"That's because I know you can do better than him. Don't waste your time with a part-time lover. If dude was around every day checking for you, then he might be worth waiting on. But that every-blue-moon dick is not worth the investment."

"Do you always have an answer for everything, Demetria?"

"Sure do. Because I've been there, done that."

We end up at Bennigan's on the South Loop near Reliant Park.

"Damn, why you gotta pick Bennigan's?" Mike asks.

"What's wrong?" I ask.

"I was banned from Bennigan's. Not this particular one, but still . . ."

"Mike, you're such a fool. How can anyone get banned from here?"

Mike shrugs sheepishly but says nothing else. Veron's first to the entrance of the restaurant, and she puts her hand on the door, but I clear my throat and stare her down, and she lets Mike go first. He swings the door open for us, and we all walk into the place, where the hostess seats us in a booth.

"What was that all about?" says Veron, who's seated next to me.

"A real woman never opens her own door. Always let the man step ahead of you and do it for you. And if you ride with him in his car, don't get in until he opens your door."

"What's the big deal? I'm pretty capable of opening my own door, Demetria, and it is the twenty-first century."

"It's not about that; it's all about respect."

"You're serious?"

"Yes, Vee. You gotta be clear about what you want, and don't back off or compromise."

"What about men who are so rude and selfish that they won't open the door for you when they clearly see you coming?" she asks.

"Call 'em out," Mike says.

"Hell, yes," I agree. "I do it all the time. I say, 'I thought God stopped creating men with no manners.' Who cares if they're pissed off—if a man can't even open a fucking door, no way he's gonna be fucking me."

Veron is staring at me so intently I shrug and roll my eyes so as not to let her scrutiny bother me.

"Get a grip, Vee. You're in training every second you're with me, so take careful notes."

"But how did you learn all this? I mean, I feel like I've been living life letting all the important things slip by me."

"Well, you know, with your mom's passing away when you were a teen, you're gonna miss out on some vital info."

"What happened with your mom?" Mike asks.

"I don't talk about it much, but she died of an aneurysm when I was fourteen. But before she died, Mama was too strict. She wouldn't let me date, go to the mall with my friends. I had to do group dates if anything, with church kids mind you, so that time of life was a bit messed up. I'm no victim, but a few things about men have totally slipped past me, and that is embarrassing, frustrating."

"Hey," I tell her. "I'm not trying to be mean, but you really think I was born knowing how to deal with men? Be for real. It takes time and experience, Vee. But that's what I'm here for. Just make sure and pay close attention so you may apply everything you're learning from this moment until you take your last breath."

"Veron," Mike interrupts. "Tell me more about yourself in five sentences."

"What?" she asks, perplexed. "Why?"

"Just do it," I instruct my girl. "Do what the man says and don't question everything. Let trust flow out of you for once." I turn to Mike. "You know, this is what I love about you. You're one of the few men out there who we can talk straight to about guys, and who will give us the real deal." I laugh. "Vee, you remember that time we asked him to give us the truth about whether size really matters to men?"

"I remember that," Mike says. "I told you hell-to-the-fucking yes! We're sensitive. That is one thing you never tease a man about. As far as you're concerned, your man is always packing, even if he's as limp as some scrambled eggs. Tell him he's got the biggest dick you've ever seen, because that's the only thing he wants to hear, on the real."

"See what I'm saying? What other man gonna tell us that, huh, Veron? Just tell him more about yourself."

Looking hesitant, Veron opens her mouth. "Well, I am a Virgo, born September first."

"Go on," Mike urges.

"I enjoy reading Japanese comic books, listening to light jazz and old-school music. And I love playing dominoes, doing karaoke, talking on the phone—and talking in person. And I get a kick out of cooking; I'm a bit of a foodie."

"Borrring," I interrupt.

Veron squirms. "Okay . . . I like to be treated well. That's what I want more than anything."

"Tell me one more thing that you wish everyone in the world knew about you," Mike says.

Veron takes a deep breath. "I want a man to be as in love with me as I am with him. I am dying for a man to spoil me, for us to spoil each other and to have a good time together no matter what is going on in our lives."

"Give me an example," Mike says.

"Huh?"

"Clearly define what you want by painting him a picture," I tell her.

"Okay, well, I want a man who comes home from a long,

hard day at work. And even if the boss pissed him off that day, he takes a moment to chill out, sip on a glass of tasty wine, and relax on the love seat in front of a burning fireplace for a few minutes, but he won't block me out. I'll let him have his private moment, but after that, we can focus on each other. He'll let me serve him his home-cooked meal, then I can rub his feet and massage his muscles with soothing oils. We'd cuddle together and laugh and kiss, and he won't be anxious to push me away if I ask him what's wrong. I'd love to vibe with my man like that."

"Great job, Veron." Mike smiles and nods. "You're cool people with a lot of decency inside. We just gotta bring you out of your shell."

"Veron's got it going on more than she realizes," I remark as if she isn't sitting at our table. "And between the two of us, I'm confident we'll whip Ms. Darcey into shape."

"Don't talk about me like I'm a charity case," Veron complains. "I just need a few surefire tips. Once I decide what I want to do, I can take it from there."

"Okay, okay." I smile at my friend, impressed with her snippy attitude.

We all order colorful, flavored drinks, tons of onion rings, and baked potatoes topped with cheese, bacon bits, sour cream, and butter.

"Okay, Mike, the reason why you're here is because I personally believe you're as real as men come," I say to him. "And I want you to answer a few questions about why men are wired a certain way. Of course, this is for Vee's info." Oooh, that was a little blunt. Vee winces and I pull back. "Uh, well, *both* of us want to pick your brain. I mean, I have lots of experience, no doubt, but there's always a scenario that catches me off-guard. That's why *we* need to talk to you, got that?" I clarify offering Vee a peace-making smile.

"I get it. Both of y'all need *mucho ayuda.*" He winks. "Go ahead, Demetria!"

"Okay, question number one. What's up with men who feel like they gotta fuck several women and keep 'em on lock?"

He thinks for a second. "Well, some men will just never be satisfied with one person. Plus, every woman is different. Woman number one might be a good listener, is sweet, brings no drama, and can hold her own during a sexual Olympics marathon. Woman number two is fiery, unpredictable, and stays on a man's dick. She won't let him get away with BS, and sometimes a real man needs that."

"Okay," Vee remarks, nodding slowly.

"Another thing," Mike continues. "Most men don't like a woman who lets him walk all over her if he's in the wrong. He respects his lady more if she doesn't let him get away with dumb stuff and calls him to the carpet."

"Pssh, I knew that," I brag. Vee rolls her eyes.

"Okay, Ms. Darcey," Mike says. "Since your girl claims she knows it all, what's *your* question about men?"

"Ooo, Mike, where do I begin? For starters, I want to know why some men will tell you they like you, ask you out, say all the right things, but then they break dates at the last minute, or always have some excuse about why they didn't show up."

"Now some men are real good at follow-up," Mike responds. "If they say they're going to pick you up at seven, you can set your watch to them because they're gonna be five minutes early. But another guy may always be goofing off and running late; that's 'cause he's unorganized, self-absorbed, or, to be blunt, he might not be that into you."

"Okay, fine," Vee says, exasperated. "If you're not into me, just tell me. Why ask me out on a date if you aren't honestly feeling me?"

"He's either the sensitive type of guy who doesn't want to outright stomp on your feelings by telling you the truth, or he just might be keeping you on lock," Mike tells Veron. "Some men just like to shuffle three or four women at all times, keeping them within his rotation. He'll call you once in a blue moon so you won't forget about him. He knows he can wrap his little fingers around your heart, but it doesn't mean the man wants to hook up every weekend. It's just that if he reminds you he exists now and then, when he's horny and ready to tap that ass, you'll be there for him, no problem, because he's put himself on your mind. It's like he's checking in on his investment."

"I can't stand playing games like that!" Veron shakes her head. "Why is it so hard for a man to just be real with me?"

"See," Mike says, "what you don't understand is there are women who don't mind if they're in the rotation. Hell, she's got her own little rotation going herself, so if she gets to see her boo once every two weeks, it's no skin off her back, because she wants to hook up with boo number two or three when her number one ain't available. Women run game, too. Y'all better at it than men."

I toss back my head and laugh at Mike's accuracy.

"See what I'm saying. This dime here," Mike says gesturing at me, "she can have any man in Bennigan's that she wants. White, black, Baptist, or bisexual." He grins. "Demetria plays the game well and—"

"That's good for her, but I don't want to have to play games; didn't you hear me?" Veron looks annoyed.

"And exactly how many men call you on a Saturday night?" I ask her, equally annoyed.

Vee hesitates. "I don't accept last-minute dates," she says.

"See what I'm talking about?" I tell Mike. "Anyway, Vee, you're lying because you did it for rusty-ass Ferris. What was that?" I ask. I'm getting angry now, because if she really thinks about it, regardless of the dead mama excuse, some of this is Vee's own fault. If she doesn't play games, she should've told corny Ferris hell-to-the-fucking no from the start.

"Look, that was different," she explains. "I hadn't heard from Ferris in a while."

"Lame excuses, Vee."

"I had no other offers on the table," she continues.

"Then let those chips fall," I tell her. "It won't be the end of the world if you don't have a date on Valentine's Day. Life ain't stopping behind something like that, right, Mike?"

"Demetria, this is so easy for you to say," Veron jumps in. "You have four or five men chasing you day and night. If you tell one guy where to get off, the next one is happily waiting in line."

"Yep. And?"

"Why can't you remember what I'm dealing with in my life and stop giving me advice based upon your philosophies and actions?"

"Hello? Ms. Veron, that's the whole point. What you're doing *doesn't work.* Period. You say you want what I have; then you need to do what I do. You've got to get in the game, even if it means playing some at first."

Veron answers in a soft voice. "Well, I am okay with the way I am for the most part. I just want a little bit of what you've got without playing the game to get it."

"I don't believe that you want it bad enough, then," I tell her. "Your mouth is saying one thing but your actions suggest otherwise."

"I agree," Mike says.

"Michael?" Vee says in disbelief, her eyes wide at Mike not backing her.

"It's like some women out here talking about not wanting men to hit on them, yet they're wearing bootie shorts, and their titties are jiggling around in those skimpy halter tops," he says skeptically. "Say what? You don't want men staring down your boobs, but you're letting 'em bounce around like you're posing for a *Hustler* ad? Mixed signals. That's kinda what you're doing, Veron. You're in denial big time."

"I am not in denial."

"Denial is the first sign of denial," I tell her. "You gotta go through all the other parts to change yourself, not just stop with Wig World. You've got to learn the game."

"I understand what you're saying, I just don't see why . . ." and her voice tapers off as if she really has run out of excuses.

"Look, Vee," I say as gently as I can. "You will never be me one hundred percent, 'cause that's just how the good Lord made things, but you can begin one step at a time. Why? Because you are not happy, young lady. Admit it."

Veron's stony face doesn't scare me enough to shut my mouth. Truth hurts, doesn't it? And truth is what we need to bring out for this girl to wake up and stop living in her fairytale world.

"Vee," I begin again. "You may not agree with the choices I make, and that's fine. But I think once you change your mindset and be open to what I'm telling you, your life will be different. You may not want to play the game—even I get tired sometimes—but I'm always thinking about the end result."

"Yeah, but it all seems so fake," Veron complains in a tired, scratchy voice.

"It's not fake," Mike interjects. "It's the way of the world. Every day we go through stuff, unnecessary stuff, just to get what we want. Can you honestly tell me you enjoy doing every little peon task you do working for the city? *Do* you? Hell, no, but you put up with the BS because you're earning your paycheck, am I right?"

Veron's eyes finally fill with understanding. Looks like Mike can get through to her, and good thing, 'cause God knows what I've been trying isn't working. Even though I've been where she is—sweet, dumb, and lonely. Existing in a world filled with unrealistic dreams. Waiting for the earth to change itself and make me be everything I felt I should be. But guess what? It never did. So I had to change myself, and now look at me. I just hope Vee has gotten the same message. Sometimes you can't just be yourself, not if you want to achieve your goals.

"Okay, Mike, Demetria. I vow not to fight against what you're saying. I just need y'all to help me institute these changes. Deprogram me. Give me the twelve steps to happiness, whatever you wanna call it, because I am tired. All excuses aside, I have messed up. I know I have."

"But today you've taken some good steps. I mean, you got rid of Ferris, and I can imagine how hard it was to do that," I tell her with all sincerity.

"Wasn't hard at all," Vee says with conviction. "To hell with him. He got some nerve asking me out 'cause Shelly wasn't around. That fool needs to keep me out of his drama. I'm a number one, dammit!"

— 5 —

Veron

I am a liar, and my biggest victim is me. I want to get rid of this inability to face hard truths starting now. I am sitting here staring at Michael West and Demetria. I'm looking and listening and making mental notes that I pray won't escape my memory. But somewhere in the back of my head, I'm hearing, "It's hard to go against type. You're a Virgo; you can't suddenly be a Scorpio. That's not you. Be *you*."

I scream at my brain to shut up and it whimpers down to silence, muted to humility. I know I can institute this new transformation. Yeah, a new life may start with the outward (the new sexy hairpiece), but eventually my inward will be chipped away. I'll break down the parts of myself that are limping and dysfunctional and build myself up into a woman who's glorious, strong, confident, and desirable. This new woman who I'm becoming won't be second to anyone. I'll draw the type of men that Demetria draws and get the kind of attention she does. That's my goal. And I'm going to do my best to reach it. I might be a little afraid now, but like Demetria, I want to face the fear until all the butterflies are chased from my belly.

"Okay, Ms. Darcey," Mike says to me. "How are you feeling inside?"

"I feel pretty good right about now. As a matter of fact, I actually detect joy inside."

"Hot damn, that's the best thing I've heard come out your mouth in a while," Demetria exclaims. "Why do you feel joy?"

"I–I don't know exactly why, but I know the fact that I feel joy without having a man in my face right now is a great thing. It's like I'm cool with where I am right this second. That make sense?"

"Perfect sense," Demetria says. "You know you got it going on and you don't care if anyone agrees with you or not. 'Cause what you think about yourself is more important than what anybody else thinks."

"Exactly," I say, feeling a bit rejuvenated.

"That's where it starts," Mike adds. "You speak it until it becomes reality."

"I'm doing it, Mike, what else do I have to lose?"

"Then, young lady, I think you're now on your way," Mike says and picks up his glass filled with a tasty Hurricane. "Let's toast. To Veron Darcey and the fabulous new woman she's becoming."

"The new woman I am," I correct him.

We all loudly clink our glasses together as the waitress places the check in the middle of our table.

I stare at the check, tempted to pick it up and look at it, but I know that it's not my job. Not anymore.

Mike scoops up the check and reaches for his wallet.

I sit back in my seat, relishing the feeling of a man who is fine with being a man, who's not being a cheapskate by asking us to go dutch. Dutch is for losers. Chipping in is for scrubs. I am a real woman, dammit, and I expect and deserve the best. Besides, it feels good to be pampered, taken care of, and treated with respect.

In the parking lot, Demetria and I wave at Mike and watch him speed away in his BMW, his tires squealing and popping as if he's trying to show off.

"He's cool people, Vee. Brother is the go-to man if you are in a pinch and need a keeping-it-real perspective."

"He gives it to us straight, no chaser, huh?" I say.

"You damn straight. And that's how it oughta be."

"So have y'all fucked?" I ask in a keeping-it-real tone.

"What?"

"Give it to me straight, Demetria. Be honest."

"Okay, I'll give you the scoop. Let's hop in your ride and you take me home."

"Cool." I slide in the front seat of my HHR and rev up the engine. We peel out of Bennigan's parking lot and roll onto the West Loop South.

"So," I say.

"Okay, so Mike and I hooked up one time. That's it."

"That's it?"

"That's all."

"What's wrong? Was it not any good?"

"Horrible, forgettable. But don't tell him I told you."

"You're serious?" I ask Demetria, trying to drive the car and scrutinize her at the same time.

"Girl, I'll put it like this: he was average. His tongue is kinda short—I think that got in the way of what could have been. You know how much I love to be eaten out."

"No," I grimace as if I'm about to puke. "I had no idea but I'll keep that important detail in mind."

"Stop acting so bitchy. I don't know if I like the new you, Vee."

"Hold up, the other me was too wimped out for you. Now that I'm acting like you, you don't like it?"

She laughs, then thoughtfully stares out the window, avoiding my questions and attitude like they're something she's not prepared to handle.

And I discover maybe Demetria is a liar, too. She's all filled with hope and optimism, preaching to me like I'm an idiot, but when I implement her advice she can't deal? Which does she prefer? This is becoming interesting, and we're nowhere close to where I plan to go. Before it's over with I want to be so different that no one recognizes me.

I've realized today that one of the first things I need to learn is how to be satisfied from within, not needing a man to hook up with on the regular to make me feel okay. Still feeling like I'm complete even though society suggests that something is missing if you're in your midtwenties and don't have a man. Anyway, I read tons of magazines and I know men are mostly attracted to single, happy women who are comfortable being who they are, not single, sad, bitter women. And when I think about it, I can't say I blame these men. I definitely want to meet a hot man who is confident, secure, and content.

Right now, the man who I hope fits that description is a man whom I've been sweet on the past six months. His name is Seaphes Hill. Like me, he works for the city, but we rarely cross paths—I've only admired his good looks from afar. And when I have run into him in the employee cafeteria, my tongue gets so twisted up that I can barely say hello. I'm sure he thinks I'm a fool.

But that's about to change.

I want Seaphes to pay attention to the new me. If he speaks to me, I plan to hold a conversation with him. I plan to have an encounter with him that he won't forget.

— 6 —

DEMETRIA

I am lying on my back on the carpet in my huge walk-in closet. Seven vanilla scented candles are gently flickering on the ledge of the Roman bathtub in the nearby master bath.

Darren, my faithful "placeholder," is crouched between my legs using his hands to gently spread them wider. He starts out tenderly placing sweet, lingering kisses on my inner thighs. His tongue is so long and moist, and I grow wetter each time he slides it up and down my skin.

"Mmm, Darren, that feels sooo damn good. Good, ohhh, good."

He mumbles unintelligible words and kisses the inside of my left thigh, then moves to lick the other. He slowly blows hot breath directly on my inflamed vagina; it tingles and I grip his head with my hands. He kisses the top of my vagina, then takes his tongue and presses it deep inside my hole, wiggling it lovingly and moaning while he fingers me.

"Keep going, baby, don't stop," I grunt and gyrate my hips for maximum satisfaction.

When he lays his head on the side of my vagina and starts sucking it sideways, I gasp for breath, and squeeze his head between my shaking and squirming thighs. "Oh, God, I love this, I love this shit. You the best pussy-eating mofo I've ever had."

He licks and slurps it over and over, like a hungry dog, making loud sucking sounds. I hump my ass up and down, creating a nice rhythm. This feels so good I could lie here forever, eyes closed, tears seeping out the corners, me feeling like I'm being loved deeply, sincerely, by a man who wants nothing more than to please me.

Darren reaches up and squeezes both my breasts in his hands. He tenderly rubs my nipples while vigorously eating me out, kissing, licking, sucking me and bobbing his head up and down like a wild man who found a fountain in the wilderness.

"Ooo, baby, I love it when you do me like this."

I feel my orgasm building up; my entire body is hotter than a skillet of chicken grease. Everything starts to shake. Fingers, legs, thighs, vagina, shoulders. I scream and twitch and reach out to pull Darren up on me so he can slip his fat, erect dick inside me. His body slumped on top of me, he pumps into me harder and harder, rocking me back and forth, while my eyes flutter and roll around and my orgasm goes on and on. Making love to him feels so good I want to die and be born again at the same time.

His dick has been hard as stone for the last hour. And I'm so happy my carpet is tan and not winter white. My fluids keep pouring outta me like an overflowing fountain. Darren drinks up my happiness, slurping and moaning as if he's so thirsty for every part of me. He is raptly attentive, and I feel better than I have in a long time.

"Whew, Demetria, I don't know what I'ma do with you."

"Keep doing what you doing, baby, that's what you need to do."

"Hey, it's all up to you."

I sit up and grab the towel that he hands to me. I sop up the sticky wetness from my neck and forehead and set the towel back on the floor.

"Darren, don't start."

"Hey, I'm here for you to give you what you need as long as you want it. I'm just saying, it ain't my fault if a brotha wants to holler at you, show you some love, and you won't hear him."

"Darren, I love how you're loving me; you know that."

"Yeah, but you still won't let a brotha hook you up every single damn day for the rest of your life. Hell, I am shocked you let me make love to you in your own house. First time for everything."

"Well, since you couldn't wait on me and went and got you a little psycho jump-off, I knew I didn't want to go to your place."

"She ain't nobody. Just a girl, some wannabe. Nothing next to your fine ass."

"I don't believe you. Why don't you show me?" I tease him with a contented and satisfied smile. Quite frankly I wouldn't care if Darren had ten jump-offs, as long as he's doing me. What the hell do I care about his little sideline chick? I just want to be fucked by a man who I know will do anything he can to please me.

"When ole boy coming back?" he says.

"Sunday."

"So can we hang all day today? And tomorrow?"

I rise to my feet, not bothering to cover my body with my silk robe.

"Mmm, I'll have to think about that. I really don't have a lot of energy, Darren baby. I gotta recuperate."

He rubs his chin and grins. His black skin is so chocolaty smooth. Suddenly I want to place my teeth on his neck and bite him and suck on him till we both come again and again. But my hot ass needs to get a grip. Darren and I have been going at it since daylight changed to night. It's now two in the morning, and I didn't eat anything for dinner . . . at least, no *food.* I actually hate the taste of semen, but I will swallow from time to time, since he is so good at eating me and never complains about licking up my juices.

I walk slowly over to my master bathroom's dual marble sinks and turn on the faucet, listening to the sound of running, cold water. I yawn and grab my favorite yellow toothbrush out of the holder.

"Here, let me help you." Darren reaches for the tube of toothpaste, untwists the cap and squeezes a dab of toothpaste on his tongue. He pulls me toward him and sticks it deep inside my mouth. I open wider and let his tongue explore me inside. Darren kisses me long and deep, our mouths minty and tingling, while he squeezes and pulls on both my hardened nipples. His presses his dick against me and nudges my ass up against the bathroom counter. We stop kissing long enough for me to hop up on the counter and spread my legs wide.

"What you doing that for?" he asks, grinning, finally turning off the cold water faucet.

"Stop playing, Darren," I say huskily.

Darren grabs my right foot with his big masculine hands and starts caressing my toes and the underside of my foot. I arch my back while he massages and squeezes my foot, and when I moan, he reaches for the other.

"See, baby," he whispers, "you could have this type of loving every day. Every damn day."

"I know," I cry out when he sticks out his tongue and licks me from the tip of my toes to the top of my knees. His wet tongue wiggles up my body, flicking and licking, teasing me 'til I squirm. I'm so wet.

"If you know all this," he asks slowly as he kisses my thighs, "then what's the problem?" He moves his head from my knees to my big breasts.

"Oooh, damn," I gasp, thankful that moaning gives me an excuse to ignore his question.

Darren covers my right breast with his entire mouth, swallowing it whole, licking, sucking, and rolling his tongue around and over my nipple. The hairs from my arms rise up.

"Baby boy, what you doing to me?" I scream, thankful my house is so big that it makes me think no one can hear my shrieks.

He says nothing. Just keeps working me over, squeezing my breasts together, rubbing his hands across my thighs, gently caressing my lips, which swell and contract, and teasing me so much I am this close to chomping my teeth into my own hand.

"Hey, baby, you get a raise yet?" I whisper, my eyes half closed.

"What you say?"

"Never mind." I watch his head bob up and down while he continues to press his lips against my breasts, sucking them lovingly like his only desire is to please me. This man is so good to me. He never hurts me, is always ready to do whatever I ask. We are so sexually compatible it's unreal. It's a shame that the most he's ever given me is fifty bucks one time. That ain't nothing, and it made me sad 'cause I was really feeling this guy. But I chilled, thanked him for being sweet, and made myself stop thinking Darren could be my all-in-all.

It's hard to find the whole package: a man who has enviable looks, sophistication, and money, one who is truly unattached and mentally stable, with a tough-boy exterior but also a tender, caring heart . . . and is a sexual stallion. You just can't have it all, not in the real world. So I've learned to take the good parts of a bunch of different guys. Ten years from now, Darren might make some pretty young thing very happy. He's just not the most ambitious guy when it comes to making and doubling his money. He is satisfied living paycheck to paycheck and thinks his dick skills will keep a woman in his life. Sometimes it makes me feel foolish, because he doesn't give me anything and I'm giving this good stuff away for free. And because I willingly do it he probably thinks he's my big daddy on the real. But Darren can think again. I have never met his family. He won't be meeting mine. I don't know and don't care about his favorite color or his favorite cologne. I just need him to be there when no one else is. Because I know he can deliver. Even so, I know it'll never work between us, because as good as the sex is, I need more than banging sex to be happy.

I need the complete package. Whether that's Thaddeus or not, I'm not sure. But I'm not worried, either. As long as Darren keeps giving it to me like I want, I am willing to accept that the quality of his fucking is the equivalent of receiving a hundred thousand dollars a month.

Darren's cell phone rings while he's eating me out. He jumps from between my legs, giving me his famous stupid look.

"I know you not about to answer that," I snap.

"I'm not going to answer that."

"So get back to work."

"Okay," he tells me, but he weakly licks my clit and I can tell he's not giving his best effort.

"Whatsa matter, Darren? Why aren't you concentrating? Don't be wasting my time."

"Why you bitching, Demetria? I'm doing the best I can. I always bring my A-game."

"You can show me better than you can tell me."

"Well, if you keep talking like that my dick won't stay hard, so remember you gotta help me help you."

I push his head from between my thighs and laugh. "How's that for helping you? What you don't seem to remember is I shouldn't have to do any work at all. I mean, it's not like you're tearing me off with any cash, so . . ."

"Hey, I told you I'm working on that. Lay off will you? Damn."

"Don't raise your voice at me, Darren Foster."

His brown eyes narrow, and I can tell he doesn't appreciate me talking to him the way I am.

"You know me, Darren," I say in a softer, apologetic tone. "I hate excuses. Either bring it on or keep it moving."

"Oh, it's like that, huh?" I can tell he's still miffed at me, which is good, actually.

I manage to stand and go to my walk-in closet to get my silk robe, wrapping it around me and pulling the belt tightly.

"Well, that's a mood killer," Darren says. "What time is it anyway?"

"Almost three. Damn, my back is hurting."

Darren's cell rings again. He gives me another stupid look.

"I know you ain't answering—"

"I am not answering, just looking. Demetria, chill out for once."

"You know what? I'm getting really sleepy. Do you remember how to let yourself out?"

"You want me to leave?" He has a fragile, hurt sound in his voice, but I wait for him to come back to me.

When he does, I look squarely in his beautiful eyes and I gently tell him, "You seem like you have other things going on, Darren, and I don't want to stand in the way of you taking care of your business. So do what you need to do. If you wanna hook back up tonight just hit me on the cell and I'll see if I can make that happen."

He stares at me for five minutes until he gets sick of me ignoring him, then he heads toward the door, zipping up his jeans.

I bite my bottom lip and wonder if he can read the yearning that swims wildly in my eyes. I know I'm acting cold, but it's 'cause I gotta be. What I want more than anything is for him to come back in and hold me until we both fall asleep.

— 7 —

Seaphes

I love to fuck and I'm good at it. Not bragging. The truth. A lot of men brag about being good in bed, but this is how to know for sure. If a man fucks a woman one time and never has to call her again, that's when you know you're good. If you fuck her right, she'll be calling you damn near every weekend saying, "Hey, my DVD player is acting up, can you swing by? I won't keep you long." Interpretation: my stuff needs to be sucked, you want to lick it?

Oh, believe me, I've heard it all. I put it on these women just one time, and all of a sudden, their car needs an oil change, their refrigerator is leaking. "My cable is acting funny," they say. You get the picture. These women couldn't care less about getting stuff fixed—they just want to fuck. They want a skilled man to love 'em like they've never been loved before. Young, old, tight body, tens, banged-up faces, don't matter. All women want a man to hold 'em at night, to listen to them bitch about their problems, a man who will be there to rescue them if they're stranded on the side of the road.

Problem is, I don't want to be the fix-it guy anymore. I think it's about time I settled down and pick the *one*. You know, the one woman in the world who captures your heart in such a way that you ain't thinking about being with anybody else. Just her.

Truth be told, I've been there before. Twice. I've met two women in my lifetime who caught my attention so tough I iced the others.

My first fiancée's name was Murenthia. Yep, a ghetto-ass name for a ghetto-ass woman. That was back when I was going through my ghetto bootie phase when I got caught up by all the trashy *BET Uncut* videos. The message in these videos was to get ass and get lots of it. And Murenthia's ass was so big she could've rented it out as a shopping cart at Sam's Club. You could've balanced two plates and a couple of drinks on that fat ass. I was blinded by her, too. Because what sane, intelligent man would've proposed to a woman who didn't have a real job? She was "in-between" jobs, and for some odd reason, that didn't bother me. Say what? All Murenthia had to offer was her juicy, fat ass. And that didn't look to be changing—she was lazy as a dog with a broken leg. She loved to lie around as if she was crippled, refused to cook, and despised housework, because "I can't stand getting my hands dirty." But the woman had tons of energy when it came to partying, smoking weed, shopping for skimpy clothes, and getting her three-inch nails done. Guess who paid for all that?

"The man is supposed to pay," she'd whine. "My mama always told me that."

"Well, what is the woman supposed to do?"

"She supposed to let her man pay, that's what. Why you getting smart? I'll leave your ass."

"Don't leave me, Murenthia! You're too sensitive sometimes." Then she'd smile and suck a brotha's dick like it was going out of style. She loved to suck me for hours, and I also loved that she was addicted to taking it from the rear. I'd get her ready and would use half a bottle of baby oil and pour it all over her big fat round ass. The oil made things so slippery you were never sure where your dick would end up. But that's about the most fun I had with this chick. Being in bed all day. We'd be in the house so long I'd get cabin fever and feel disoriented, bumping into walls and needing to sit down and get myself situated. And that's when I realized I couldn't marry a woman like Murenthia. Why I gotta marry her just to get a piece of that fat ass?

I asked for the ring back.

"My mama said never give the ring back, why you trying to play me, Seaphes?"

"You knew you weren't going to marry me. Just be nice and give back the ring."

"You must think my mama raised a fool. I'm taking this bitch to the pawn shop. Hell, I need money for nails and hair since you ain't hooking me up no more. A sista's gotta do what the man won't do."

I never talked to her dumb ass again and feel embarrassed that I actually used to tell her I loved her.

The second woman's name was Sapphire. I called her Fire. She was about five feet one inch, but walked like she was six feet two and strutting down a runway. She had her own life, made six figures, kept busy with her social circles, earned two degrees, had A-1 credit and no babies in her part of the family tree, and didn't live with her mama and daddy plus her extended family. Fire cooked for me when she felt like it (which was usually every Sunday afternoon), and she got her nails and hair done every two weeks. No matter how much I fussed at her, she'd disagree with me if I was wrong, she'd ignore me if I was right, and she never emotionally broke down if she didn't hear from me in three days. Fire could suck dick, too (not that dick-sucking is number one, but she had insane skills). This woman made ear-shattering noises when we fucked, too, and that's much better than humping on a woman who is silent and stiff for two hours. (I mean, what's *that* about? Give me something to work with, clap your hands or whatever, to let me know you're having an okay time!)

When you added up everything she brought to the table, Fire was all that. Made this boy run for the nearest jeweler, plunk down seven grand for a diamond engagement ring, the whole nine yards. When the big day came, I took her out on a dinner cruise and she acted unimpressed. Said she'd been on cruises much better than the one we were on, but when I asked if she ever got an engagement ring better than the one I'm giving her, she was like, "Seaphes, don't play. What you talking 'bout?"

"Here, woman," I told her. "I love you. Will you be my wife?"

"You can't do better than that?" she asked, but I could still see her fingers trembling as if she was freezing cold. Fire held out her hand, and I slipped the ring on her finger. Thank God it fit perfectly. Thank God she said yes, thank God . . . but just because a woman says yes doesn't mean she's your wife. Fire wore the ring, flashing it proudly like it was a Rolex, but this woman took her sweet time about making wedding plans. She was on a career track and needed to stay focused, so she said. She told me, "We can be engaged for a couple of years, no need to rush."

I said, "What the fuck?"

She said, "You heard me. Let's take our time."

I said, "Why? You not sure you wanna do this?"

"Yeah," she said, "you know I wanna do this, but I wanna do it correct."

I didn't know what that was all about, but I took her

advice and took a crack at chilling, not getting my drawers in an uncomfortable bunch, and let my woman have her way. First sign that something was twisted was when I'd introduce Fire as my future wife, but she was still calling me her "significant other."

"Fire, why can't you call me your fiancé?"

"I just hate how it sounds."

"Well, I hate how 'significant other' sounds."

"Oh, man, stop whining. You sound just like a woman."

I shut my woman-sounding ass up. I could only hope she was going through a temporary insanity phase. That she'd wake up, think long and hard, and realize how good she had it.

Check out my résumé.

1. I am an employed African American man who doesn't live with his mother.
2. I do not have any wayward children running around.
3. I am not attracted to my sex.
4. I pay my bills on time, no repos, no foreclosures, none of that.
5. I pay for dates, no going dutch, no letting her pay taxes or tips. I pay it all.
6. I know how to take a woman someplace to eat besides Luby's or Red Lobster. I'm not opposed to Ethiopian, Jamaican, French, soul food, Italian, seafood, or sushi.
7. I have never been arrested. I pay my speeding tickets. There are no warrants. I don't punch in for weekend jail time.
8. I know how to switch out a lightbulb and fix a flat tire. (Don't laugh. Some so-called men act like they can't do anything on the maintenance tip and won't lift a finger to even try.)

9. I still open doors for women instead of letting the door slam in their faces because I foolishly think women are so independent that they don't require a man to have manners anymore.
10. I love to fuck and I'm good at it.

Now, I stopped at ten but could have added at least ten to twenty more. Bottom line is I have umpteen admirable qualities that any woman can see. But Fire? Fire still dragged her feet. She was moving so slow that after eleven months with still no more talk about a wedding I said, "Fuck it." I fucked her one last time, then I broke our engagement. Told her to keep the ring (she did), and I took a couple of months to reevaluate the situation. What did I do wrong? Why wasn't she rushing me to the altar like most normal women?

And I figured it out—she was just *too* independent. There's something to be said for someone who can show you a little vulnerability, who can feel like someone who might want or need you around once in a while. Her mind wasn't even on me, and it certainly wasn't on our wedding. I like a girl who's got her own thing going on, but not when that's all she's got room for. Well, I found out the truth a few months down the road.

I was at a crowded Greek restaurant with one of my boys. We were having a good time, and it was something I needed and I was feeling real good just talking to my boy. Later on, who struts inside the restaurant but Fire with two other people? All of them sit at a table near us. I see her, but she never sees me watching her sit comfortably close to someone who I now realize is her significant other.

The two locked eyes several times, smiling widely and laughing together.

They sat shoulder-to-shoulder and ate gyro sandwiches and pork chops from each other's plates.

And when they moved their heads in together and kissed each other on the lips, sticking wet tongues inside each other's mouths, that's the moment I got over Fire.

Because if a woman I love is kissing another woman in public, then she's not the woman for me. So Fire did me a favor, with her undercover lesbian/bisexual/carpet-munching ass. The end.

So that's the past. Terrible. I need a different type of woman, someone who can appreciate a good brotha like myself. Someone who won't take advantage of my kindness, dogging me out just because she thinks it's her God-given right. I need a woman I can fall in love with, stay in love with, and know she's not on a mission to disrespect me and break my heart. I've got some rules:

> No stalkers (meaning no women who call me twenty times a day and do drive-bys to find my car because they want to know where I'm at every second).
>
> No women who know the ins and outs of DNA tests.
>
> No women who won't work because they're "too cute for all that" (no woman is *that* cute).
>
> No women who go from sugar to shit in five seconds (at least pretend like you're emotionally stable).
>
> No women who judge me solely based on my zodiac sign (I'm an Aries by, the way, and yep, we've got to be in control).
>
> No women who have the nerve to ask for money and I've only known them for a few days (do I have *stupid* written across my forehead?).

I could go on and on until the sun reverses the way it turns, but you can figure it out. I have these standards, my little wish list: I want a woman who's honest, has integrity, and is a good listener. I want a woman who has the sweet side but knows how to speak up if I say something certifiably stupid. Basically it just adds up to this: I want a woman whom I can love and respect and who will love and respect me back. That's where I am right now. Expunging the old and preparing for the new.

I think it's time for your boy Seaphes to date smarter. Take my time and find a woman who once and for all deserves to be part of the Hill family.

And I won't stop until I find her.

— 8 —

VERON

I am an active member of a book club and have been for the past three years. Our next monthly meeting will be held the third Sunday in March, and I'm hosting, so I get to pick the book we're going to discuss. And it'll be fun sprucing up my apartment so it is comfy for the twelve members.

Of course, Demetria is the one who invited me to visit the club in the first place. "It's the bomb, girl. We just sit back, let our hair down, eat good food, and spread all our business. It's very therapeutic." I was skeptical at first. I don't exactly consider spreading my business something that's therapeutic. But I was hooked from the moment I walked in the door.

The thing that makes a club successful is the members. The main chicks are Gladys, a sassy, shapely sista who has been divorced two times, so she knows all the ins and outs of dysfunctional relationships. Then there's Tweetie, who's always smiling, positive, demure, and considerate. Tweetie has the huge shoulder you gotta cry on when you're going through hell—no judging, just loving. I've also bonded with Mia, a Puerto Rican cutie who acts as if the world revolves around her. I don't think she's ever paid a bill in her life, and believe me, she wants to keep it that way.

Every book club has a member who loves to spread negative energy. For us that would be Fonya. (Who the heck would name their child *Fonya*?) She never agrees with anything the other members say, even though she rarely finishes reading the books. She's often broke and always begs us to pass along our books to her.

And who can forget Elle? If I could trade places with anyone besides Demetria, it would be Elle. She's confident, stylish, upwardly mobile, and is engaged to a gorgeous hunk of a man named Darius. They make the perfect couple. Neither of them has ever been married. They're fresh, unspoiled, and ready to support each other. Their love for each other sickens me at times. But I force myself to watch so I can model myself after people who are doing the damn thing the right way.

So today I sent out a group e-mail to let the book club know that my pick for March is *Why Men Love Bitches*. I've already started reading the book and figure it will make for great discussions.

Demetria agreed to come over and talk about the book with me tonight—it's Sunday, one of the rare days when she takes a break from Thaddeus and her other men to spend time with friends.

"Girl, I am not dumb," she told me one time. "I know better than to always lay up with my men, neglecting my girls, and only coming around them after I've kicked a guy to the curb."

"Well, thank God for that," I told her. "I know I'd never get a chance to see you if you didn't specifically make time for me."

"I lost a really close friend because I chose a man over her," Demetria said. "Her name was Wanda. She begged me not to get too chummy with this guy, but I figured she was a hater and I iced her. Imagine how bad I felt when only two short months later, my dumb-ass boyfriend was busted for selling two pounds of cocaine to an undercover cop, got arrested, and had to do a bid. I tried to reconnect with Wanda, but she never answered or returned my messages. I was really hurt, and I learned my lesson. So now I always leave time to hook up with family and friends, and if my man is too possessive or can't understand, well, too bad for him."

Now, when I see this other side of Demetria, the caring side, it makes me able to tolerate her more snarky side. I know she has a good heart, even though her bluntness jars me at times. At any rate, I am having fun today reading my book-of-the-month, and I can't wait to discuss these relationship issues with Demetria.

I manage to read and outline four chapters when my cell phone rings. I look at the display and smile a little. I take the call, but don't say anything.

"Veron, stop playing games," Ferris says. "C'mon, baby girl, I didn't mean to act like an ass. I'm sorry, I'm sorry, I'm sorry."

I quietly giggle and settle back on the couch, pressing the phone close to my ear.

"I miss you. I haven't even been able to eat, sleep, nothing since you dumped me."

"I didn't dump you," I say.

"Baby girl? You finally talking to me?"

"I just wanted to hear what you had to say. But I'm not talking to you."

"Awww, baby, it's so good to hear your voice. But look what you've done to me. I've lost three pounds, haven't been in the mood to go to church."

I roll my eyes. "Don't let lil' ole me come between you and your God. Plus, big as your church is, there are plenty of single women. I'm sure you can find someone else."

"Don't want anybody else. I want you."

"I don't believe you."

"Why else would I put myself through this? You hang up on me all the time. I waste my minutes calling you and leaving long voice mail messages."

"Oh, so calling me is wasted minutes?" I say, insulted.

"No, I didn't mean it that way. It's just that trying to win you back is costing me. I–I even got you a real nice present, but you not even decent enough to let me bring it by. You acting so different you got me wondering that you might pack a gun now or something."

"Ferris, why would I waste my time shooting you? Huh?"

"Why you treat me so bad after all we've been through? I mean, what have I done?"

"You know exactly what. You disrespected me."

"If you think I did then all I can say is I won't ever do that to you again. I promise. Shelly is through, anyway. She was just some crazy girl who begged me to take her to the concert. But I ain't got time for all that. She's not my type. And she can't compare to you, for real though."

I thoughtfully chew on my bottom lip. But no, if the girl hadn't gotten sick on Valentine's Day, Ferris wouldn't have called me at all. And that's unacceptable.

"I don't like playing second fiddle to any woman, Ferris." I spoke clearly and strongly. "I must be number one."

He gasps. "That's the only way I would have it, Veron. You are my number one."

"Your number one what?" I ask, feeling a mixture of strength and weakness. *Number one fool? Doormat?*

God knows I've found myself in this sickening position countless times before. It's when you swear on your grandfather's grave you'll never, ever speak to a man who's treated you poorly, yet a few days later your knees wobble the second you hear the man's sissy-sounding, begging voice. You make up excuse after excuse for his poor behavior, mistakenly believing that one day he'll shape up, rationalizing he didn't mean the awful things he said, assuring yourself that he was having a "bad day" instead of recognizing he's just a bad man.

"Baby girl, you're my number one everything," Ferris says.

"Hey, Ferris, I gotta go. I refuse to listen to this." And I hang up in the middle of his repetitious apologies.

A couple hours later Demetria and I are comfortably lounging on my concrete patio in two aqua and white lounge chairs. We're enjoying a picturesque view of Richmond Ave., one of the busier streets on the southwest side of Houston. Demetria has her legs crossed, chilling out and sipping on an ice-cold strawberry and banana smoothie that I made.

"Okay, now I wanna slap you," she fusses

"I know, sis. I deserve to be slapped."

"If you get tempted to act a fool, just call me."

"I'll remember that next time, Demetria. It's just that . . . what do you do when you actually miss that man? It isn't always easy ignoring his calls. I mean I can do it sometimes, but being strong day in and day out gets hard. But then I thought about it, and I realized he lied to me on Valentine's Day, and I can't accept that. So yes, I was tempted for a moment, but I hung up on him."

"Well, good, then! Some guys pride themselves on being good liars. I'm glad you're starting to realize that. Without trust there is no love. And how can you trust him if he never tells the truth?"

"But what if he lies to spare my feelings?" I ask. "Does that count?"

"Well, it's like this. I might BS and tell a female coworker that her hair looks fly even though her style reminds me of Woody Woodpecker, but I doubt the woman will hate my guts for lying. Her pride is at stake. There's a difference. But when a man lies about proven, undeniable facts, we have problems."

"Demetria, let me ask you something. Do you lie to Thaddeus if you're out with another guy?"

"Nope."

"I don't believe you."

"So?" She laughs.

"What do you tell him?"

"Nothing. When it comes to things like that, I'd rather be silent than tell a lie."

"Oh, that's smart."

"Sure it is. You can always say 'no comment' if you don't wanna get into certain details. I mean, it's hard enough trying to be creative and remembering all the details, lying to cover up more lies, you know what I'm saying?"

"Do you think Thad is all right with your silence?"

She squirms in her seat and briefly glances away. "I really don't know. But if I stay silent on the subject, he knows not to ask anymore. He just has to believe what I do choose to tell him."

Just then a horn blows. A yellow Hummer bounces by with a hand waving frantically from the barely cracked window.

"Damn, this sumbitch is checking on me?" Demetria scowls, standing up.

"Aw, man, so Thad *doesn't* trust you!" I laugh.

"What the hell is he doing on this side of town? That

wasn't cool at all. I never did drive-bys, even when Marilyn was still in his crib. I told this fool I'd be chilling with you, what the hell? Without trust there is no love."

"I think it's cute," I remark in a delighted squeal.

"Stalking is cute?"

"He misses you. You're on his brain. He wants to be with you."

"He's insecure, that's what he is. I'm paranoid that I have hidden cameras on me now." Demetria shudders and rubs her shoulders. "Let's go inside, Vee. I'm starting to feel a draft."

We hurry inside my apartment and settle in my bedroom, sitting on the black and white quilt that's spread on top of my queen-sized bed. I flick on the TV but mute the volume. BET is airing *The Jamie Foxx Show* reruns for the millionth time.

"Question for you," I say to Demetria, who is lying comfortably on my new fluffy pillows.

"Shoot."

"How exactly did you and Thad start liking each other? I know you told me you met him at a jazz concert. You were impressed that he didn't appear to be with anyone."

"What? Oh, yeah. Right. I think it takes confidence to show up at a concert solo. So I sized up Thad and took that opportunity to ask him if he was enjoying himself. He said, 'I'm doing even better now that a pretty woman like you is talking to me.'

"I told him thanks for the compliment and asked why he was there alone, if his girlfriend and he were fighting, and I found out he didn't have a girlfriend . . . because his wife wouldn't be pleased. We both laughed," Demetria says, staring into space. "I was shocked he admitted he was married. Most guys might've swept that little detail under the rug. But

I followed Thad's lead. If he wanted to talk about her it was okay. If he didn't, that was cool, too. We liked each other because it seemed we had a few things in common and shared an easygoing flow from the beginning. He taught me a lot about things I didn't know, and I enjoyed listening to him, something his wife evidently wasn't too good at. But honest to God, I didn't let him get in my panties for a long time. He had to earn it. He had to chase me. And he had to prove that he was headed for divorce. The best thing is they have no kids. That eliminated any guilt. At least on my part."

"So y'all didn't have sex until she moved out?"

Demetria frowns. "Well, technically no. He told her he was leaving, that he wasn't happy and knew they'd grown apart and she agreed. We made love soon after that. It was absolutely in-cre-di-ble. But while he was with Marilyn, he would never, ever mention me. That would've been a major mistake."

"Why's that?"

"A man should never leave his spouse for someone else. He should never say, 'I've fallen in love with another woman and we're very happy and want to be together.' You're asking to get killed when you do that kind of crap. And anyway, he wasn't leaving her for me—he was leaving her 'cause it was just time to go. He set her up in a nice loft right downtown. She has no complaints."

"Does she know about you?"

"I sure as hell hope not. Put it this way, I've never had any obscene phone calls or strange cars driving by my house, none of that."

"Well, that's good to know for your sake. I don't think you're that much in love with the dude to endure confrontations with his wife."

"No, definitely not. I don't even know if I love Thad. He

was kinda like an experiment. I felt if I could pull him, I've stepped up my game. I mean, dude cosigned for me to buy a car and I haven't paid a single dime. He pays it all."

I stare at my friend for a long time. I don't know how she does it. What is it about her that a man is willing to buy her a top-of-the-line SUV? And give her tons of loot?

"Is he super rich?"

"He's got more money than me and you together, and he travels constantly. So his little tokens of love are his way of keeping me by his side. I don't mind at all." She laughs; a sparkling gleam fills her eyes. "You see, Vee, I always act like I'm a prize. I know there are many more men like Thad out there. And Thad knows, too. He's scared I'll dump him in a second and pull another man that same day. I always remind him of that fact. He believes it and compensates me accordingly."

"When I think about what you've achieved, it just makes me feel like I have such a long way to go."

"Listen, I faked it until I could make it. I looked in the mirror—" Her voice breaks, and she sighs heavily. "I forced myself to look in that mirror every single day, and I'd tell myself, 'Demetria Elayne Sparks, you are *beautiful*, you deserve happiness, you're a queen, you won't settle for less than what you deserve.' It's all about inner strength and attitude. And now I know that I am the baddest chick in Houston."

I'm discovering it's easier to slap a wig piece on my head than it is to transform my entire psychological state of mind. That's the part I fear. But I'm going to face that fear because I want to be a queen. I want to be a queen.

I *am* a queen.

Queen.

— 9 —

Demetria

"So, queen," I say, changing the subject. "What you wanna talk about? Anything else on your mind?"

She smiles. "I want to talk about work."

"Work?"

"And the guy who attended the March of Dimes planning meeting."

"There were a lot of guys who attended our meeting."

"But none like this one."

"Vee, what are you talking about?" I ask her.

"Well, he's the distinguished gentleman who came to the meeting a few minutes after it started. I remember he actually blushed like . . . he felt embarrassed. I thought that was endearing."

"Ahhh, okay. I've seen him before. You want to push up on that?"

"Well, not saying all that. I barely know him except for an occasional run-in. But I didn't notice a wedding ring, so my curiosity is aroused."

"I'll bet that's not all that's aroused," I say, smirking at my girl. "Well, go for it. Step up to him."

"I plan to, I am. I just don't want to seem overly aggressive.

So far he hasn't approached me. I mean, he's friendly but just says hey and keeps going, like he's always in a rush."

"You call that an excuse?"

"Oh, Demetria," she whines.

"Look, I don't know anything about this man, but I'm positive one of my many sources can give me the four-one-one."

"No, I don't wanna take that approach, either."

"Well, I can tell you like him. You're blushing. Be careful, Vee. You know nothing about him except that you're attracted to his blushes—you don't even know his name."

"Oh, I do, it's Seaphes Hill. I looked him up on the employee directory. He's an architect."

"Hmmm. An architect. Very nice. Means he's educated and has money."

"Yeah, but will he be interested in—"

"Stop it, girl, yes. You're a queen, remember? Queens can have anyone they want. From the limo driver to the prince. A queen has her pick. Jeez, I'm gonna have to slap this into you for you to get it." I am just playing with my girl, but her low self-esteem is starting to get on my last nerve.

"Okay, Demetria, pretend like you're me. How would you approach Seaphes?"

"I'd walk up to him and hold out my hand, and say, 'Hi, forgive me for being forward, but I'm Veron Darcey. I work in Finance and Administration. I just wanted to compliment you on that sharp-looking suit you're wearing. It really makes you stand out so much I couldn't help but come say hi. And you are?' "

"Okay, so men don't mind the direct approach."

"It depends. Check him out first. Just watch him without letting him know you're watching. If he's the type that looks you directly in the eye, go for it."

"God, I'm going to need a rule book. Oh, speaking of, I'm about halfway done with *Why Men Love Bitches,* and I love the heck outta this book. I think I'm learning. Like the day I hung up the phone on Ferris, he was so shocked. He kept calling back. He didn't hear my voice in real time for days. He left me like ten voice mails. I loved hearing him beg and whine. He even started singing me a song on one of the messages."

"And how'd that make you feel?" I ask her.

"Powerful. In control. Like I was being pursued."

I smile and nod at my friend. "You wanna keep feeling like that?"

"I sure do."

"Then keep doing what'cha doing. Don't forget. You're the queen, the boss, the head bitch in charge." I hop up from her bed. "Where's your book?"

"Right next to the toilet. I'll go get it."

Vee rushes back, plops on her bed, and opens the book. "I *love* this part. 'Never start what you don't want to continue.' That's genius. I know I used to date a man named Woody. And I made the mistake of making him some oatmeal with raisins and walnuts one morning. Oatmeal turned into homemade biscuits or waffles with strawberries and whipped cream. And when I'd beg him to give me a break and take me to IHOP, his punk butt refused to do it. Said my cooking would put IHOP outta business."

"And like a fool you believed him, huh?" I ask.

"How'd you know?"

"Easy. I know how women think." Like I said before, Veron is the old me. The dumb me who had to turn smart. I shiver when I recall how desperate I used to act. A man disrespecting me was like the Detroit Lions not making the play-offs. It's just something everybody expected. So once I got sick of the routine, the routine had to be overhauled and I forced myself to change. And I have to be careful because I don't want to revert back to my former self. I'd rather die than return to who I used to be.

"Well, anyway," Vee continues, "I had to grab the rules book, take my yellow highlighter and highlight the hell outta that one sentence. Because I plan to start out how I want to end up. I am not following my instincts from now on—each move will be carefully planned. I am making a list of what not to do."

"That's a good start. Like what don't you want to do with your new man, Seaphes?"

She blushes, but recovers. "Yep, my new man, Seaphes. That's right." She stops for a second. "Oh my God, now I'm getting nervous. I feel like I'm scheming to get him. He's supposed to chase me, not vice versa."

"Reverse psychology can get a man to do the things that you want him to do. Don't even sweat it."

"Okay. So I am going to have a conversation with him for the first time in my life, this week. Because you know we have another planning meeting. The March of Dimes Walk America event is coming up and we're going to organize that for our unit."

"Well, I can't wait to meet this guy. Anything to get your mind off that weak-ass Ferris."

"Ahhh ha, you never hold back when it comes to men, Demetria. And I love you for it."

"I got cha back, girlie."

Vee's phone rings. She blushes when she looks at who it is and makes a silly-looking face.

"Screw off, asshole," I scream at the phone. "She don't want cha. She's a queen."

"And that's why he's calling me."

"Yep, that's why the lame-o is calling you. And what do you do when a lame-o calls?"

"I don't pick up."

"Why?"

"Because I am busy. I have a life. I keep myself unavailable and do things only if it fits into my schedule."

I start clapping. "Go ahead, girl. And when will you be available, Vee?"

"In the year two thousand never."

"That's what I'm talking about."

And we high-five.

— 10 —

Seaphes

Because I don't let things bother me, I am asked to do favors for people a lot. Things like watching my infant nephew while my sister goes to a bridal shower. Or holding the elevator for some women who are so busy gossiping they aren't ready to hop in when the door opens. Or helping comanage the March of Dimes Walk America campaign for several departments within the City of Houston. I might be kind of a sucker, actually. No, I was probably asked because everyone at work heard that my nephew Tupac (don't laugh) was born prematurely. He weighed only three ounces. But now he's almost eight months old and is doing fine. He's a little trouper. He's spit up on me several times, so we've bonded. I can't abandon him, even if his mom can. And if she wants to go hang out with her friends so she can ooo and ahhh over her girlfriend's bridal gifts, that just means Tupac and I get to hang out.

Really, I am honored to be involved with this fund-raising campaign. We're about to go into a brainstorming meeting to figure out clever ways to get people to part with some cash, so we can help out babies like little Tupac. I hope they hurry up, though. Almost lunchtime. My stomach is growling, and I'm in the mood for some heavy grub, since I didn't have time to get breakfast this morning.

"Hey, you guys, let's get this meeting started," Ursula Phillips says. She's a fine-ass administration manager who wouldn't throw a bucket of water on me if I was on fire.

"First I want us to come up with different ideas on how to raise money for the March of Dimes," Ursula says. "I'll just jot down your ideas on the whiteboard. There is no wrong answer. Just toss out something. I want to ask every single person in this room, so we won't leave anyone out. Okay, Percy, you go first," she says to Percy Jones, an intern who works with me in Engineering and Construction.

"How 'bout we do a bootleg video sale? You know, how we've already seen the video and know we not gonna watch it no mo'?" he asks looking around the room as if anyone else is stupid enough to admit they actually buy bootleg movies. I shoot him a look—as a black professional, he's got to learn how to behave in certain settings so white people won't think we don't know how to handle ourselves in professional situations.

"Hmm, interesting," Ursula says without writing down Percy's idea. "Next, how about you, what's your name?"

"Veron Darcey with Finance and Administration."

"Great. What's your idea, Veron?"

"Well, people love to eat."

"Amen, sista," says Percy with his loud, ignorant-sounding voice.

"And I love to bake. I'm great at making carrot cake. I'm sure we could sell loads of baked goods twice a week until the campaign is complete."

"Hmmm, sounds good," Ursula says. She smiles and writes down *bake sale.*

Ursula continues going around the room, jotting down various ideas like selling Beanie Babies or raffling off tickets for corporate-sponsored small electronics items and department-store gift cards.

"Good, thanks, people, I love it. Let's take a moment to vote on the top two fund-raising picks based upon all the ideas you've given today. We're almost about to get outta here for lunch," Ursula says.

She distributes notepaper, and we jot down our top two picks.

I walk up to the front of the room and stand in front of Ursula, holding out my paper toward her. She's busy writing.

"Just put it on the desk, please."

"But what if I prefer you to take it from me?"

"Look, Seaphes—"

"Oh, since when were we on a first-name basis?"

"Mr. Hill, if you don't mind, I'm busy," she says with sharpness in her voice that makes my cheeks turn red. I can tell the room has gotten quieter and my stomach is growling even louder.

"Uh, well, I didn't mean any harm," I tell her in a soft voice. But she still won't look at me. And I don't know why I'm letting this bitch talk down to me.

"I need to talk to you directly after this meeting," I tell her.

"I don't have time for—"

"You don't even know what I want to say."

She sighs and finally looks at me. "You're right. Whatever you need to say, say it now."

Other people are now bringing up their fundraising choices, which Ursula gladly retrieves with a smile and a soft "thank you."

"Fine then. Why are you so mean?" I ask in a quiet voice.

"I beg your pardon?"

"I barely know you, and you've always had a nasty attitude. I just want to know why."

"I'm sorry, but this is not the time or place."

"You just asked me to say whatever I needed to say right now," I say, my voice increasing in volume more than I expect or want.

"Hey, hey, now you two quiet it down," Percy cuts in. "We trying to get up outta here."

I hold my tongue and slither back to sit down, my face red as some Georgia dirt.

"Okay, sorry, everyone. It is getting a little past twelve. So I'll just e-mail the results to the group this afternoon with further instructions. Thanks for your time and participation. Have a great weekend."

Ursula begins scooping up papers, her head lowered while she stares at the table. Most of the meeting participants jump up immediately, flying out the door and loudly gabbing about nothing.

"Damn, she was the bitchiest bitch I've ever seen. Don't even waste your time on that sista."

I look up. It's that carrot cake baking woman. She has one hand on her hip and a book lodged under her arm. Only word I can make out in the title is *bitches.*

I glance at Ursula, who's still pretending to gather her stuff, obviously waiting for me to leave before she'll look up.

"Yeah, I hear ya," I say to the woman. "She's got issues. So, what's that you're reading?"

"Oh, this," she says, blushing. "I'm a member of a book club, and this is what was picked. It's pretty cool. Gives great info about men and women and our relationship challenges."

"Oh, yeah." I glance at the book she's holding up. "Shoot, I could've written that book," I say, looking back at Ursula, who is now talking to Percy.

"I'll bet you can," she says, flirtatiously. "You look like you probably know a lot about relationships."

"Yeah," I say, taking a closer look at this woman. She's standing an arm's length away from me, appearing bored and casual. She's killing the dress that she's wearing; it's purple, my favorite color, and shows off a great pair of legs in black leather boots. All that makes me wonder what's underneath the dress, and I have no idea why my mind is going there about her so soon.

"Well, women are something I have a lot of dealings with, but I don't always understand them."

"Mmm hmmm. In what way?" she asks, tilting her head.

"Huh," I say. "Well, take for example my bonehead sister. She has a good man at home, the father of her child, but she still has to party every Friday night like if she doesn't the world is coming to an end. Dude always lets her go, too."

"'Lets her'?"

"I mean he doesn't ever tell her he has problems with her going. Probably because she starts whining about how she's stuck in the house all day and needs to get out and be around someone that she can hold grown-up conversations with."

"Ahhh, she sounds like a mom with a young kid. First-time mom?"

"Yeah."

"Figures."

"You got kids?" I ask.

"Mmmm, why do you ask?"

I cough and clear my throat.

"I mean," she explains, "I was hoping that my figure doesn't suggest that I have kids. That's what I meant by my question. You see my hips are wide and sometimes people think I got my wide hips from kids. The answer is no—I was born with these suckers."

I laugh and nod approvingly. I look back up at Ursula, who's actually following Percy out of the room.

"Hey, you wanna do lunch?" I ask the woman a little too loudly.

"Really?" she asks, eyes widening. Then she catches herself and looks nonchalant. "Uh, shoot, I would love to but I forgot. I promised to meet a friend."

"Well, hmmm, okay, it was nice talking to you. Do you have your card on you? I've run out."

"Hold up a sec, let me look." She fiddles around in her purse but pulls out nothing.

"Sorry," she apologizes. "I'm all out, too."

"Oh, well. I guess I'll stop hogging your time so you can go meet your date."

"It's not—well, I guess it is getting late. See ya later, Seaphes."

"Okay, I gotta run too—I need to drain the vein."

"Excuse me?" she asks, looking confused.

"Men's room," I mouth.

She laughs and blushes, and I take one step forward, then stop.

"You know," I say to her, "in the old days no one depended on handing out business cards. If they still wanted to continue a conversation or further get to know someone, they wrote down numbers on a piece of paper."

"Uh, yeah. Why don't you give me your number?"

"Are you going to do anything with my number?"

She looks like she's about to say something again, but catches herself. "Why, you want me to use it?"

"Listen, you look pretty in your dress. Your legs really stand out in that outfit. I want to see you wearing that one again."

"Ah ha. Thanks," she says, allowing a grin to spread on her face.

"Here, take my number," I say and hand her a receipt I used to scribble my cell number.

"Thanks again. I gotta go," she says, holding the receipt.

"I gotta go, too," I tell her and rush into the men's room.

What was *that* about?

— 11 —

Veron

Demetria is waiting for me at the entrance of the building. "You did well, little grasshopper," she says.

I beam at her. I was so happy that she let me do my thing with Seaphes without having to intervene—she just stood a few feet behind him and listened.

"Where ya wanna go for lunch, boo?" Demetria asks after we hop in her Dodge Nitro—it still has that intoxicating new-car smell. I inhale and let the aroma fill my nostrils. I sit back and relax, unzipping my boots.

"Girl, your feet betta not stink."

"Please, they're fine. Just hot."

"That's what women do for beauty. Gotta suffer. You needed to wear something that aroused your man's sense of sight."

"You're so right. He complimented me on my legs, I couldn't believe it. But . . ." I chew thoughtfully on my bottom lip.

"But what? Hey, where are we going?"

"I dunno. Surprise me," I tell her.

" 'K," she says and grins at me. "Finish what you were about to say."

"Well," I tell her wistfully. "I was dying inside, as you can imagine. And I think I played it cool enough, even though I almost messed up a couple times. But I don't know; it just doesn't feel like me! And anyway, I can't tell if he was really sincere."

"Sincere about?"

"He gave me my props about my legs and dress and whatever, but how can you tell if a man is just going through the motions? Almost like he's obligated to give me a compliment but not that he really means it."

"Don't even worry about it. Men lie about that kind of stuff, but we do it, too. Hell, if I can twist my lips to tell Percy Jones he looks nice, then, hey."

I giggle. "Why on earth would you tell that clown anything good about himself?"

"He needs that nurturing, too. As annoying as Percy is, we gotta be sweet. He is someone who can help us out one day if we're in a pinch. I'm telling you, be nice even to the most trifling of guys, and they will do whatever you want. The goal is to get what you want from whomever you need to get it."

"Damn, Demetria."

"Gotta up your game, girlfriend. You're off to a good start. But there's one slight problem."

"What's that?" I ask her.

"This Seaphes guy doesn't know who the hell you are. I noticed that he never once called you by your name. I was tempted to say something to you, anything, as long as I called you by your name, because I could tell he wasn't paying any attention in that meeting. He was too busy trying to get in Ursula's panties."

"And that's an insult. So what she has a big-time position? So what she dresses in a different outfit every day? So what? She's mean as hell. And he was all over her, anyway! Men piss me off with that. They always fall in love—"

"—with *bitches.* Bitches that don't give a damn about them. Happens all the time. But guess what, Vee."

"What?"

"If you wanna tag this man, you're gonna have to pull an Ursula."

"I was afraid you were going to say that." I sigh.

"All the things you're doing now, keep doing them. Don't act excited about him. Be nonchalant. Show him you're a challenge. You want him to hound you like he hounds Ursula Phillips."

"Do you know anything about her on a personal level?"

"Not really, but I can still size her up enough to see she's a true bitch on wheels. She's gotten a few people fired, I know that much. Here we go," she tells me as we pull up to the side of a restaurant.

I look out the car window and want to pump my fists in the air. I'm dying for some Greek food, and Demetria must want some, too, because now we're here on Montrose Street at Niko Niko's—one of the most popular Greek restaurants in Houston. Their gyro sandwiches are second to none, and if you love thick, hot, salty French fries, this is the place to get them.

When they call our number at the counter, Demetria goes to pick up our food, and it feels good to let her. Usually I'm the one who gets up to get stuff when we go get lunch. I thank her when she gets back.

"No problem, but you're not going to believe this. Your boy Seaphes is up in here, and he is not alone."

"Demetria, please tell me you're playing one of your jokes." I suddenly lose my appetite.

"Just chill out, it'll be okay. No matter what, you gotta act like you do not give a rat's ass. Because you don't, right? You have a life, you are a woman who has things to do, and it doesn't bother you if you see your man with another tramp."

"Oh God, please don't tell me he's with . . ."

Demetria simply nods and stuffs gyro and pita bread in her mouth.

I just sit back and stare at her. And it amazes me how you can go from standing on top of a mountain to being sprawled out in a valley in less than thirty minutes.

"Hey, keep cool. It's not over. Let them do lunch. That is your man, you got that? Ursula Phillips doesn't give a damn about him."

"That's what I'm scared of!"

"One thing you gotta understand about men. They love all kinds of women, they don't have a type. So that is why you'll see a man with a light-skinned woman one day, a hefty one the next, and a dark-skinned skeleton a week later. They could care less about if she's ranked a ten or a two; as long as she was born with some trim between her thighs, he can be attracted to her. She can be sweet, mean, Christian, Muslim, smart, or a GED candidate, it does not matter. Once you understand that, you won't waste time wondering why he's trying to get with this Ursula chick."

"Well, that sucks."

"So what it sucks. Things suck. Get over it."

I blow out a long, depressing breath and try to listen to Demetria. But what she says worries me. "Okay, Ms. Know-It-All, if men don't have types, then all men would cheat, wouldn't they? They wouldn't be picky. They would have you and anyone else they think they want."

"Well, some of them do," she says. "Listen, girl, just be you."

"Meaning?"

"You continue the game plan of acting nonchalant."

"I feel like walking up to them and giving him his stupid phone number back, tearing the paper up in little pieces."

"That's childish. You're a grown-ass woman, you don't roll like that. You gotta be confident and oblivious."

"But I don't feel it."

"Be it anyway; it's not about feeling it."

"Look, Demetria, with all due respect, what if you walked in here and found your wonderful Thaddeus chilling out with another woman?"

"Girl, it's already happened."

"W-what?"

"Hell, yeah. A few months ago I was out conducting some business, and I wanted to grab a bite to eat. So I rolled over to this popular spot called Baba Yega—they make the best turkey burgers in town. I walk in the restaurant and place my order and decide to venture outside to the garden area, since I knew the wait would be a good ten minutes. Girl, yes, I go outside, and who's out there but Thaddeus with this anorexic, stringy-haired brunette. He was squirming in his seat like he was about to crap on himself. And I am pissed off, because I consider Baba Yega just one of *our* spots. That's just plain rude and doesn't make me feel special. So to see him in the restaurant with this bitch, Vee, I was tempted to pick up a knife and slash him across the throat. But I just walked up to their table and said, 'Hey, Thaddeus. It's been so long since I've seen you. How'd that STD test come out?' "

"No, you didn't."

"Yeah, I blurted it out and quickly changed it up to make it look real, but this lady gave a wide-eyed blank look like she didn't catch on, so it didn't matter what I said. And so I get my food and I go eat it in the car, waiting to see how long they stay in the restaurant. Girl, they came out of that joint five minutes later."

"And then what?"

"Oh, he was blowing up my cell phone, leaving messages, trying to explain who she was. Said she was some woman he works with. I believed him, because when I was out there in the parking lot he didn't see me, but he still didn't hug or kiss her or anything. But I still let him sweat it."

I roll my eyes—I have my doubts about his story. Maybe she trusts her non-trustworthy man, and I don't blame her, but I hate when she preaches to me but doesn't have the license to do so.

"I gotta make my bladder gladder," I tell Demetria. I rise up out of my seat and head for the women's restroom. I pass by Seaphes's booth. He's alone. Surprised, I wave at him as I walk by.

"Hey," he says, raising his eyebrows. "Why are you here?"

"Probably the same reason as you. Love me some Greek food."

"Something in common."

I smile but don't say anything.

"You met your boyfriend here?"

"Uh, I'm here with someone. And you?" I wonder if it's okay to ask that.

"Well, I actually ran into Ursula. She came in for carryout and she actually sat and talked with me for a second, which was shocking."

"Y'all make a great couple," I tell him, trying to look unconcerned. "She's a cute gal." I hate this so much, so much, so much.

"Why you say that? I don't even like her, she's not my type."

"Why *you* say *that*? It's very apparent that you're attracted to that woman. Everyone can see it."

Seaphes frowns in disgust, and I wonder if he's playing things off or if he is genuinely repulsed.

"Well, everyone may think they know what they see, but it doesn't mean I like her. But hey, I'm glad you told me."

"I'm glad I told you, too. Look, I gotta run to the ladies' room real quick, plus my lunch date is probably wondering where I am."

"Sorry to hold you up. Now don't forget to call me sometime."

"Hey." I smirk. "If I called you, would you even know who I am?"

"What? Why do you think I don't know who you are?"

"You never say my name."

"What? W-well, that doesn't mean anything."

"Hmmm, never mind. I gotta run."

Blushing, I hurry to the ladies' room and look in the mirror. Jeez, why do I have flyaway hair right now? I smooth it with my hands and then empty my bladder, hoping that Seaphes will be gone by the time I walk past his booth. Damn, I wish we'd have gone somewhere else for lunch. But then again, it feels good to have had that conversation with Seaphes, and I hope that he's telling the truth about not being attracted to Ursula. One thing I've learned is a man will always deny liking certain women, but if everything about his behavior screams that he's feeling her, then I believe what I see and not what he says.

I take an extra-long moment in the ladies' room trying to pull myself together. I know we're creeping up to the end of our one-hour lunch break, but right now I just don't care. Finally I storm out, make a sharp right around the corner, and walk briskly with my head up, the thick heel of my boots clicking against the floor. I don't even know if Seaphes was still in the restaurant or not.

"Damn, what took you so long?"

"Let's go, Demetria."

"Okay, be that way."

"No, chill girl. Everything is under control."

I request a to-go carton, pack up my remaining food, and we leave Niko Niko's.

We head north toward downtown, rushing back to work as fast as the synchronized traffic lights allow.

"So," Demetria asks, "how'd things go back there? You keep your cool?"

"Yep. It probably helped that Ursula wasn't actually eating lunch with him. She just happened to be in the restaurant. And they talked. And that's fine. But I can't shake this feeling that there's more to them than he wants to admit."

"Why you say that?"

"It's like what you told me. Go with your gut. Well, my gut is telling me all kinds of stuff I don't want to hear."

"Listen," Demetria says. "There are times when we sense things about men that we really don't want to face, but that are true. For example, my boy Darren—he's sooo good at making love that I can't help but wonder how many women he's slept with. I mean we always use a condom, but I still don't like to think that he is too experienced. Yet it's a catch-22, because he's able to give it to me like I love to get it." She actually shivers and reaches for her cell phone.

"Hmph," she continues. "Thaddeus is flying to Connecticut, so hey, why I gotta be lonely?"

"So is Darren your standby?"

"I call him my placeholder. He's always game, and I could use some attention right about now."

"And you don't feel guilty?"

"For what? Girl, I *deserve* having a man that does everything I want him to do."

"Shoot, it's been so long since I've had sex . . ."

"Okay, we're going to have to do something about that. We'll start with finding someone you can hook up with just for sex."

"Demetria! I'm not that kind of girl. I'd rather be in a monogamous relationship than have bed buddies."

"If that's how you feel . . ."

"That's exactly how I feel. I want the whole enchilada. Nothing else will do."

"Well, then, you're going to have to take matters into your own hands."

"What do you mean?"

"Girl, you've gotta call him."

— 12 —
SEAPHES

"Hello," I say into my cell phone.

Silence.

"Hellooooooo."

"Is this Seaphes Hill?"

"Who's asking?"

All I hear is a long sigh. And I would hang up, but I know it's a woman on the other side of this attitude. And I wonder, what the hell? It's Friday night. I'm supposed to be celebrating getting through another work week, and this is what I'm forced to deal with?

"What can I do for you?" I say in an even tone.

"You can answer a question for me," says the soft, tender voice.

"Wait, *who* is this?"

"Let me just talk first, and I'll tell you who I am in a minute."

I pause. "Okay."

"What type of man are you?"

"W–what? Who is this? How'd you get this number?"

She laughs. I could have sworn I heard her whisper *idiot.*

I hang up.

The phone rings again.

"Hello?"

"I'm sorry, Seaphes. I-I really just want to talk to you, and I know I'm not doing a very good job of it."

That softens me up. "And you are?"

"It's . . . V-Veron."

Veron, Veron, Veron. Oh! The lady who bakes. Nice round patty-cake ass, smooth set of long, shapely legs. Calm, cool demeanor. Soft feminine voice. Gentle personality, but really baffling sometimes—this one is as mysterious as a Raymond Chandler novel. And that intrigues me. Hell, I've been around so many types of women that I've discovered they all fall within a few basic categories:

1. Sluts—Doesn't take much to get them to spread their legs. To anybody. Anywhere. 24/7. For them, responding to a booty call is like sucking in oxygen. Happens on a constant basis without much thought. Sluts equate sex with love, which means they love some of *every*one's body. They're searching for love in all the wrong places: the workplace, the club, cruise ships, bars, BlackVoices.com, MySpace.com, HerSpace.com, you get the picture.

2. The Hypnotized Dumb Chicks—Have you ever seen a goat herder who has to lead the goat wherever it goes? If the herder doesn't pop the goat on the head every once in a while, the poor little goat will stand around isolated from everyone, happily grazing in the field, looking about as dumb as a . . . well, a goat! That's the characteristics of the Hypnotized Dumb Chick. This type of woman cannot think for herself—she only believes what her man tells her. Even though she holds a master's degree, has a good job, and may be the head of her department, she never investigates the foolishness her man feeds her. This is the type of woman that backs her man even though everyone knows her lover is sleeping with any woman who smiles at him. Yet poor Dumbo isn't catching on, because she thinks her guy is so friendly and handsome that women can't help but smile back at him. Her dumb ass dangerously believes that just because a woman is ugly she doesn't have to worry about her man pushing up on "that fat, black, and ugly woman," but usually it's the ones who he always bitches about, accuses of being "crazy," and claims aren't his type whom he's really kicking it with. Yet Dumbo is too hypnotized to wake up and face reality: she doesn't have half of what she sadly believes is hers.

3. **Very Independent**—These chicks don't have a man, don't need a man, probably earn more than you, are good at making their own decisions, and are able to hop on a plane to Paris for the weekend just because. They wear the latest designer everything, are very well put together, educated, refined, and wouldn't dare TiVo soap operas. They rarely date—no time for it. And if they do get cheated on, they won't believe it if you tell them. They stupidly assume the world revolves around their expensive pussies, not realizing that they're not the only women who have those. After years of climbing that corporate ladder, they have the funds to buy the 5,000-square-foot house, the Lexus, and join the investment club, but she's manless, childless, and wonders why no man is running after her trying to wife her.

4. **Gold Diggers**—These skanks expect you to pay for everything (jewelry, vacations, rent); they want you to rescue them from every crisis; they pretend to be dumb and weak so they can make you feel as if you're smart and strong. You gotta pay to play with this one—so break out the checkbook and the

credit cards, because she eats lobster and filet mignon and caviar and drinks *bottles,* not glasses, of Pétrus at five grand a pop.

5. **Wounded, Bitter, Bruised Sista**—She's been hurt so many times that she doesn't trust anybody, including herself. She thinks all men are dogs and she won't even let you go to the corner store without imagining you're really scheming to meet a woman to have sex in your car for five minutes. Her baggage is so heavy that her shoulders are always sagging, and she can't see the future for the past.

6. **The Scandalous Wench**—Scheming, conniving, can't tell the truth even when it's obvious, she falsifies documents to get whatever she wants. She'll steal money out of your wallet and claim she won the money by playing the lottery; she'll learn all the passwords to your e-mail accounts and snoop out info; she'll do drive-bys on a Friday night just to see who's parked outside your crib, so she can accuse you of screwing other women. And she'll stoop low enough to use her kids' social security numbers to apply for another credit card. But she won't feel guilty because "it's all about me. So deal."

7. **The Beauty Queens**—They do not leave the house unless their hair, nails, feet, and makeup are intact. They have zero depth, and instead of sleeping with a man, they sleep with a mirror, a comb, and tubes of lipstick that they stash next to their pillow. They know nothing about politics or foreign affairs or the economic climate; they lack the patience to read the *New York Times* ("there are too many words and the print is so small"), and you'd never catch them watching MSNBC for hours. They haven't voted in years, because war, poverty, a national health care system, and the world economy are not their

issues. Because the way they see it, if a fingernail gets broken, all hell's gonna break loose.

8. The Psycho—She is paranoid, overanalyzes everything, gets depressed if you don't call every hour, and will whip out a knife and chase you with it while screaming obscenities—but won't even explain what you've done wrong. She'll give you her house key on Sunday and ask for it back on Monday. At twelve noon, she swears she loves you, but by 12:10 she's yelling, "I hate your black ass!" She's an emotional rollercoaster whose middle name is "Drama," and the worst thing is she never believes she's at fault.

9. Women Who Try Too Hard—She is a man pleaser to the *n*th degree. She will overdo everything. Buy you expensive gifts thinking that you'll be so moved by her generosity that you'll vow always to stay by her side. If you get mad at her, she blames herself, even though you were clearly at fault. She is scared to lose you, even though you haven't given her anything to lose. Her self-esteem is so low that she doesn't believe she is worth loving as she is, so she does things to please you without ever taking the time to please herself. This woman really needs to learn how to say (and mean), "Screw you. Good-bye, asshole."

10. The Kind of Woman a Man Wants to Kick It With—She is supportive, secure, and doesn't expect you to call her every five minutes. She trusts you when you do right, she calmly questions you when you fuck up. She can take you or leave you; she's happy whether there's a man in her life or not. She's powerful and confident and doesn't apologize for being strong. She has a popping personality and shines no matter what challenges come her way. She doesn't play high school games, gets straight to the point, doesn't expect you to read her mind, and never assumes anything (something that causes all kinds of problems in relationships). She understands what men like and how men think and doesn't try to change the way God made us; she just learns how to effectively deal with us. She's thoughtful and generous but doesn't overdo it to the point that you take her kindness for granted. She doesn't wave drama in your face, and she wouldn't dare start trouble just to be doing something. You get along well with her, and you enjoy being around her because she's laid-back and has a positive attitude. She strokes your ego and lets the man be the man. The sex is so off the rafters she makes you want to suck your thumb while she sucks your dick and then hold her close in your arms until you both peacefully fall asleep. This woman keeps it real, keeps her man in check, and doesn't get things twisted. She's exactly the type I'm looking for . . . if only I could find her.

Now, the problem is trying to identify which category this Veron chick falls into. I mean, as far as I know she could be a straight-up 8, a 10, or a combination of several. I can't tell right off the bat, and I'm curious.

"Well, hello, Veron," I say. "I'm glad you identified yourself."

"Me, too," she says in a voice that sounds like she's blushing. "Look, Seaphes," she continues, "I appreciate that you were straight with me about Ursula, and I'm choosing to believe you."

"That's cool, I guess. But why are you calling?"

"Why do you think I'm calling?" she asks. Is she trying to be cute? This is annoying.

"Why are you talking in riddles?" I ask her. "Why can't you just say what you want to say? Look, I'm over thirty, and when you are a mature person, you don't have a lot of time to play games. I don't want to play games with you, and I'd appreciate it if you felt the same."

"Well, I'm glad you feel that way, Seaphes." She sounds surprised, which makes me wonder more about her.

I tell her, "Look, I'm okay with talking on the phone, but I prefer face-to-face. Can you meet me somewhere?" We agree to hook up within an hour at Panera Bread in Memorial City Mall off the Katy Freeway.

— 13 —

Veron

If I could clearly see into my future, I'd know right now if I am making a mistake or not. He asked me to meet him so quickly and unexpectedly that I abruptly said yes—but it's so last minute I'm afraid I'm messing up.

And I don't want to screw this up. God knows I am attracted to this man. I like that he is a black, professional, degreed male who seems strong and in touch with who he is. I love the sound of his voice, a voice that is slightly baritone, that is friendly and welcoming but still no nonsense, not down for tons of BS. There's something about Seaphes that makes me feel safe. And I want this safe feeling to continue, to wrap its arms around me and squeeze me tight. I kinda wish I had Demetria's brain and instincts inside of me right now. She'd know exactly what to do and wouldn't have any problem executing it. But when I attempted calling her an hour ago, she told me she couldn't talk. She was in the middle of something, and she'd get back with me tomorrow. So I'm on my own. But I think I got enough of this book in my head now that I'll be okay.

When I finally walk into Panera restaurant, Seaphes is casually browsing *USA Today*. The aroma of freshly baked bread and bagels fills my nostrils and gives me a sense of peace and satisfaction. I immediately feel more relaxed than I initially thought I would. Maybe it's because he's offering me a warm, connecting smile.

"Hey, there. You look nice," he tells me with a nod.

"Oh, thank you," I say, blushing. "So do you."

"So what did you want to nibble on? I'm getting that cheesy French onion soup and a sierra turkey sandwich and am going to wash it down with some honeydew green tea."

"I'll have the same."

Seaphes invites me to go have a seat while he attends to our order.

I find a brightly lit corner spot near the front entrance and sit down in a seat that allows me a chance to stare at Seaphes. He's dressed casual tonight, in some tan Dockers and a black short-sleeved polo that shows off his arms' bulging muscles. When I was getting dressed to meet him, I made sure to wear a twirly black and white skirt in that same cut as the purple dress, with a short-sleeved white blouse and some cute black strappy heels.

Seaphes juggles our drinks in each of his hands and approaches me. He walks with a little strut, which greatly turns me on.

"So," he says. "Let's get to know each other."

That's so quick. Again, I'm caught by surprise, and what I've actually been wondering about all day bursts out. "How many women have you been with?" I ask.

He just stares.

I cough and clear my throat. "I guess that info is none of my business, huh?"

"Veron, even though we're just getting to know each other, you can take one look at me and tell I'm not a virgin."

I blush. "I know that. I'm not, either."

"Okay, so we're even."

"I beg your pardon. For all you know I just gave up my virginity a year ago."

"For all you know I could've done the same."

I nod slowly, staring intently at this intriguing man.

"When were you born?" I ask, deciding to shift gears.

"March twenty-eighth."

"And you're in your thirties? Never married?"

"Why are you looking at me like that? I've been in love but haven't found the right woman yet, but don't worry, I'm one hundred percent pure man."

"I can see that." I laugh. We loosen up, and soon the conversation turns to past loves. He tells me about his ex, Murenthia, that they were going to get married but things didn't work out. She took the breakup hard, especially when he asked her to return both the engagement ring and a secondhand car that he was nice enough to let her drive.

"She kept the ring, fine, but ain't no way I'm obligated to give her a car. It was the first car I ever owned, a Mazda RX-7. Very old but in tip-top condition."

"What color?"

"I don't care if it was pink with white polka dots, it was my car and I did her a favor by letting her drive it."

"So the million dollar question is . . ."

"Did I get back my car? Let me tell you, Veron, I had to go through hell to get it back."

"What happened?" I am still smiling at him, not because I am gleeful about his past drama but because I love to hear him talk. He has a tendency to stare deep into my eyes while he's explaining himself, something that I find intoxicating and reassuring.

"Murenthia may not have been the sharpest cheese in the dairy section, but she was very much a routine person. So after politely asking her for the car for the tenth time, I decided I had to do what I had to do. It was a Friday night, and I knew she'd be at Supercuts. So it was in November, you know, when it gets dark early. I had my buddy drive me. Sure enough, there was my car sitting a few yards away from the front entrance of Supercuts. Thankfully, I had an extra key; I hopped out of his ride, quickly popped open the locks to my ride, started the car and drove outta there like a volcano was erupting behind me."

He actually throws back his head and starts laughing so hard his shoulders shake.

"Well, I'm glad to see you're laughing about it all now."

"At the time it wasn't funny. She pissed me off, you know? This is a woman who claimed to love me and she acted foul like that? Love does crazy things to people."

"Tell me about it." We are having such a good time talking that I can barely enjoy my sandwich.

"Seaphes, did this Murenthia chick scare you away from being with women?"

"What?" he scowls. "Never that. I love women."

I skeptically raise one eyebrow.

"I *love* women," he insists, looking into my eyes.

I smile and feel heat warm my face. His pure boldness and confidence arouse me. He refuses to apologize for who he is, and I respect that. He's not trying to hide himself from me.

But at the same time, I wish Demetria could see this man in action. She could probably assess him in ten seconds and determine if he'd be a good match for me.

"I am not afraid to fall in love," he continues. "At this point in life, my philosophy is to let the woman be herself, tell me what she needs me to know, good or bad, and I'll do the same, and we'll figure out whether we're meant to be. That's about all anyone can do, you know what I'm saying? No point in playing games, pretending to be something you're not, wasting everybody's time. 'Cause one thing that's never going to change is tomorrow is not a promise, so we gotta make the most of the little time that we're given."

Suddenly my stomach feels queasy. I wonder if Seaphes considers me a fake. But I don't want to drop the games—Demetria and the book and everyone else have been telling me I'm wrong, and I want to be right with this man.

His cell starts ringing, but he doesn't even look at it. Instead he stares intently at me and says, "Now, if it's okay, may I ask you a question?"

"Go ahead."

"What exactly made you want to call me?"

"I, uh, jeez, it was just something to do," I say tapping my foot against the floor as if I'm listening to a fast song. I am being nonchalant. Can't tell him. Can't tell him. "I was, hmmm, bored, I guess and . . ."

"Sorry, but I don't believe you, Veron." He grins at me with reassurance. "Tell me the real answer."

"I beg your pardon," I squeal.

He pauses for a beat. "Do you like me?"

"Oh, my God, I can't believe you're asking me this."

"Look at you, you're blushing, you're covering your face with your hands, you look like a cute young high school girl. Your body is telling me what your mouth won't."

I stand up on wobbly legs. "Uh, I'm so sorry, but I need to go to the ladies' room. I'll only be a few minutes."

I can hear him loudly chuckling behind my back while I sprint to the rear of the restaurant, my heels noisily clanging across the floor. Thank God, no one else is occupying any of the stalls in the ladies' room. I barricade myself in one of the empty ones and breathlessly lock the door. I reach inside my cell-phone pouch and manage to dial Demetria. The call goes straight into voice mail. I dial Michael West. When a woman picks up the line, I hang up.

What would Demetria do? What would she say? How would she make herself come out on top in this situation? I allow myself three minutes to dwell on what happened and what needs to be happening, then I emerge from the stall.

When I get back to the booth, Seaphes is turning the pages of the *USA Today*.

I calmly sit back down and clear my throat.

"Seaphes, to answer your question, I just find you intriguing. That's it. That's the truth. And that's all I'm gonna tell you for now. Is that cool?"

He just grins and nods his head, and I am happy that I knew not to say too much or go too far. This is so hard, but I am managing to keep my instincts pushed down and do right.

— 1 4 —

VERON

It's Friday, exactly one week since Seaphes and I met at Panera Bread. Our March of Dimes subcommittee agreed that I'd bake and sell delicious slices of frosted carrot cake, so after work I head to the HEB Pantry to buy ingredients, as well as supplies for our book-club meeting, which I'm hosting on Sunday.

When I get there, I see there's only one available shopping cart. I rush to grab it, but another hand lands on the cart at the same time as mine.

"Michael?" I gasp.

"Veron!"

I laugh and give him a hug. "What you been up to?"

"I've been around, doing my thing."

"So you wanna share this cart? I don't have too much stuff to get."

"Hey, I don't need it. I saw you and was just messing with you. I only gotta get some washing powder, some of those dryer sheets, bleach, and some furniture polish. All that can fit in two hands."

I giggle. "Dang, Mike, you sound so domesticated. What happened to the player-player?"

"Even players gotta wash clothes sometimes."

We start walking toward the fresh-vegetables section. "So."

I clear my throat and peer about my surroundings. "Is it safe for us to be seen together?"

"What you mean?"

"You know exactly what I mean." I pretend to crack a whip.

"Awww, don't even try it." He chuckles. "She ain't got *that* much control over me."

"Hmmm, then why did she answer your phone when I tried to call you last week?"

"Say what?"

I don't know if I should buy Mike's look of surprise. I know how prideful men are. They will deny the truth just to save face and seem like they're on top of their game.

"What you talking about, Veron?"

I explained how I called him on his cell last week and the person who answered the phone definitely wasn't Mike.

"I didn't know that. I had my phone all the time and never heard it ring."

"That doesn't make sense."

"You're right, it doesn't make sense. Man, there's some weird shit going down lately with my phone. It didn't ring all last weekend, but a bunch of friends told me they tried to call."

"Well, I'm pretty sure it was her who answered when I called."

Suddenly Mike stops walking. "Damn, you know what? On Monday, Francine was acting real funky. She had attitude all up and down her face. And when I asked her what's wrong, she tells me, 'You know exactly what's wrong, you liar.' And I didn't know what the hell she was talking about!"

"Well, I did notice that I got a couple of hang ups on my phone from a private caller the next day. You think she . . ."

"Francine is the queen of pulling stupid mess. She

probably got ahold of my cell when I didn't know it and forwarded my calls to her number. She probably figures I'm messing around, 'cause a bunch of my friends that tried to call were females."

I giggle with amusement. "Can men and women be just friends, Mike?"

"You wanna know the truth? Ninety-nine percent of the time it's gonna be a fuck naw. Men are always thinking about sex. The minute a man meets an attractive woman he's figuring out if he can get in the panties. No man wants to be just a friend."

"Mmmm, I find that hard to believe," I say, my eyes glazing.

"Why's that?" he says, craning his neck to stare at a cute Vietnamese woman wearing a thin line of sky blue eyeliner.

"Because," I say loudly, irritated. "There are men that you meet who never make a move on you. You feel that they aren't attracted to you. They don't even try to kiss you, let alone try to have sex with you."

"Awww, boo. That make you feel rejected?"

"Well," I pout, "of course it does. Who doesn't want to be desired?"

"Listen, little mama, don't be upset just because a man may not want to do the nasty with you. That's nothing. A man can have sex with any woman. So let me hip you up on something," he says leaning in closer. "Sex just don't matter. Now if the man wants to make you his wifey, that's what's up."

I stare at Mike while he continues talking. And in those few seconds I realize that I have been undervaluing myself. I've been thinking that getting to have sex with my dream man equates the largest achievement in life. Horrifying! I barely want to think about it.

"Have you ever been married or engaged?" I ask.

"No, ma'am. Never will."

"Why not?"

"My folks divorced when I was three. Daddy had four other kids by three women and two of his women weren't black. Both my brothers divorced, and they are paying child support out the ass. One lives in a halfway house 'cause he can't afford rent. The other can't stand his ex and he hates women, doesn't even have sex anymore. If marriage does that to people, destroys them to the point that a man can't even raise his head proud 'cause his life is stripped away, I don't want any part of it."

I nod my head, realizing that men harvest deeper feelings about love, family, and sex than I thought. "I feel bad for your family, Mike, but just because . . ."

"No, Veron, I know what I want and what I don't. I can live to be fifty without a wife, and they can call me gay as Richard Simmons, I don't care."

"So what do you want from life?"

"I love women, period. I want to find a chick that backs me, builds me up, and lets me be the man."

"I hear you say you love women, but you don't love them enough to give them your last name."

"I don't need to be married to have banging sex, to laugh with my woman, to take her out. That's just how I feel, Vee."

"But, Mike, a few minutes ago you just told me that marriage is honorable, more honorable than just having a sex partner . . ."

"Listen, I'm just not going to get married. It's fine for other people, but if you do it, do it right. That's all I'm saying. Make sure it's with the right person for the right reasons. I guess more than anything, I haven't experienced that yet. Don't know if I ever will." And he once again glances at another young woman, barely out of her teens, sporting some tight

Apple Bottom jeans. He smiles for a second, but when he turns back to look at me, his face bears such a sullen, empty look, and my mouth can't form anything appropriate to say to him.

But he speaks up. "Enough about me. How's your love life going? You kicking ass and taking numbers?"

"Well," I say feeling more relaxed, "one of the two."

"Meaning?"

"A guy that I really like gave me his number. We both work for the city. Last week we hooked up and everything was cool," I tell him, my voice tapering off.

"But?"

"But this week while at work he was oddly polite. Said hi to me. Made small talk. I mean like 'how you enjoying this weather' talk. It confused me. As if our date didn't even happen."

"Did he consider it a date, or is that just you?"

"Look, Mike," I say, my face feeling warm with humiliation. "We ate at a restaurant."

"Did he pick you up?"

I look down and don't say anything.

"Veron, wake up. I hope you didn't think that just because you meet up with a man and y'all chitchat and share a cup of coffee that that's a date, especially if he hasn't called you since."

I place my hands over my ears. Mike removes my hands from my ears.

"Listen up, Vee, I know it's hard to understand. But forget this dude. If he hasn't followed up, he ain't anybody to be following. Always let the man chase you."

I swallow deeply, and my vision becomes cloudy. Why does this man mean so much to me when I barely know him? I really felt something special the other night and I can't imagine that he didn't.

With that Mike takes my shopping cart and says, "Okay, I'm helping you shop. Let's go."

I reach in my purse and hand him a lined sticky note that lists the specific items I need to purchase, and we go. Mike ventures down the aisles and waits for me to point out my preferred brand of confectioner's sugar, cinnamon, and granulated sugar. When he's done with the spices he continues rolling the cart and picks up two dozen eggs, opening the carton and making sure none of the eggs are cracked. On the produce aisle, he places carrots in my cart and then takes a deep breath and faces me.

"You really want this man?"

I nod vigorously.

"Then ignore him. Lose his number. Don't talk to him at work. Always have something going on, like you don't have time for him."

"But that just feels so wrong, especially since I want to talk to him all the time!"

Mike reminds me of everything that I've told him about Ferris. "Remember that the more you ignored Ferris, hung up on him, and cussed his ass out, the more he called."

I hate this, I hate the games. "Okay, I do remember that," I finally agree. "But Ferris isn't my guy."

"You gotta treat your guy like he's Ferris, though. I know it makes no sense and it'll be harder than hell, but trust me on this one."

We walk to the checkout line. Mike pays for all my groceries, walks me outside with them, loads them in my car, and then asks for my keys and starts the car for me.

"You make me feel like Demetria," I tease him.

"If you wanna really feel like Demetria, treat that dude like you don't give a damn about his ass."

— 15 —

Demetria

Attraction Principle Number 24: Every man wants to have sex first; whether he wants a girlfriend is something he thinks about later. By not giving him what he wants up front, you become his girlfriend without him realizing it.

I put the book down and look up at the other members of the book club.

We are all spread throughout Vee's living room, some of us comfortably plopped on her couch, others perched on dining room chairs. There's a nice little spread of fried and seasoned salmon patties, Spanish rice, onion-laced green beans, oven-baked rolls dripping with margarine and bowls of pure honey on the side, plus fresh strawberry shortcake with whipped cream for dessert.

"Well," I say. "Y'all agree with that principle about sex?"

"I wish I'd had known that before I gave some to my man," says Mia.

"Hey," Gladys speaks up. "As I see it, if he became your man then you lucked out even though you didn't hold out."

"That's what's up." I nod.

"And that's rare," Tweetie says, smiling like she's amazed, "but I definitely think that particular attraction principle is one of the most important ones women need to focus on. From what I hear, most women give it up within a week or two, and sometimes they open their legs on the first date."

"From what you *hear*?" I ask Tweetie and frown. "You don't know about quickly giving up the goodies from personal experience?"

"Nope, never, ever," Tweetie says, still smiling. "I try to get to know a guy first, and we will date for a long time before I'd even considering going to bed with him."

"Damn, that's different," Fonya says sarcastically. "And old-fashioned. But I don't believe you, Tweet. All women got a freaky side even though you won't twist your lips to admit it."

"Fonya," Gladys cuts in, "if Tweetie says she waits then don't be trying to slander her. How you know what she does behind closed doors?"

"Because I was behind those closed doors. We used to be roommates, remember? And I've heard her wild screams before." Tweetie looks horrified and jumps across me to place her hand over Fonya's mouth.

"Fonya, girl," Tweetie says with hurt cutting her voice. "I can't believe your big fat mouth. That's exactly why we aren't roommates anymore."

"Like I care," Fonya snaps after removing Tweetie's hand off her face. "You can't tell the truth half the time."

"And you can't pay your bills a hundred percent of the time."

I am the one smiling now. Tweetie rarely shows anger, and it feels great to see her stand up for herself.

"Hold up, Tweetie baby," I say. "Go sit yourself back down and cool off. Y'all are getting off topic. We're talking about *Why Men Love Bitches,* not why bitches can't be roommates. Let's stick to the book."

"That's what I was trying to do, Demetria. I was trying to

answer your specific question, but I got attacked. Why can't we all just get along?" Tweetie asks, frustrated. But then she breaks into her signature smile and holds up two fingers to make the peace sign, her way of restoring order to the meeting and letting bygones be bygones.

"Okay, anyone else have comments about this principle?" I ask. "Vee, you're very quiet. Speak up, girlfriend. I know you got something to say. She loves this book y'all—she really needs to be moderating this meeting instead of me."

"Well, I read the book from cover to cover. And I don't know if it works, but that principle is something that I'd want to try," Vee says. "Holding out just to see if the man will become my boyfriend."

"Yeah, I heard it works—I just can't do it," I say, giggling. Everyone knows good and well I love to fuck too much to keep my desires locked up for long.

"Good that you're bringing that up," Vee says. " 'Cause to be honest, Demetria, it seems like you break all the rules and still get everything you want, and I just don't understand."

"What you mean? I don't break all the rules, I go by the rules."

"Girl, be for real, since when do you follow rules?" Vee says. Her attitude is suddenly so nasty that I actually stand up.

"Let's take this out of the room," I instruct my friend. "Sounds like you have something on your mind."

"Let's do it," Vee says, just as arrogantly. The other women become very quiet, but I yell at them, "Y'all continue discussing the book, we'll be right back."

Vee follows me to her bedroom. I close and lock her door, turn around and face her with my arms folded under my breasts.

"What the hell's wrong with you, Vee? Don't you ever try

and loud talk me in front of anybody. I haven't done anything to you and don't appreciate you getting nasty with me for no reason."

Vee flops on her bed and turns her back away from me. She curls her body into a tight ball, and I notice her shoulders shaking.

"Damn, girl, I'm sorry," I say, touching her on the arm.

"It's not you," she wails and hisses.

"If not me, then who?"

"It's me. I messed up, and I don't know how to get things right again."

"Talk to me." I lay right next to her, grab her and hold her in my arms as if she's my child.

"I got weak last night," she sniffs. "I got so weak that I called Seaphes. He didn't sound happy to hear from me, but he didn't sound outright rude, either."

"I told you not to be calling him too much!"

"I know, but it's over and done with now."

"Damn, Vee. You letting good advice go to waste. So what happened?"

"He is a different kind of brotha. He started out kinda cold but after we got to talking for a little while, he warmed up and was asking me advice. You know, asking me questions about women. So I was happy at first, thinking he wanted to know what I thought about relationships and cared about my opinions, but ultimately he . . ." She stops talking and sits up in bed, wiping a few tears. I want to laugh at this girl, so overly dramatic. Men are *not* worth crying over.

"Go ahead, Vee. Ultimately he what?"

"Well, I was trying to play all coy and whatnot, but I must have messed up again, because he had the nerve to ask if I really thought that he and Ursula would make a good couple."

"Oh no, he didn't." I jump up from the bed, cursing up a

storm and pacing the bedroom. "That is so rude it's not even funny. I didn't know Seaphes had that much game in him. I mean, he sounds like a hard nut to crack, that's for sure. But baby, don't despair. He may be hard, but no man is impossible. As far as I'm concerned, you can have him and any other man if you handle this exactly the way I tell you and stop ignoring my good advice." Veron sniffs and sits up. "Whew, the things women do for love. I wish to God you didn't care about this prick, but it's much too late now." I sigh deeply while trying to get my think on. "You gotta crank things up a whole other notch. You call *me* if you feel like calling him. You gotta *ignore* him, Vee." She sniffs again, but nods.

Damn, did I actually used to act like this pitiful child? Thank God for transformation, strength, and a haughty attitude, because truly it's gonna take all three for Veron to get this man where she wants him.

"Okay, I won't mess up anymore, I swear. From now on I will listen to every single thing you tell me to do, and I will do it no matter what, Demetria. I am tired of feeling foolish and disrespected, so whatever you need me to do let's do it." She stands up and wipes her face. I stare at her and she retrieves a comb from her purse and begins prettying herself up like she has it going on. "Mmm hmmm, nobody is worth all this trouble. I don't know who he thinks he is, but he isn't the only man on earth."

"Now ya talking."

The next day we're eating lunch in my office. I manage to eat one quarter of my Reuben sandwich and drink two sips of bottled water. Veron offers me some leftover strawberry shortcake, but I decline.

"On a strict diet."

"What?" she asks. "Since when?"

"Uh, recently."

"Must be 'today' recently because just yesterday you ate two portions of this stuff and tried to get a third, and I wouldn't let you."

"And that's exactly why I'm dieting. I oughta know better. It's almost summertime, and I wanna make sure I can fit in some fly bikinis. You know I'm supposed to be going on a cruise with Thad."

"Mmm hmmm," Vee says, sounding unconvinced. "You haven't talked about him lately, what's up?"

"Everything's cool. He's busy with his businesses, and I always keep it moving. Like the good book says . . ."

"The Bible?"

"No, the *Bitch* book, fool. It tells women to always act like you got better things to do."

"And so you've been acting real, real busy right? And has Thad even noticed? 'Cause it seems to me he still running all across the country and hasn't even invited you to join him."

I roll my eyes, and luckily, she gets the hint and changes the subject. "Demetria, I passed by Seaphes's office the other day and couldn't help notice a picture of a little baby on his desk."

"Girl, I've seen that picture. That baby doesn't even look like him. Besides, so what if he got kids? That's a good thing these days . . . least you know he's not gay."

"Well, that's true," Vee says. "I'm more worried about him liking Ursula."

Suddenly, I see the man himself walk past my office with Ursula. I look at my watch—fifteen minutes past one. Just about the time that a lot of people stroll in after lunch break. I run up to my door and continue watching them. They're headed for the employee lounge. They're doing it openly. That could be good or bad. If he's really trying to roll up on her, and he's the discreet type, he wouldn't want to be seen walking with her, especially since it's now going around that office that he's sweet on her. Or maybe dude likes her so much that he doesn't care who knows it.

"I have an idea," I say, returning to my desk. "What's his cell number? Call him but make the discussion be about work. Try not to mention you and him."

"And why would I do that? All I want to do is tell him how I feel!"

"No, girl, you need to seem all business like you have no interest in chasing him. These things get kinda tricky, but you train yourself. Do what the *Bitch* book advises."

"Okay, dang. This is so exciting, but it's scary, too."

"Stop wearing your emotions on your sleeve and start acting like you're Vivica Fox. Act the part and you'll become the part. So call, go 'head," I say, picking up her phone and thrusting it in her hand.

"Now?"

"Do it!"

"Okay, okay, okay."

Veron calmly presses number one on her phone. I whisper, "Put him on speaker." She does.

Seaphes answers, "What's up."

I smile and wink at Vee.

"Hi, Seaphes, what are you up to? How was lunch?" Vee says.

"Hey, how's it going? Uh, I actually didn't go today. I may slip out in a little bit."

Vee pauses. "Oh, that's too bad. I wanted to talk to you about an important work-related issue. But that's okay, I'll find you some other time." I'm impressed. She really sounds like she's about to hang up.

"Hmmm," Seaphes says. "Would you want to come with me? I'm just going to grab some carryout real quick."

Vee pauses again, like she's considering. "Sure, that's cool."

Seaphes stops. "Well, you don't have to, Veron. Just thought it might be nice to get outside for a minute." He sounds kind of distant, but she quickly speaks up. "No, I'd love to come. Meet me by the front door in five?"

"I'll be there."

Vee hangs up.

"I'm sooo shocked. You did good, girl. Gotta think on your feet. And it's great that he is open to seeing you. If he wants to meet you then I think he likes you."

"Or maybe he did it because Ursula was there, and he's trying to make her jealous," Vee says with a frown.

"Whatever the reason, you got your invite. So ride with your man and do your thing."

— 1 6 —

VERON

When I get downstairs, Seaphes is yapping on his cell. But as soon as he sees me, he quickly ends the call. Every time I envision Seaphes talking to Ursula or even walking down the hall beside her, I can't help but feel sad and disturbed. It's going to be hard trying to cloak my feelings.

"Hey, you ready?" he asks. I nod, and we go up to a Nissan Armada and get in.

His ride is very neat and has tan leather interior. Cinnamon air freshener fills my nostrils as soon as I inhale.

"I like your car," I say.

"Yep, me, too. I'm leasing to own, so we'll see what happens." He seems so honest and open—most guys I've been with would have bragged that they bought the thing with cash. His honesty makes me want him even more. He's talking to me and telling me about himself without me having to ask. And I also like how he carefully backs out of his parking space, unlike younger men I've dated who make it a point to burn rubber and drive recklessly, as if I'd be impressed with their immature hotdogging.

"So, Seaphes, I'm trying to collect all the registration forms and wanted to know if you're going on the Walk?"

"Oh, yeah, I'm going, yep, yep. I never did fill out the form though. Will you do it for me?"

"Sure." I blush.

"Sorry about not paying attention to your deadline. I've been kinda busy lately. But I'm making it a point to do this event; I have personal ties to this kind of thing," he says, looking away. Then he turns to glance at me. "How was your weekend?"

"Oh, mine was very busy. I rarely have a moment to myself. Ripping and running, you know."

"You got family here?"

I explain that my mom died when I was younger, and I keep in touch with my brother and father mostly during holidays or when family emergencies arise. "But," I tell him, "my way to relax is through quiet time. I love to read all kinds of things. As a matter of fact, I'm an active member of a book club and we met at my place yesterday. We discussed that book that you've seen me with before."

He has a blank look on his face but says, "Oh, yeah, right. So how was the meeting?"

I cough and clear my throat. "It would have been great if you and some friends could have been there. We were discussing men," I explain.

"I'll bet you were." He grins mischievously and pulls up in the drive-through lane of a Pappas B-B-Q located off a busy intersection. "This joint is always crowded, so we may be in line for a half hour, but that's cool with me if it's okay with you. I can just talk to you."

I try not to grin as I nod. It takes everything inside me not to reach for his hand, which is casually resting in his lap.

"Seaphes, I'm starting to discover that you are so easy to talk to. Why is that?"

"What?" He hunches his shoulders. "I dunno. I didn't even realize it."

"That's another thing. You seem so . . . I can't put my finger on it."

"Are you observing me? Is this a test or something?"

"Oh no, not a test. I'm sorry. I go overboard sometimes analyzing stuff that shouldn't be analyzed." I slyly glance at Seaphes. "For example, I get a kick out of examining people's hands and finding their life lines. May I?"

He shrugs.

I carefully lift his large hand and place it in mine, flipping it face up so I can study the brown, arched lines.

"Ahhh, yes, you have a nice life line. See that extended line that comes all the way here? You're gonna live a long time."

"Well, young lady, thanks for telling me. Is it because I don't let nasty nicotine and pig intestines touch my lips?" he teases. "Or is it because I haul ass and run five miles every morning?"

"Could be all that and more," I tease back. As much as I want to continue holding his hand, I release it. But I savor the brief warm feeling that it gives me. I manage to turn the conversation back to the Walk America event and listen to him give a funny description of how hard it is to get coworkers to even give a dollar to a worthy cause.

We finally reach the take-out speaker. And sure enough, even though we're at a barbecue joint, he orders a baked potato with turkey meat.

"You want anything, young lady?"

"That baked potato sounds delicious, but I'm good."

"That you are," he tells me, smiling. He drives forward to the next window to pay.

"So," I continue. "You're easy to talk to, not half bad looking, yet you have an ex that chose not to continue her life with you. Are you concealing all your bad sides?"

He shrugs. "I don't think I am. I mean, hey, everyone has skeletons and no one is totally perfect. But I just think my ex and I weren't meant to be, and I've accepted that. I've moved on. And I am searching for the right woman who I wanna kick it with outside the bedroom, you know what I mean?"

Oh, God, do I. His heart is finally being revealed.

"I do know what you mean, Seaphes. But you'd think that it would be easy for a decent employed black male to find a wife. Not just you, but any eligible man," I say, trying my best to try to keep the conversation general.

"You'd think. I mean I guess I could ask any old body to hook up with me, that part is easy. But finding one that I really connect with, body, mind, soul, and spirit, that takes time, careful consideration. Marriage is a serious thing; even dating is serious as far as I'm concerned." He's staring into my eyes, but I make myself break his gaze and giggle.

"So I love to discuss these kinds of things with men. Can you tell me what type of woman you like?"

He looks disappointed for a minute but recovers. I have to remind myself that this is the way I have to do things. It's so hard; I'm playing completely against my nature.

"Well, she can't be a dummy, of course. It helps if she's educated, with common sense, nice looking in the face and body, a woman that has her own thing going instead of totally revolving her life around me. And if we can talk about subjects from A to Z, that's a plus. I've been around whores who—"

"Excuse me?"

"What? You don't like that word? All chicks aren't ladies."

"And most chicks aren't whores."

"Believe me, these were. They were only good for one thing. They were beautiful from the neck down but could care less about me as a person. They were just throwing the ass at me, and, hey, I'm a man."

"So you accepted that type of woman just because she threw herself at you?"

"I was a young thing then, about your age. As long as I wore condoms—which I always have since day one—I didn't see any harm in wilding out. But it helped me to get to know all kinds of chicks and decide what works for me in the long run."

"Hmmm," I say. I sit up as a woman sticks her hands out the window to hand him his order.

"Thank you, ma'am. Have a great day," he tells her, driving off.

On the way back to work, he makes small talk. But when he turns off his ignition, he turns to face me. "How's *your* love life?"

"Excuse me?" I ask, sincerely surprised by his question.

"No excuses, I answered your questions. Now you answer mine."

"But," I say and squirm uncomfortably in my seat. What would the book say? "Don't you have to get back upstairs?"

"I got another five minutes to spare. So go on and tell me."

"Well, I don't know how to answer."

"Just do it. What? You getting it on with somebody? Someone at the office?"

I laugh and shake my head. "Mmmm, I don't want to answer that."

"So who is he? Anybody I know?"

"Are you teasing me, or are you serious?"

"I'm curious . . . I'm curious as to why you don't wanna

answer me when I've answered everything you've wanted to know."

"Not everything," I tell him.

"What else you want to know?"

"You . . . ," I say toying with my hands. "You, uh, got kids?"

"No, why?"

"I noticed a baby seat in the back of your car."

"Oh, that's for my toddler nephew, one of the most special guys in the world. We hang out on play dates whenever his schedule allows," he says and winks. "And when I get a free moment, I ride him around with me showing him all the hot club spots of Houston."

"I see," I say, feeling relieved. "Okay, then."

"Okay nothing. Can you answer my question please?"

Damn. I hate this. What am I supposed say? Do I lie to make myself look good? I don't think Demetria would be too pleased if I told him he was really my only prospect right now and I spend most weekend nights hanging on my own. I think for a minute.

"Well, all I can tell you is I'm single, no kids, no rings on my finger, but I definitely date."

"Good, what was so hard about that? Women make things so hard sometimes."

"I just didn't expect that question from you. You shock me at times. I can never predict what you're going to say."

"Well, get used to that—I'm unpredictable!" And he laughs like it's a private joke.

When he unlocks the SUV, I'm pleased that he walks around to my side of the vehicle and opens the door. But I want to scream when I see Ursula slowly walking by with her eyes boldly glued on us. Seaphes nods hello at her but continues to focus on me, and Ursula frowns at us and rolls her eyes again. I wonder what he sees in that kind of woman.

"I think someone is not too happy right now," I murmur once she's finally gone.

"So? She had her chance."

"What's that supposed to mean?" I ask.

"Just like it sounds. When a woman clearly isn't interested in me, I roll out."

"Ahhh, okay," I tell him, wondering what exactly happened between them but knowing I couldn't ask. I'm starting to hate the *Bitch* book.

"Seaphes, forgive me for being presumptuous, but it's my understanding that men enjoy a woman who's a challenge."

"A man always wants what he can't have. The chase in itself is what's exciting. But I'm a grown man, and I'm not going to wait around while someone is rude to me and is obviously not going to come around." I notice that his eyes have left me and are now watching Ursula, who's in her car and driving slowly past us.

She rolls down her passenger side window. "Hey, Seaphes. C'mere. I need to talk to you for a minute," she tells him, ignoring me.

"I'm busy right now," he says, and places his arm around my shoulder to walk me up the stairs of our building.

I remove his hand from my shoulder as soon as we get inside. "Look, I don't know what's going on between the two of you, but please don't use me to make Ursula jealous. That wasn't cool," I say. I hope my taking up for myself is the best thing to do but somehow doubt it.

Seaphes looks taken aback but also weirdly amused. "I wasn't trying—"

"Now, Seaphes, don't deny it. Would you have put your arm around me if she hadn't been there?" He blushes. "I thought so. Thanks for being true to your unpredictable side," I tell him and briskly walk away.

"Hey," he says, but I ignore him, trying to respect myself.

I'm shaking once I get far away from him. Damn. Why does doing the right thing sometimes feel so wrong? I shouldn't have let him know that that incident upset me. But I'm not gonna stand there while he pulls some crap like that, no matter what the damn book says.

— 17 —

Seaphes

"Veron," I call to her, frustrated. But she continues walking down the long stretch of hallway with her head held high.

"I don't care," I mutter to myself and stagger down the hall, my legs feeling as if weights are attached to them.

Finally in my office, I sit down at my desk and glance at my work phone—no message-waiting lights flashing. I pick up my BlackBerry and dial the last number that called me. It rings two times, then quickly goes to voice mail.

She gave me the busy button! I dial her up again right away, but voice mail kicks in, kicking me out. Sighing, I pull my humongous baked potato from the white paper bag. I only eat these when I'm very hungry. But this time I take only two bites, then push the food to the side.

Using my BlackBerry, I swallow my pride, and dial up this woman again, but she busy buttons me a third time. I don't like this at all. I pick up my work phone and dial Veron's cell number.

"Hello," she says with slight hesitation.

"This baked potato is some kind of big, you want some of it?" I say, sounding like a chump.

"I don't want any of it," she says, and hangs up.

All that afternoon, no matter what work I am doing, my

mind is on Veron. Although her rejection hurts, I think about her sweet soft voice and how she genuinely listens to me when I talk. I notice how she stares at me even though she doesn't realize that I'm hip to that. I enjoy our easy banter, and I love that she's a feisty little one if I get on her bad side and that she won't let me get away with anything. But I wish she would be more up front with me—it's like she's always playing games and pretending to be someone she's not. Effective communication is what I'm looking for in a woman, because God knows I've been around too many of them who are too afraid to tell me what's bothering them. I know she says I used her to make Ursula jealous. But I don't even like Ursula anymore. So why would I do that?

I wait until four o'clock and spontaneously make a quick run to a florist shop on Fannin Street to buy a single white long-stemmed rose. I return to work and insert the rose in the window wiper of Veron's HHR. And I get in my car and drive toward home, waiting and nervously wondering what will happen.

At 10:00 p.m., I'd already watched *24* and lots of Court TV then tossed and turned in bed. But my anxiety kept whispering to me, dividing up my mind as well as my heart, and when the phone rang I answered it. Now I'm sitting on the edge of my bed staring through the dark shadows at her body. The outline of her round breasts makes my dick expand ever so slightly, but will it be erect enough to get the job done?

"What's wrong?" she asks softly.

"Nothing." I lay back until my body meets the soft covers of my bed. A few minutes earlier some Will Downing was softly transmitted via the clock-radio CD player that sits on the night stand, but it felt too sincere for this so I turned it off.

Although every other piece of her clothing is messily covering my carpet, she's still wearing a pair of panties. I guess it's just as well.

"I can't believe we're doing this," she exclaims as though shocked, but she smiles as she's speaking. The musky scent of desire glistens on her body. She rises up to position herself between my legs, kneeling, with her hands spread out like a slave willingly offering itself to its master. I'm lying flat on my back, one hand resting lazily on top of my head, looking at this attractive creature with mixed feelings.

Ursula leans in closer and awkwardly tries to press her thin lips against mine. Her breath smells like Smirnoff Ice.

I turn my head away from hers. My mind is preoccupied.

"Why no kiss?" she whines. "We were kissing real nice not too long ago."

"No."

"Okay, then, I want to fuck," she pleads.

"Go ahead," I tell her, thinking about Veron and how badly she hurt me when she refused to talk to me.

Ursula sighs but crawls over me, placing her wide hips on top of me and pressing the weight of her ass on my lower half.

"I love being on top," she proudly whispers.

"Not surprised."

Using two fingers, she seductively slides her panties to the side and mounts herself squarely on top of me, pulling and twisting on my dick several times, then moving to insert it between the lips of her dripping vagina.

"You still not ready. How long it's going to take? My husband is supposed to be home in an hour."

"I think we have time." *Veron really messed up.*

"Then you need to hurry it up and find a better way of staying erect."

"Girl, how can I stay erect with you rushing me and saying ignorant shit like that? Wait," I say. "No. No, girl. Hang on." I gently stop her movements down there.

But I still care about Veron.

"What the fuck ever," she cries, lifting herself up off me. An anguished sob bursts through her lips. Crying shakes her naked body, which she twists over so that she's lying in my bed facing the wall. My hands tell me to reach for her and caress her shoulders, but I don't do what my hands say.

My heart can only think of the woman who has touched my heart. As upset as I am with her, my desire is to call her one more time, and it's what I plan to do as soon as Ursula finds the strength to get up out of my house and return to her own. I don't know why I gave in to her and let her swing by. Maybe it was the sultriness of her voice when she said, "I'll only be a minute. I really wanna see you." But I'm not positive she's any more into me than I'm into her—she just didn't like seeing Veron and me together earlier. And the hubby part! She let that little detail slip out a few minutes after she got here. Even though I'm undeniably lying flat on my back, I don't feel comfortable sampling another man's meat.

But it almost happened, you almost let it happen, my mind tells me. And I agree. Terrible. I'm weak—am I that upset about Veron? I couldn't have justified this to myself. I'm just glad I caught myself in time.

As soon as Ursula pulls herself together, gets dressed, and finds her way out my front door, I return to my room, lifting my phone from underneath my bed and dialing *67.

I listen while the phone rings, waiting for the answering machine, which soon connects. She's still not taking my calls.

"Damn, she's straight up pissed," I say to myself. I

wonder how her face looked when she saw the rose on her car. Did she smile at my apology? Or does she now think I'm a pest? I want to right this wrong so bad, I get on my knees and ask the Lord to forgive me for what I almost did and beg him to straighten out the mess I've created with Veron.

The next morning I have to attend a design meeting off Highway 290, so I don't get to work until almost 10:30. My heart jumps when I see the message-waiting light on my work phone. But my heart falls when they're all messages from Ursula: "Where are you?" "You are so wrong for what you did," and "I brought you some donuts this morning, they'll be in my office."

"Oh, hell." I have no one to blame but me.

My phone rings.

"You finally are answering your phone," Ursula says.

"I just got here. Listen, don't leave those types of messages on my work phone. Nothing is private anymore. What do you think you're doing?"

"I didn't think you'd answer your cell, and I wanted to talk to you."

"Talk to *me*, okay? Not my answering machine."

"Baby, can we do lunch today?"

"Lunch won't work," I tell her.

"Why not?"

"We probably should talk now . . . on the phone."

"But I want to see you face-to-face."

"That's not gonna happen."

"Why?"

"Because I remembered that I need to do a few things. I

don't know exactly when I'll be able to get out of here, and, uh, I wouldn't want to have you waiting on me."

"Oh, so you do still care about me?" she asks with hope weaved in her voice.

I don't answer. I'm too busy tripping out over how just two weeks ago, I would've given up a kidney just to bask in this woman's attention, but now that I have it I realize she's not worth it.

"Look, Ursula, let's keep things professional. I was wrong for what I did. I'm sorry for doing it. Let's just move on, okay? I don't think it's a good idea for us to do lunch or talk."

"Nope, no, no. You chased me, muthafucka, you got my heart all twisted up, and now you want it to stop all of a sudden?"

"I-I, you aren't even . . ."

"I'm not what?" she cries, hurt mangling up her voice as if she's on the verge of a meltdown.

When I don't answer, she shrieks, "I gotta go," and slams the phone down.

I gladly hang up, but then I just sit there staring. Women are complicated as it is, and this one here hides her issues underneath her stylish clothes and cool-as-ice demeanor.

"Hey," she says walking in and quickly closing the door of my office.

"Ursula, you can't be doing this. What'd I just say?"

"Just this once. I want to talk to you to make sure you mean what you're saying."

"Why you gotta look at me to tell? I mean business. It's not you, the whole situation just isn't quite right. You're a lovely woman, but we can't be seeing each other."

"I'm so sorry. My spouse and I had broken up, but we recently got back together, and I'm having second thoughts.

It's so confusing," she says and takes a seat in my guest chair, holding her head in her hands.

"Maybe you should take the rest of the day off," I tell her.

"No, I'm not that bad. I'll be okay," she sniffs. "I understand where you're coming from. But I still want us to be friends."

"Yeah, that's exactly what we are, what we've always been. I'm just looking for a situation that's going to work for me."

She nods and sniffs. I stand up from my chair and reach to pull her up so I can grasp her in a solid, heartfelt hug, something she needs; she trembles a little bit and briefly closes her eyes. She squeezes me so tight that I'm eager to release myself from her grasp, but I want to do it in a gentle way so as not to hurt her but at the same time get my point across.

"I can't believe it's over before it ever started," she whispers, placing her head against my neck while I hold her around the waist.

Just then Veron walks in while Ursula and I are still hugged up. "Excuse me," she says curtly and quickly disappears.

My heart stops.

Inside I'm screaming, but I don't let it show. I shrug and calmly ask Ursula, "What were you saying?"

"I was saying that we never really got a chance to do what I dreamed we could do together. Like fate stepped in and snatched away my happiness," she replies in a despondent voice.

"It's like that sometimes," I remind her.

"Well," she says with a conclusive sigh before she releases me from her grip. "If you ever want to talk or even hang out, just give me a buzz."

Months ago I would have said, "I'll do that" or "You got it." Now, I just hold on to the gift of silence.

The rest of the week Veron is always flying past me in the hallway without a word, and she never returns even one of my phone calls. So by the beginning of the new work week, I cave in and confront her friend Demetria.

"So you say she's gone where?" I ask. I am standing in the doorway of her office, trying to cull any information possible about Veron's cold behavior.

"Vacation. She'll be back next week."

"Did she mention me before she left, or . . . ?"

Demetria attempts to look at me, but her eyes don't quite meet mine. "Look, if you want me to tell you everything I know, I can't. That's my girl, and I'll do anything and everything to protect her. Just know that she's worth the wait."

I contemplate her words, then slowly allow, "I see." Demetria calmly begins typing, her fingers rapidly clicking across the keyboard. I hesitate, then come in and sit down in her guest chair. The aroma of roses fills my nostrils, alternately soothing me and making me feel agitated.

"That smell," I start out, "it reminds me of someone I used to date."

"Oh, yeah?" Demetria says. When I don't answer she stops and looks at me. "Keep going, I can type and listen at the same time."

"You never forget certain things, the scent of a woman or something that jars a long ago memory," I tell her, crossing one of my legs over the other. "As much as I want to forget, sometimes nature doesn't allow me." When she doesn't reply, my face reddens with warmth. "I hope that makes sense."

"Sure it does. I know exactly what you mean. I can ride down certain streets, recognize familiar buildings, and am instantly transported back into time, even if it's a bad memory and I don't want to be there." She finally stops running her fingers across the keyboard. "And in those moments I am grateful to have just the memory of the pain and not be still affected by the actual pain that I felt while going through those situations." She shudders and smiles. "And if you want to avoid having to put roses in women's windshields, you'll learn to stop causing other people that kind of pain." She starts typing again.

I nod, satisfied that her girlfriend has mentioned me and the gift I left her. Now, whether she spoke well of me or with disdain, that's something I need to find out.

"How can I get to her heart?"

"Excuse me?"

"Demetria, you don't impress me as being slow in the mind. Not by a long shot. You know what I want and what I should do to get it."

"And you don't impress me as being slow in the mind, either, so what?"

I stand up and advance closer to her, so close that I feel her body tensing up.

"Demetria," I say, softly singing her name.

She again stops typing and looks me squarely in the eyes. I notice gentleness, a sincerity that makes me feel hopeful. "Veron is good people, but she doesn't stand for BS forever. You gotta come to her correct or don't approach her at all."

"That doesn't quite sound like her . . ."

"Look," she snaps. "Do you want me to help you out or not? I oughta know what she likes. I mean, don't insult me."

"Hey, hey, chill out. Give me a minute to me take in all that you're saying. A lot is at stake here."

She frowns and looks unimpressed, but I still sense that she accepts my words as truth.

"What do you want from Vee?"

"What I want," I respond, "is another chance. I feel like I haven't totally put my best foot forward. I need her to know that I can admit I screwed up, and she should give me a chance to see that I'm a decent brotha who's not out to intentionally hurt her." I wince as a vision of Ursula's tear-stained face dashes across my mind. "I mean, it's not like a woman hasn't ever been hurt by me, but I try to be as fair as possible."

"Well, that's good," she says. "Veron is a sweet girl."

"Yes." I smile and nod. "From the little time we've spent together, I can tell."

"And she doesn't have loads of experience with men, but you shouldn't hold that against her. You'll have to be patient and understanding."

"Hmmm, I think I can manage." I laugh out loud. "You won't believe this, but I've been thinking about this woman every day. I gave up on calling her since she doesn't seem too willing to talk to me, but I am hoping that time and now distance will heal any hard feelings. Where'd she go? Is she alone?"

"Seaphes, I am not going to go there. I tell some things but never everything."

I peer at her thoughtfully, studying her apple-shaped face. "Why's that?"

"You gotta do what works for you. Everyone does. I mean, do *you* tell it all?"

"Eventually."

"I don't believe you."

"That's your prerogative."

Demetria looks intrigued. She moves a little closer to me, raking my body with her eyes. "I'd have to see it to believe it."

"Keep your eyes open," I advise her.

She looks at me. It's an interesting look, a hungry, flirtatious one. But then she says, "Are you serious about Veron?"

"Why would you wonder that?" I say, puzzled.

"Because she told me you were all over what's-her-face the other day."

"I wasn't all over what's-her-face. And to answer your question, of course, I'm serious about Veron."

"Alright," she says. "So what's your game plan?"

I study her curiously. "You always have a game plan?"

She shifts in her seat and breaks eye contact for a second. "I'm not the topic here. Let's stick to Vee."

"As you wish. Do I have a game plan? I'm not sure. It's been a long time since I've been serious like this. I know what I would do if I just wanted to get some from her, but I don't quite know how to go about getting her to like me again. And that's the truth."

"Why are you so into the truth? That's different from most men."

"Listen, I've been around a lot of women and some were cool as hell, smart, sophisticated southern sweethearts, but others were straight-out hos. If people would just be up front with who they are, a man like me could avoid all the nasty-ass hos we don't wanna deal with."

"That's cold, Seaphes." She stares at me a second. "What do you see when you look at me?"

"I don't really want to go there."

She gets up and sits in the chair next to me, her leg touching mine. I slightly scoot over.

"No, go ahead, Seaphes, tell me what you think of me. I'm curious."

I lean toward her so close that I smell the mint fragrance of her warm breath.

"I've had you before, Demetria. You're a woman who outwardly expresses confidence, vitality, and obvious beauty. You try extra hard to make people think you're the shit, and usually that's a red flag that something else is going on underneath the fancy wardrobe, the dangling jewelry, the sexy and bold talk. You've been hurt. And there's more to you than meets the eye, admit it. Well, let me drop some truth on you. The part you're hiding is the part that people really want to know. No man is gonna give a fuck about a woman who doesn't have flaws or feelings." I'm looking her straight in the eyes. "Listen, I would finish this conversation, but I need to go back upstairs."

On my way back to my office, I remember the expression on her face. I wonder if I was too harsh. How many people is it gonna take to lift that woman up off the floor? I'm totally convinced that not even twelve people will be enough. That's Veron's friend. Why do I keep fucking up with this girl?

The next morning, Ursula stops by my office again. "I, um, stopped and picked up some pigs-in-a-blanket."

"You know I don't eat pig."

"I know that. You didn't let me finish. I also got you some of those strawberry-covered donuts that you love and two steaming-hot cups of coffee are sitting on my desk. I can't possibly eat it all . . ."

"That's very thoughtful, Ursula, but I'll pass."

A hint of anger flashes in her eyes. "I'm trying so hard with you."

"And you're wasting your time." That was harsh. "I'm just being honest," I explain as gently as I can.

She folds her arms under her breasts. "You played me!" she screams.

"Please, let's not start." I grab both her shoulders, gently shaking some sense into her.

"Hi, Seaphes, hey, Ursula." Demetria passes by, and I keep my hands on Ursula's shoulders, not because I want to, but because it will look too obvious if I remove them immediately.

"Now, Ursula, you going to be alright?" I ask, staring at her and ignoring Demetria, whose eyes are burning on me. Ursula just gives me a sad, dejected look. Demetria finally walks on down the hall, shaking her head.

"See," I tell Ursula, letting her go. "You've gots to chill. I appreciate the offer of breakfast, but that's the past, okay? Can you tell me if you're gonna be alright with that?"

I don't wait for her to answer. I'm headed out of my office. This is just great—nothing is ever going to go right on this one.

— 18 —

Demetria

"What happened, girl?" asks Veron. I'm outside sitting at a picnic table, talking to her on the phone.

"I just think you should know that your catching him hug Ursula wasn't a onetime thing. This week while you've been on vacation, he's been all over that girl. Your boy lets her bring him breakfast, and he was giving her a back rub right there in the open, so everyone can see that they're screwing. Vee, why would you want a man who openly disrespects you like that?"

"But two days ago you told me that he misses me."

"If he missed you so much, why his hands gotta be crawling all over her?"

"Awww, Demetria, he gave me that beautiful white rose. I know he was remorseful. It doesn't make sense."

"Sometimes things just don't make sense, but they still happen."

"Hmmm," Vee says. "I guess you're right. But I am not giving up. I'll bet that Ursula throws herself at him, and he's such a gentleman that he's trying to be polite and not let her down too hard. He told me with his own mouth that he's dealt with situations like that with other women."

I start to get angry. This man is disrespectful—he even

dared to disrespect me! I tell her, "I know you like him, Vee, but I'm wondering if you're wasting your time with this one."

"Well, I really don't know what to say."

"Just say no. If he comes up to you next week, lying and trying to sweet-talk you, tell him to fuck off."

"I'm not going to do that."

"Why not?"

"Because I'm not that mad. But it sure sounds like you are."

"What? I'm trying to look out for you. If he screws you over, it's just like screwing me over. So we're both screwed as far as I'm concerned."

"Calm down! Jeez, Demetria, maybe the book would call me a fool, but I want to trust that man."

I make myself calm down, placing my hand over my chest until my breath gets measured and my heart stops beating wildly. That mutha doesn't know who he's dealing with. How can he sit and judge me? He knows nothing about me. I've got to make her see that he's wrong.

"Vee, this man only shows you the sides he wants you to see, but the dickhead part of him is kept hidden."

"Girl, you make him sound like a monster. I have a bad side that I don't want to show. I get in bad moods and snap at people, whatever. Seaphes is probably the same way."

"Believe that fairy tale if you want. I'd rather see you with Ferris than Seaphes."

"Oh no, mmm mmmm, I want someone like Seaphes way more than Ferris. Oh, speaking of Ferris, he actually called me last night. I didn't pick up but he left me a voice mail message, singing that song by Klymaxx called 'I Miss You.' I love that song, but I wish that Seaphes would've left it on my voice mail instead of all those hang ups. Why doesn't he just talk to me? I mean, sure I was mad at him, but it's not like I never want to hear from him again."

"Pricks don't talk. They just screw you over. That's why. Wake up, girlfriend. You've just landed yourself a high-salaried, educated, SUV-driving asshole." I'm so mad. Why is she refusing to see the truth? He's a judgmental bastard. I tell her that I'll call her back.

I go upstairs and tell my boss that I'm leaving for the day because I've got an emergency to deal with at home. And on my way to my crib I think about Seaphes Hill and how men like him convince a lot of women that all men are assholes. And it's not just a joke, something that someone repeats because they've heard someone else say it and wants to make someone laugh. Many women think this, deeply in their hearts. They don't understand how a man can be so emotionally detached from what is important to a woman.

And so we end up reacting in ways that men don't like or understand. Because we are trying to protect our hearts, sustain our dignity. But if there's one thing I want to keep, it's my power as a woman. I want to show that I can rise above any circumstance no matter how badly it irks me. There's no way I'm letting this man get to *me*.

When I call Vee that night to continue our conversation, she pleads, "Don't quit on me now. I still need you. And I want him, too."

"I know you do, boo," I tell her. "So let's rethink this and try to make it work. Actually, you're in a good position. But we're not totally there yet. So let me regroup, and I will work my magic on his ass tomorrow. I'll keep you posted."

"Sure, do whatever you need to do. I want him to be a different man by the time I get back to work."

We hang up, but the phone rings again almost immediately. It's Thaddeus calling to let me know he's back in town. But I just tell him, "That's nice," and then explain to him I'm tired and want to get off the phone. He's hurt, but not shocked. He knows I always have something going on. In fact, I wouldn't be surprised if he does something extra special for me, since he has been a bit neglectful lately, doing things like staying gone for days and forgetting to inform me. And his divorce proceedings have been delayed because the court docket is too full. As usual, I roll my eyes and keep things moving. Like with Darren, who washed my feet again, and not only did my feet feel clean and soft, but I could just close my eyes and think of him and get wet.

I remember watching Darren blow hot breath on my feet. My toes curled up, he filled his mouth with hot tea and thick honey, placed his lips against my feet and started sucking on my toes until wetness came gushing out of my vagina. I cried and whimpered as he licked his way up my body, planting sweet kisses on my inner thighs, and kissing all around my cunt, teasing me until I grabbed his head and mashed him against me. "Damn, Darren," I whispered, and I wept as waves of pleasure washed over me time after time.

I actually didn't want to see him go that time. I enjoyed having him stick around, turning off his cell, and lying against my breasts, us enjoying some nice pillow talk until we both fell asleep. But when we woke up hours later and I discovered that my desktop computer was acting funny, I had to make him bounce because he "doesn't know anything about computers," and I sure know he doesn't have the money to take me to the computer-repair shop. That burned me up, all that good dick going to waste in a man who can't do anything for me.

The next day at work, I decide to change strategies and I send Seaphes an IM over the company messaging system.

DESparks: Can you come see me when you get a moment?

SHill: What's this about?

DESparks: I need your assistance.

SHill: K.

Seaphes walks in my office a whole freaking hour later, rubbing his eyes and yawning.

"What's the matter?" I ask. "You had a late night?"

"Not really. I've been so tired lately that I overslept today."

"And you didn't shave, either. I see some stubble on your chin. Looks nice though."

"Thanks. Now, how can I help you?"

"You know anything about computers?"

"Sure. What's wrong with yours?" He approached my desk and glanced at my PC.

"Oh, it's not the one here. It's at my house. Can you come take a look tonight? I've been working hard on my taxes, and I do not want anything to happen to my files."

"Hmmm, I dunno." He hesitates.

"I thought you said you know about computers."

"What's it doing?"

"I really can't describe it. Just come over and take a look."

"Where you stay?"

I pull up MapQuest on the Internet and print out directions from the office to my house.

"Oh, you want me to come there directly after work? Can't a brotha go home first, change and shower?"

"Sure, that would be best," I tell him, smiling.

He winks and starts to leave my office, but then stops. "What's your phone number?"

I call it out to him but am disappointed that he just writes it down instead of inputting the digits into his phone. He says bye and I let him go without a fuss.

"Okay, girl." I call Veron. "It's all set. He'll be dropping by my place tonight."

"Wow, you're good. So what do you plan to do?"

"He and I just got off on the wrong foot. I'll be putting in a good word for you," I say. Meanwhile, I'm thinking, I'll make him forget all about Ursula, that's for sure.

"I know you will, girl. Thanks. You're the best. I wish I could be a fly on the wall."

"Oh, you don't wanna do that." I giggle. "Talk later. I'm about to get off work. I need to go home and make sure the place is decent."

" 'K, do your thing."

My place is sparkling and clean and smelling fresh like usual. I got up an extra two hours early this morning and rubbed down all the walls with Pine-Sol and hot sudsy water before I left for work. I also defrosted some salmon so I could bake it later on and picked up some delicious vegetable dishes from Whole Foods.

After I'm done preparing dinner, I draw a hot bubble

bath. My phone beeps twice, indicating I have a voice mail message, but I continue soaping up my vagina with a sponge and squeezing hot water and bubbles on my breasts. It feels so good I almost don't want to get out of the tub. But I finally make myself get up, pat myself dry with a thick cotton towel, and lay naked on my bed while I listen to the voice mail.

"Hey, Demetria. It's Seaphes. Something has come up. A family issue. So I won't be able to swing by. Give me a call so we can reschedule."

I sit up. "No, he did not."

I am pissed. I turn off the oven and store the salmon in the refrigerator. Then instead of doing something destructive, I decide to just go to bed early with my headphones attached to my ears. I fall asleep for an hour and a half, but then my bladder wakes me up. I remove the headphones from my ears, then pick up my BlackBerry. Voice mail message. I get it on my way to the bathroom.

"Hey, Demetria, girl. Call me back when you can. I wanna know how things are going."

"They're going just perfect," I say out loud and delete Vee's message.

Still naked, I use the bathroom and run my fingers through my hair, which is wild and tangled with a bad case of bed head. Suddenly the doorbell rings. I go downstairs and, figuring it'll be Darren or Thad or someone else coming over to cheer me up, I sleepily open it up without first looking to see who it is.

Seaphes's eyes pop wide open.

"Oops," I say and slam the door in his face. I run to my closet to find my silk robe, pulling my arms through the sleeves and twisting the belt around my waist as I run back to the door. When I open it, he's facing the street.

"Sorry about that. It's okay to look now."

He lifts up his chin and walks on into my place.

"Seaphes, I thought you had some emergency. I didn't expect you to swing by."

"Well, sorry, things turned out okay, and I called but I guess you fell asleep. I decided to come by anyway since it's only nine."

"Whatev."

He follows me into the house, and I turn on a couple of lights so we can sit in my sunken living room.

"Nice crib."

"You want some wine? I have some Chablis."

"What about vodka?"

"Got that, too. Be right back."

I find some long-stemmed glasses and pour him some Grey Goose.

"Hold up," I tell him. I light three vanilla candles that are sitting on the mantel of my fireplace.

"Nice. This tastes good," he says, sipping on his drink.

He sets down his glass and peers at me for a minute. "Your hair."

I'm not wearing my weave. "Oh, my God, I'll be right back."

He stands up. "No, Demetria, no need to do all that. Just relax. Be yourself. Let me see the real you."

"Well, the real me would have every hair in place."

"No, she wouldn't."

Fuming, I snap, "How do you know what I normally do? Huh? You don't know me any better than I know you, yet you've told me things about myself that have no basis."

He slowly sits back down and nods. "You're right. My bad. But I still insist on seeing you natural. I mean, women get so afraid to let a man see if she's carrying extra baggage, unsightly hair, unpainted toenails." He glances down at mine. "Ah ha, but not the great Demetria Sparks."

"Okay," I say suspiciously. "Tell me something."

"Go ahead."

"Why do you have a split personality?"

"I have a split personality?"

"And why do you repeat things? That drives me crazy. It's like you can't hear straight or something."

He laughs out loud and takes another sip. "I'm sorry, no one has ever told me I have a split personality."

"Maybe I'm using the wrong terminology, but sometimes you seem like a decent man but other times . . ."

"I act like an asshole?"

"You said it."

"Look, Demetria, I guess you got hurt when I tried to assess you the other day. But I got the feeling you were fishing for a compliment, and I hate that. If you needed me to tell you that I think you look fine, just ask. I want to do that when I want to do it, not because I'm coerced."

The light from the candles is hitting Seaphes in just the right way, and he looks hot. I love what he just said, but how do I get him to keep complimenting me? When I say nothing he breaks the silence.

"You just hide behind a curtain that anyone can see through. I didn't mean to insult you—I was just trying to say that I've dated all kinds of women. And all of y'all fall into some basic categories. You, young lady, are no exception."

I pout, staring at Seaphes. "What you mean?" I whine, trying to be cute.

"Listen," he says. "If you are feeling me, why don't you just say so instead of playing all these high school games?"

"I beg your pardon?" I say, standing up. "What nerve. My man is fifty times better than you. I need you to help me with my computer, and believe me, if the stupid thing was working properly you wouldn't even be sitting inside my house right now. So before you come to more incorrect conclusions, let me show you my office so you can take a look. If you can fix it, fine. If not, no big deal."

He laughs while I'm fussing, and I want to throw him out on his ass, damn the computer. I wring my hands and start pacing back and forth. "I really think it's unfair for you to judge me like you have. You're a hypocrite of the worst kind, because the thing that you accused me of is the thing that you do."

"And what is that?" he says softly.

"Point blank? You don't know me, Seaphes."

"I know your type."

"But you don't know *me*. Admit it."

"Technically you're right."

"Technically? Why are you so stubborn? I could never be with a man like you."

"Does this mean you've thought about it," he grins, "or am I asking for too much information?"

"You know what, I think you should leave."

He stands up and takes a large gulp of his drink. "Demetria, tell me something. There really wasn't a computer problem, was there? Do you even have a computer?"

"Man, you are insane. Get the hell out my house. You got some nerve insulting me."

The smirk finally vanishes from his face, and he walks out the door. I fall back on the couch and hold my head between both my hands. What just happened here? I couldn't even handle a man like him. How in the hell does Veron think she can?

— 19 —

VERON

Men don't respond to words, they respond to no contact.

"Now I understand what the book is talking about," I say to myself. It's Friday and I'm in my HHR, on my way to work. I told Demetria I'd be back on Monday, but I decided to go in a day early. It's strange—I haven't known him for long, but not being able to talk to Seaphes these past few days made me feel like Jesus bleeding on the cross. But even Jesus rose from the dead, so now's a good time for me to make an appearance and test whether or not leaving a man alone for a while is really how to get his interest. I hope my absence has caused Seaphes to think hard about his actions, and I am curious to see whether he's remorseful. If not, I'd say he has a missing sensitivity chip.

When I pull up to the employee parking lot, I see that the only two empty spaces are near the far end of the perimeter. Great, I think. I'll have a bit of a walk. Grabbing my leather hobo bag and my briefcase, I shove a copy of my favorite book under my free arm and get out of the car. Immediately, I hear a horn honking and I look up. Seaphes waves and pulls in next to my vehicle.

Oh, no, I'm not ready for this yet.

I quickly pull out my cell phone and press the instrument to my ear.

"Hey, Mike, what's going on? Sorry to just now be calling you back," I say aloud, pretending to be chatting.

I hear footsteps behind me and feel a tap on my shoulder.

I glance back at Seaphes, who's gesturing at my briefcase, asking if I want him to hold it. I shake my head no and turn away with the phone. "Yep, it was good seeing you too." I laugh loudly.

When my phone actually starts ringing I stop walking.

"You gonna answer that?" Seaphes asks, stopping right next to me. I try to smile at him, but my eyes don't totally meet his. I press End on the phone and cut Demetria's call off.

"What's up, Veron? Why won't you talk to me?"

"I'm just kind of busy right now." I attempt to start walking again.

"I won't let you alone until you talk to me." His voice is loud enough to make my legs stop moving. "Are you really that angry with me? Or are you playing a game?"

"Oh, Seaphes, I've just—I've been busy."

"Too busy to return my calls?" He reaches inside his briefcase and pulls out another white rose and hands it to me. "I may not have all the right words to say, but maybe this will help communicate to you that I'd love nothing more than to have peace with you, and maybe a cup of coffee. Now you go get settled in your office, but I'll be coming to see you within the next twenty minutes, okay, Veron?"

"O-okay."

"See you in a bit." He leaves my side, confidently walking away from me with his head held high.

After I put my stuff down in my office, I take my rose and head straight to Demetria's office and shut her door. She is sitting at her desk and looks up at me with widened eyes. "What are you doing here?"

"Never mind that. Tell me what to do. He's making it easy and hard at the same time."

"He who?"

"Who else? He told me he's coming to see me in a few minutes, and he is actually behaving very sweet," I say and blush. "I like it, but I don't know how to react to this, especially since you told me that you saw him hugging on Ursula again while I was gone. Is this a trick?"

"Of course it is. Smoke and mirrors, girl. You've got to wise up. Stay here; let him come to your empty office. And we should talk anyway. I need to tell you what happened last night."

"Can't it wait?"

"No! I started to call you last night, but it was so late I thought you'd be sleep."

"Oh, yeah?" I say, eyeing her closely and sniffing my flower. "What happened?"

"Um, don't be impressed with all those flowers Seaphes is throwing at you. If a man is giving you flowers, it's usually because he feels guilty."

"Well, sure." I shrug. "He's trying to make up with me for using me to make Ursula jealous and all the misunderstandings."

"Girl, don't be naive. There's more going on between him and Ursula than he wants you to know."

I just stare at her openmouthed.

"They fucking!" she blurts.

"How you know?"

"She told me."

"And you believe her? I don't. She's lying."

"Girl, she and I had a long conversation last night—"

"How'd you end up talking to her?"

"Listen! And she described in detail how Seaphes has a mole on his left calf. She said his nipples are very taut and sensitive to the touch. She said he doesn't ever kiss her 'cause he has mono."

I sit down heavily.

"I'm sorry you have to hear this about your boy, but you need to know what you're dealing with."

"But . . . women lie."

"So do men." Demetria's eyes start glazing. "This one here, oh, he's a real piece of work. But you don't own him, so technically he can mess around with whomever he wants."

"Yep, that's true, I guess . . . but it's not what I want to hear." I start pacing and stare down at the ground. "If he doesn't really care for me, why doesn't he just leave me alone?"

"Men have a hard time explaining what they really feel on the inside, especially if it means they're going to have to face an angry woman when they do. Remember, Michael West told us how some men will lie just to spare your feelings?"

"Well," I say, looking directly at her. "I think I want to talk to Ursula face-to-face."

Demetria shrugs. "What good will that do?"

"She can tell me what happened . . . in her own words."

"What, you think I'm making this up or something?"

"No, never that. I'd just rather talk to her directly, just like I plan to talk to Seaphes directly."

"No, girl—don't talk to him directly. Bad idea."

"What, you have to run interference for me?" I ask. She just nods. Right—the book. "Okay, fine. Well, maybe you can get him alone and find out what he wants. It sounds like he's showing you his real side."

"I guess. I'll try running into him today and see if he still has that rotten attitude that he showed me."

"By the way, what exactly happened with y'all last night?"

"Nothing more than what's already happened."

Puzzled, I ask, "Can you be specific?"

"No, I gotta go," she says, glancing at her ringing phone. "I'm sure you need to get to work, too. We'll meet up later, alright?"

"I guess I have no other choice," I tell her. Too bad. I'm sure she's going to tell me what Seaphes said about me when they were hanging out last night, and I'm impatient to hear.

As I return to my office, my mind is like a busy, clogged-up expressway. There's so much going on—I'm trying to decipher Demetria's words, analyzing Seaphes's behavior and wondering what is really going on with him and Ursula. I want to trust him so much, but everyone is telling me not to and to do things against my instincts. I'm starting to really freak out. I wonder if I should have even come back to work today.

It just feels so familiar. It's like every time I meet someone, there's something or someone more worthwhile who captures his attention. I'm feeling that fear . . . but I'm not going to let it get to me. I'm not going to mope around this time, letting despair convince me that I'm not worthy to be loved. I'm going to ignore that negativity and face this.

I've survived so much. I'll survive this, too.

With that thought, I rush to the bathroom, close and lock the stall, and pray. And once peace wraps its fingers carefully around my heart, I emerge—sane, strong, and ready to take the next step, no matter where it leads me.

— 2 0 —

SEAPHES

Later that afternoon, I stand outside Veron's office. The door is open, but her back is turned and she doesn't know I'm here. I watch her as she opens and closes several drawers in a gray metal file cabinet, swinging her hip to close it. She's wearing a brown belted dress that tightly wraps around her backside. Her leather high heels are resting next to her feet. A pair of honey-colored thigh-highs is also strewn on the floor.

I swallow hard and tiptoe into her office, walking behind her to cover both her eyes with my hands.

She gasps. "Who's that?"

"Who do you want it to be?" I say, disguising my voice. I smile and move in closer so that the back of her head tickles my nose and the side of my face is pressed against hers. "You like how this feels?" I whisper.

"Mmmm," she giggles. I enjoy the feel of her wiggling hips pressed against me as she tries to balance herself on her feet.

"Why weren't you in your office when I came to see you?"

I feel her body stiffening up against mine. I want to reach out and hold her, but she pulls away.

"Seaphes?"

I remove my hands and ask, "You're disappointed it's me?"

She slowly turns around, her eyes narrowing. "I can't really answer that."

"Well, I'm happy to see you, too," I say, slightly sarcastic. "How was your break?"

"Not long enough." She turns her back to me and opens up a drawer.

"It's like that, huh?"

"No, I'm just kinda busy right now."

"I told you I was coming to see you this morning, but you weren't there. Didn't answer your phone. Why are you avoiding me?"

"Seaphes, we're cool. I just had a lot of things going on this morning." She repeats words that sound hollow, like her heart isn't in it, but she feels obligated to say them, anyway. Sometimes it's like this girl is two different people.

"Here, I have something for you," I say. She doesn't react at all. "Can you turn and look at me? I feel better if I can look in your eyes."

She turns to face me, her body contorted as if she's in anguish, and finally looks directly in my eyes. I stare deeply, trying to find the woman who I first got to know not too long ago.

"Here's my form for that Walk America event. Hope it's not too late."

"Never too late." She clears her throat. "I don't tell people this, because I want them to commit to coming, but you actually could have shown up on the day of the event and still walked. The paperwork isn't that important. But thanks, anyway."

"Is there anything I can do to get you to talk to me? Really be straight with me?"

"I am talking to you."

"But you're acting brand-new with me, Veron. Like we never hung out, never connected. And I don't like it."

"Well, what do you like, then?" She smirks at me, as if she's full of skepticism.

"I'd like," I say, kneeling down to pick up her thigh-high stockings. "I'd like to put these back on your legs."

She gasps and breaks eye contact. But I won't give up.

"Go sit on the chair, please."

Veron moves away from me, walking backward, until her bottom falls on the chair and she scoots back.

"Thank you," I tell her, and, holding a thigh-high in each hand, I approach her, getting down on one knee only inches away from her legs. I set aside the stockings and take her right foot in my hand, caressing it and watching her face all the while. She bites her bottom lip and grunts.

"Ah, ah, ah," I tease her. "I'm not even finished yet and you're making noise."

She groans again and I quietly laugh.

When I roll up one of the stockings and slide it onto her toes she catches her breath. "That tickles . . . but keep going."

I roll the other stocking over her left foot, up her calves, her thighs. "Now," I tell her, letting my hands rest on her thighs and gently rubbing the soft fabric. "Is there anything you want to talk to me about?"

"Um," says Demetria real loud, walking into the office. "What y'all two doing?"

"Not now, Demetria," Veron pleads. "Girl, let me get back with you in a few minutes."

Demetria just stands there. I continue to discreetly rub my fingers across one of Veron's thighs. She bites her bottom lip.

"This is embarrassing. Can you give me a moment, please, Demetria?"

"This is all wrong," Demetria complains. "How can you do

stuff like this in the open? Anyone can just walk up in here. Better be glad it was only me. Girl, you have a lot to learn."

"She'll be okay," I speak up, moving my hands off Veron's body. I'm suddenly embarrassed about my actions. I shouldn't be taking advantage of this lady, not at work. "And you're right; anyone could walk up in here. I'm sorry, Veron."

"Seaphes?" Veron says.

"I try not to conduct myself this way in the workplace. So let me get on outta here. And it was nice talking to you, Veron. Demetria. 'Bye."

"But—"

Veron's voice rings in my ear. But I keep going.

Later, my phone lights up and I see Demetria's name on caller ID. "Yeah."

"Seaphes, you gotta start using your brain."

"Meaning?" I ask.

"Veron isn't used to men like you. She gets caught up easily, and I don't want to see her get hurt."

"What makes you think I plan to hurt her?"

"It's just getting obvious that she likes you, and I want to make sure that when y'all do get involved, that you treat her the way she needs to be treated."

"And have I done anything wrong so far?"

"That's what I'm trying to point out to you. You gotta stop fucking up. I can help you out."

"Wait, hang on. If you're so worried about me hurting her, why are you trying to help me reach her? What are you getting out of this?"

"I have something to prove to you."

My ears prick up. "Like what?"

"I don't like how you sized me up and think you know me when you really don't. I want to show you how I can be and at the same time school you on how to handle my friend. She wasn't all that impressed with those white roses, hadn't you even noticed?"

When I was silent, Demetria says, "I told you. You need to listen to me. As a matter of fact, what are you doing tonight? Let's meet."

"Uh, I have something to do."

"Cancel it," she commands. "You still never fixed a sista's computer, so you can kill two birds with one stone."

"Maybe that's not where I want to be tonight, Demetria," I say.

"Then you won't know what you're missing," she says, and hangs up. I'll have to think about this one.

When I ring her doorbell, she calls out that the door is open, and I hear the sound of water steadily running in her bathroom. Unable to resist, I walk toward the splashing noises and stop to stare at her, laughing as she furiously runs a sponge over and around the porcelain sink and countertops.

"You don't have to do all that."

"Oh, but I do," she explains. "Some old toothpaste is still glued to the counter and it just annoys me. I should've wiped it up a while ago. Sorry."

"See, that's why I like you, Veron. Why are you apologizing? And anyway, a messy counter is nothing."

"Can you go back and repeat what you said?"

"I said a messy counter ain't anything to worry about."

"Seaphes!" And her lips spread into a smile that bubbles up through the surface of her heart.

I reach out to her, take that soggy sponge out of her hand, toss it to the floor and grab her precious face between my fingers. Looking down into her engaging eyes, I enjoy the feeling of her looking back up at me.

"I've wanted to do this for a long time." Closing my eyes, I move my face nearer to hers. I can feel her heart beating out of her chest.

But I think twice about my actions—I don't want to move too quickly with this. I don't want to scare her away. I move away and open my eyes.

"That's enough."

"It is?" She gasps.

"It is. Let's go sit back on your couch."

She nods her head, lets me take her by the hand, and we go sit down.

"Thanks for the carrot cake," I say. "How'd you know it's my favorite?"

"A lucky guess?"

"You guess well, young lady."

"Thanks."

"So, I have to say, I'm shocked you let me swing by."

Veron nods. "I guess I was curious. You said that what you wanted was so important that it couldn't wait or be done over the phone."

"Not everything can be done over the phone."

My cell rings and I see Demetria's name pop up. "I'll let it go into voice mail."

Veron says, "You could've gotten that. I would have excused myself." But then her eyes harden, and she seems to be having some kind of inner dialogue.

"We're disconnecting, Veron. What's up?"

"It's just that I get conflicting responses from you. It makes me feel on edge. And I don't know who might be calling you, you know? Oh, let me be quiet, sometimes I talk too much, just like you."

"No, talking is good. Silence can hurt. At least I know where you're coming from instead of trying to guess. I want to know how you feel."

I scoot closer to her and finally kiss her. She smells like sandalwood, something I didn't expect. I push my tongue into her mouth, and she responds, rolling her tongue on top of mine then pulling out and giving me a few sweet kisses on my lips before she leans back.

"I am getting hot," she grunts, wiping her forehead with the back of her hand.

"I'm hot, too," I admit, adjusting my dick.

She blushes deep red and looks away. Suddenly I realize that Demetria was right—this girl is vulnerable, maybe doesn't know how to handle this stuff. "I really see what she's talking about now—" Shit. I can't believe I let that slip out.

Veron stands up. "I'm sorry, what? What was that? How would you like it if I was mentioning other men around you?"

"Hey, calm down. I didn't mean to do it."

"Well, don't, then. It hurts." She sits back down.

"I'm sorry, Veron." We sit quietly for a few minutes, and even though I want to break the silence, I resist the pressure to talk. I take her hand in mine and play with it for a moment. Her hands are warm. Within minutes, we resume kissing, and this time, she initiates.

Her landline rings but she doesn't get up.

Her talking caller ID machine says, "Call from Landers Ferris. Call from Landers Ferris."

Amused, I watch her hop up and run to her answering machine, which is sitting on top of the breakfast bar between the kitchen and the dining room. She fumbles around with the machine, frantically pressing on buttons, but a male voice screams out.

"Hey, baby girl, it's me. You get that money I sent you?"

"What?" she shrieks. "Aw man, I don't believe him."

She lowers the volume and looks like she wants to come back and sit next to me but changes her mind.

"Who was that?" I demand.

"You're kidding, right?" She laughs in amazement.

"No, I'm not. I need to know what I'm dealing with. Is that a husband?"

"Seaphes, don't get your panties in a bunch. It's nobody. Just a friend."

"A nobody friend that gives you money."

She looks apologetic but then straightens her shoulders and hardens her face. Her voice changes. "I can't help it if men want to pamper me."

I can't believe it. This girl really is just like her no-good friend. I thought she was different. "I think I've seen, and heard, enough." I stand up. "It's been good."

"C'mon, Seaphes, please don't do this."

"I just want you to be honest with me."

"Okay, then, you be honest with me, too."

"I have been."

"Can you honestly say that?" Her voice chokes with pain. This night is getting stranger by the moment.

"Veron, if you need to say something, just say it."

"Have you ever slept with Ursula?"

"What?"

"I've seen you hugging on her at work, and I've heard about what you do with her from others."

"You believe everything you hear?"

"Not really. But I do believe what I see."

"And you're telling me you've seen me sleep with Ursula?"

She pouts. "I catch on to body language. And it amazes me that you can be all over her yet deny that you are attracted to her. That's just plain wrong."

"Things aren't always the way they appear."

"And sometimes they are. I'm inclined to go with my gut on this one."

There's no changing her mind; she's made that clear. And with that dude calling and what she said about men and money . . . I'm done. "Okay," I tell her, throwing up my hands. "I'm out."

I leave Veron's place and stop by Demetria's.

"I tried to warn you, but you don't listen to me," Demetria says after I finish telling her what happened. It's 11 p.m., later than I realized, and I should be with my nephew, since they're rolling out tomorrow to drive to San Antonio. But obviously I need some help on this.

Is it my imagination, or did Demetria look envious when I confessed to her that Veron and I kissed for the first time?

"Seaphes, I told you she ain't used to prime beef. She has messed around with so many knuckleheads that I'm scared her insecurities might run you away. But I know your type and I think you can handle it. But you have to quit messing up like you've been doing. She really is pissed at you because she busted you and Ursula."

I feel nauseous at her words but manage to sip my drink and watch her confidently stride around her living room, lighting a match and holding it against the wicks of several vanilla and cinnamon candles. When she's finished, she casually combs her fingers through her thick hair as if she doesn't give a damn about anything.

"Okay, so you were saying that you give in. Does that mean you're ready to do what I tell you?"

"Well, I don't know about that. But I want to ask you some things about Veron, so I can decide what approach I need to take." I look around, uncomfortable for a second. "So she's mad at me, huh?"

"Extremely."

"You think she'd be okay with me being over here?"

"Actually, she doesn't mind at all, because she realizes I've got to help her out, filter info for her."

"If you say so," I murmur.

"I know so."

"Okay. So. Can you tell me who this Ferris dude is?"

Eyes widened, she grins like she's enjoying herself. "Did he come by or something?"

"Who *is* he?"

"Ferris is the impetus. He caused Veron to figure out what she really wants in life."

"So he's someone who treated her bad?"

"I guess you have him to thank for her being open to a man like you."

I laugh at the irony. "I guess I'm a lucky guy that Ferris has done whatever he's done to her."

"He's done more to her than you could ever imagine," she says, a mischievous look in her eyes.

"Such as?" I ask leaning in.

"You know, dog—oh, I shouldn't be telling you all this. It feels strange."

"You're a tease, you know that?"

"You know you unfairly judged me. Teases are attention

whores. Do I look like the type of woman who's desperate for attention?"

"To be honest, I don't give a lot of thought about how you look."

"Say what?" she asks, insulted. "Are you implying that I'm ugly?"

"Look, Ms. Demetria Sparks. I wasn't trying to imply that you are unattractive. And since you're forcing me to say it, you are one gorgeous woman. But you know it, and that's half the problem."

"And what is the rest of my problem?"

"You ready to hear truth? I think you're used to men falling all over you, and if they don't, for some reason you get bent. You can't deal. The controlling part of you emerges."

"Okay." She pouts and twists a chunk of her hair into a circle. "I don't know that I totally agree with you, but thanks for explaining yourself. I guess I can act mature and officially forgive you."

"So you're not mad at me anymore? We're cool again?"

"Well, Seaphes, I don't allow people I don't like in my home."

The tone of her voice is serious. She refills my glass. Then she drops to her knees, sitting next to my feet. She grabs one of my legs and props it on the glass coffee table. Removing each shoe, she asks, "That feel better?"

I nod, "It's alright, I guess."

She shakes her head. "See, now if Veron were me, and you were sitting next to her like you are with me, this is what I'd tell her to do." Looking into my eyes, she takes my foot in her hand and starts rubbing one slender finger against the underside. "I'm a master at caressing feet," she tells me. I want to tell her to stop, but I let her keep going. I tell myself it's just to see what else she's going to do, how far she's going to go.

"Pretend like I'm Veron." She smiles at me.

"Uh, sorry, but I can't do that," I apologize. "You and she are total opposites."

"Look, Seaphes," she says, exasperated. "Don't make things so difficult."

I just shrug.

"Stay with me." She clears her throat and talks in a soft, sweet voice. "Oh, Seaphes, Demetria told me everything I need to do to capture the attention of a man like you. Do you think she's done a good job so far?"

"Nope."

Demetria drops my foot. "You're such an ass."

"Does that mean you've got to stop massaging my foot?"

She rolls her eyes and sighs, gesturing at me with her finger.

"You're asking me to come closer?" I ask. "Veron?"

"Yes, Seaphes, come closer to Veron."

I shrug and move in closer. She puts her arms around my neck until we're cheek to cheek. Her soft skin is warm, and against my wishes, I feel something stirring down below. We're both silent, listening to each other breathe.

"Demetria."

"You mean Veron."

"Thing is, you're not Veron. You're Demetria."

"Well, yeah, we're just playing."

"Are you?"

"Damn, forget it. Why do I even go through all this?" She moves off me, glaring with an icy stare. "I'm telling you what I'm doing. Why I'm doing it."

"I'm not so sure you are."

"Oh, wait. I forgot, for some odd reason you think every woman is in love with you."

"Not every woman," I say solemnly.

She stares at me, and by the look on her face I know I'm about to get thrown out of the woman's house for the second time in a week. I cannot believe this.

"Why are you laughing?" she asks, staring at me. "What's so funny, huh? You're something else, Seaphes."

"Why, thank you. Now, I do gotta be going."

She looks up at me, genuinely sad and hurt. This is a girl who is not used to a man leaving her house of his own free will, and she looks embarrassed. "Listen," I say, getting up from the couch and draining the last remnants of my drink. "You ain't gotta worry about thinking that you're unattractive or anything like that."

"If what you're saying is true, prove it to me."

"How can I prove it?"

"Stay with me tonight."

— 21 —
Demetria

"Listen, woman. I'll stay here if you need me to, but it's just 'cause I'm worried about you." Seaphes follows me back into the living room, and I hope to hell he can't see me smirking.

"I'll be right back, okay?" I tell him. My voice sounds shrill.

Damn, why did I say that? I know I shouldn't do this, but I can't stop it. What's the real reason that he's staying? Is it really because he's worried, or does he want me like I want him? I shouldn't do this. I shouldn't do this, but it's hard when you've been through what I've been through.

I go to my main hallway and open a closet door. I hesitate for a few seconds, fighting with myself, but then reach up and pull out two goose-filled comforters and several throw pillows.

When I return to the living room, Seaphes has removed his shoes and socks and is running his hands over a two-inch stack of magazines that are neatly lying in a wooden rack. "*Vogue, Vanity Fair, Cosmo, Hype Hair, Essence, Glamour, Ebony,* and *O,*" he says, sounding skeptical.

"What about them? I'm big on reading and keeping empowered with knowledge."

"So would you say you are a product of the advice of these magazines?"

"Partially. Some of what I've become is through hard life experiences, or other women I've observed. Basically I know enough to use what works for me, and the rest I don't worry about."

"Ah ha."

"Seaphes, women have the burden of always being on top of their game. I gotta do what I gotta do."

"Is that why I'm here?"

"I'm hoping you're here . . . because you want to be." I feel weird trying so hard to get this man to notice me, but I can't help myself. I guess we always want what we don't have.

"Okay," he says. He walks up to me and helps me spread one of the comforters on the couch facing my HDTV, which I barely watch. I continue talking about myself for a few seconds, but then I switch gears.

"Are you sure you're okay with this?"

"What? Okay with sleeping in here while you comfortably rest in your big ole bed?"

"How you know how big my bed is?"

"I don't. A wild guess, knowing your type."

Seaphes hesitates for a few seconds, then walks up to me and places his arms around me, giving me a hug that doesn't quite allow him to press himself against my titties and hold me tight. It feels nice, and I forget all about being good.

"Let's act like I'm Veron," I nervously whisper into his ear, trying to take his hand in mine and attempting to lead him into the bedroom.

"I can't do that, Demetria." He lets go of my hand. "Like it or not, I'm pursuing Veron, and I don't want to fuck that up."

I can't help myself. "But she doesn't even want you, Seaphes. I didn't want to tell you, but Veron thinks you're bad news and sleeping with Ursula, and anyway she got Ferris calling her all the time." His face is falling. I am awful, but

I just can't help but give in to my throbbing pussy. All I can think of right now is what's gonna get this man in my bed. "She told me you don't have a chance. She's just keeping you around to watch you squirm."

"That . . . that doesn't sound like Veron." He sits down on my couch, head in hands.

"No? Well, who knows her better, you or me?" I sit next to him, run my fingers over his scalp, down his neck. "Didn't you hear that phone call from Ferris earlier tonight? He's been giving her money to keep her on lock."

We sit in silence for a minute, me playing with his ears. He's looking hurt, then mad . . . but then he starts paying attention to what I'm doing. I kiss his neck.

"What do your magazines say about being attracted to a man like me?"

"Uh, actually I've never really met a man like you."

"Awww, c'mon." He groans loudly. "According to you, you've had lots of experience."

"True that, but you're kinda different."

"How so?"

"You just . . . I mean, you never asked me out, never sought me out, even though we've been working in the same building for the longest time."

"Huh. Well, I don't know why I didn't. That hurt your feelings?"

I nod. "It made me feel invisible. Undesirable. I am not used to feeling like that."

"What are you used to?"

I take both of Seaphes's hands and maneuver them until they're gently lying on top of my breasts. He closes his eyes, looking like he's in pain, but it passes. Staring at him, I hope to God that he feels me and doesn't shut down what I hope to do to him. I take one of his index fingers and begin circling it around my hardened nipple. I look down at my shirt then back up at him. I love how quiet it is right now; it adds to the anticipation. I let go of his finger and smile when he continues circling and caressing my nipple on his own. He takes his other hand and massages my other breast. Even though I still have on my blouse, his hands feel electric, and my eyelids start to flutter.

"Are you used to this?" He begins to slowly unbutton my blouse, removing it so that my bra is exposed. He unfastens it from the front, and my breasts bounce out. I want to scream when his fingers finally make contact with my nipples. He strokes the hardness over and over, making them even more rigid, and it feels so good that I begin whimpering.

"Are you used to that?" he whispers.

I know it's wrong, but I place my hands around his head and push his mouth toward my breast. He opens his mouth, sticks out his long tongue, and begins licking me like a thirsty cat. His teeth gently tug at my nipple, then he hungrily sucks on it with his warm mouth. I squirm, moving my hips, and groan, and squeeze his head tight. "Are you used to that?" he moans.

I position myself so that I am lying on the floor. He falls down with me, his teeth never letting go of my breasts. I reach down to unzip, then begin pulling my blue jeans down my legs. He stops long enough to help me pull them all the way off, then resumes licking and sucking my breasts, rubbing my thighs at the same time.

I'm completely naked, and he still has all his clothes on, which is such a turn-on . . . for him, too, I can tell. The smell of sex and desire is strong. I cross my legs, afraid that the aroma mixed with my throbbing wetness will cause me to orgasm before his big, hard dick is ever inside me.

"Demetria," he whispers, "you're fucking beautiful."

"*That's* what I'm used to," I moan, tears suddenly gushing out of me like water from a running faucet.

He presses his lips against mine, his whiskers tickling my top lip, and we hungrily explore each other's mouths. His hot hands continue caressing me: my legs, ankles, ass, the sides of my breasts, my neck, nose, cheeks, and eyelids. I love it when a man kisses my eyelids. It feels like I'm relinquishing my power, yet maintaining it, too.

I reach for his body, and he stops touching me so he can remove his own shirt and pants. I press my nose against the strength of his neck. He smells like soap. Part of my mind is only thinking about how I'm getting satisfied, but there is a small part that's wondering how the heck I let myself go this far with this man. I want to stop, but I can't. I can't stop until the need is fulfilled, the need to be awash in total pleasure with another person, someone who wants me, our bodies surrendering to the euphoria. Seaphes gets his pants off and maneuvers himself above me, ready to enter my warm wetness.

But then he says, bewildered, "I can't believe we're about to do this."

"Let's stop talking about it and just do it," I complain, reaching for his neck.

"Damn, I dunno, Demetria . . . I feel . . ."

My phone starts ringing, loud and close to my head.

"Fuck," I say, sitting up. I glance at the caller ID. "I need to get this," I apologize to Seaphes.

I cover my shoulders with my blouse and retreat to the privacy of my bedroom. "Hello?" I say, trying to maintain normal breathing.

"Hey, girl, I'm so sorry that I called you this late, but I can't sleep. I'm so worried."

"What happened?" I asked.

"Seaphes came over and at first things were good. But then I began to question him, and we had words and he got upset and abruptly left. I hate when that happens, Demetria, but I do not want to keep repeating the same mistakes with guys. So I let him go, trying to act like it doesn't bother me, because I'm a strong woman who has a life, like the book says, yada, yada . . . but you don't know how bad I wanted to go after him. And now I want to call him, I want to make sure he's feeling me as much as I'm feeling him and tell him that I don't want my stupid mistakes to come between us."

"Okay," I tell her. "You know you can't call him. You gotta stay in control by letting him call you first. Even if it's your fault. Just give it till tomorrow or through the weekend and *do not* contact him first. You know this!"

"I know, I know, but sometimes it's so hard. I know you're right, though. There have been plenty of times guys were pissed, and I called the man just for him to treat me worse."

"There ya go. Learn from your mistakes."

"Yeah. Maybe . . . maybe you can talk to him for me. Or call him and ask him what's going on, like you don't know anything . . . just see what he says. Will you do that for me? Tomorrow?"

"Girl, no problem whatsoever. Uh, can you give me his number, though? I think I have it, but give it to me again just in case."

"Yeah, here it is."

I can't believe the lengths I go to. I should be ashamed. Am I? Don't know. We chat a bit, then hang up.

When I look up I see Seaphes standing beautifully naked in my doorway.

"How long you been standing there?"

"I just got here. It took you so long I felt kinda weird. You were talking to your man or something?"

"No, it wasn't like that at all. Just something I had to handle that couldn't wait."

"But I could wait?"

"Don't be mad. I'll make it up to you." I walk over to him and try to grab his dick, but he steps back out of my reach.

"Oh, okay," I say. I nod at his penis.

"You were on the phone for a long time."

"It's probably just as well," I say, to my own surprise.

"You're not in the mood?" he asks, sounding shocked yet relieved.

"To be honest, nope, I'm not. That phone call took a lot out of me," I admit wistfully, grateful to have that telephone interruption as my excuse for what's really going on inside of me.

"Then don't answer it next time," he says in an unconvincing voice.

"I'll remember that." I gesture at him to follow me back into the living room, but he grabs me around the waist and holds me tight, making me feel happy and secure.

"I'm glad we didn't do it," he murmurs. "I'm sooo glad we didn't go there."

I stiffen. "You are? Why not? You don't want me?" I ask, letting my pride get the best of me.

"I just think it wouldn't have been the right move. Don't get me wrong, I could fuck the life out of you and it probably would have been real good, but this here is the best outcome. We weren't meant to be."

I grit my teeth. Slowly, I say, "I think you're right."

And as I'm walking him out, I'm thinking about Veron and wondering what I'm going to do the next time I talk to her.

— 22 —

Veron

I sit behind the wheel of my car, shaking, until I can no longer see the SUV, until its taillights disappear in the darkness.

"Let me get this over with," I say to myself. I take a deep breath and walk up the sidewalk and ring the doorbell.

"Veron?" Demetria says, squinting and rubbing her eyes. She's wearing a wrinkled blouse and some slacks.

"You were asleep?"

"Uh, I was . . ." But that's all she says.

"May I come in?"

She hesitates for a second but opens the door.

"Did I interrupt something?" I ask, a bit sharply.

"What, you giving me attitude? Aren't you the one popping over to my crib without warning?"

"Yep, I am. Why was an Armada parked outside your house just a few minutes ago?"

"W-what?"

"What nothing. I just rolled up but noticed his ride. What was he doing here?"

"He who? You mean that lame-ass Seaphes?"

"So he *was* here?"

"Girl, yeah, you told me to ask him what was up. I asked him to come by to fix my computer."

"I didn't mean to have him over that very second! And does fixing your computer mean having a blanket and some pillows lying on the floor?"

She sighs heavily. "Girl, you are tripping big time. Darren was over here, too. When Seaphes arrived Darren got pissed, so he rolled out."

My hands are trembling and so is my heart. I hate fussing with anyone, let alone my best friend. When she walks over to me and wraps her arms tightly around me and pats me gently on the back, I take deep breaths and am able to regain my composure.

"Girl, have a seat. You want something to drink?"

"I see you've already been drinking," I say looking at the two glasses sitting on her coffee table.

"You know, I wanted to find out some of his likes, et cetera, so it was very good info. I killed two birds with one stone. Oh, and he doesn't have mono—"

"How you know that?"

"Don't yell at me, girl. I asked him about Ursula, and he said he isn't sick, he just didn't want to kiss her stupid ass."

"Oh my God, so he *has* been intimate with her? I feel so dumb."

"Don't feel dumb. You know he was trying to push up on Ursula. As much as you don't want to think about it, yeah, they've done things . . . but it was before this. Don't let that bother you."

"Why shouldn't I?"

"Because he knows about Ferris, right? I mean, you can't deny your own past."

I nod. "That's one of the reasons we kind of fell out, because Ferris has bad timing. He called and left this voice mail message that Seaphes never should have heard."

"Like I said before, don't even let that factor into things. We all have pasts; trust me when I tell you."

Demetria brings me a glass filled with alcohol, but I shake my head. "I'm straight."

"Now, why are you over here at dark-thirty?" she asks, glancing at her watch.

"Like I told you before, I was so upset I didn't know what to do. I tried to get to sleep after we talked, but I couldn't. I had to get out of the apartment."

"Well, you'll be alright, just give it some time. Calm down, and I'll help you get through this."

"What else can you tell me about him? Did he talk about me?"

"Girl." She pouts and rolls her eyes. "I can't get the man to stop talking about you. Veron this, Veron that."

"Really? Don't lie, Demetria."

"I swear 'fore God you always come up in the conversations."

"That's amazing."

"Yeah, but he seemed pretty pissed about the Ferris thing. I tried to calm him down some, but I don't know, girl."

"You were talking to him about my ex?"

"I know. I had to change the conversation, because it was too weird fucking."

"What?"

"I mean too fucking weird. That I was the one telling him about Ferris. You know what I'm trying to say." She laughs.

"Well, thanks for talking to him. I hope he's not totally pissed at me. I want to see him again."

"I'm sure you do. Hey, let me go back to bed, and by the morning I can come up with a good plan. Y'all need to take it to the next level." She yawns again and raises both her hands toward the ceiling, stretching.

"Demetria, why is your bra lying on the floor?"

She shrugs casually. "Girl, you know how much I hate those things. I took it off."

"In front of Seaphes?"

"I turned my back around and took it off and dropped it." I stare at her. She continues, "What? He was in the bathroom when I did it."

"Then why would you turn your back around?"

"What?" She laughs. "You so sleepy you aren't even sounding logical. You ready to crash? I sure as hell am." She staggers like a drunk toward her bedroom.

"You wanna spend the night with me?" she yells.

"No, I do not," I say, following her into her room. She has pulled off her blouse and is now sitting in bed with her breasts exposed.

"Do you mind?" I ask.

"Girl, stop acting like a prude. You've seen the twins before."

"Some of everybody has seen the twins," I murmur under my breath.

"What you say?" She laughs.

I finally sit down. "How are you and Darren doing? And whatever happened to Thad?"

"I don't feel like talking about them."

"Why not?"

"Hello, don't you see me sliding up under the covers?" she says, jumping in her bed. "I'm sleepy, Vee. Damn, catch a hint. Either chill out here with me or go home to your own bed."

"Fine. But I have too much energy to just go straight to sleep." I sit on the edge of her bed and remove my sneakers and socks.

Demetria says, "Will you be a sweetheart and turn off the lamp for me?"

"Sure," I say and turn the knob on her bedside lamp. It feels like the room's darkness has placed a wall between us. I get in bed, but she's already breathing deep. When I'm sure she's fallen asleep, I look for her BlackBerry. And when I look at the most recent numbers dialed and received, it's weird that none of the calls include Darren. What's even stranger is the call she placed to Seaphes before I talked to her tonight, even though she said she doesn't have his phone number.

— 2 3 —

Demetria

When I wake up the next morning, I roll over and glance at the clock: almost 10 a.m. I groan, go make my bladder gladder, then brush my teeth so that my mouth feels fresh and not so gummy.

I walk out into the living room to look out the bay window. "Good," I say aloud when I don't see Vee's HHR.

Later I decide to text Darren Foster. I send him a message that says "Call me." And thirty seconds later, the phone rings

"Yo, baby, what's happening? You want me to come over and fuck you?"

"Maybe later. I want to know why you left like you did last night. And why you pop over here without calling first? You know my situation."

"Yeah, but I thought ole dude be outta town all the time. And I had your fine ass all on my mind, and it wouldn't rest until I could see you again. That okay?"

"It's cool you wanna see me, but you need to be calling a sista first. You never know," I say, smiling over the fact that he wants to be with me so bad.

"I see that. Now who was that corny looking dude that swung by?"

"He's just a coworker. We were working on something."

"You better not be fucking him."

"Man, you don't tell me who I can or cannot fuck, what the hell is your problem?" I say, secretly happy that he's so jealous. I kinda dig that he wants me all to himself. I love being valued.

"Damn, I was just messing with you."

"Well, you oughta know better than to do that," I say, gently fussing. "Darren, don't mess up a good thing."

"Now, you know I ain't trying to do that." He pauses. "Did I do alright on the cash tip last night?"

"What? Those two bills you slid to me before you left? I kinda think you did that just to show my coworker that you got me like that or something. But hey, whatever motivates you to tear me off with some is cool with me."

"Was it alright?"

"It was alright, Darren baby. I appreciate the support." Although I give him a hard time I really do love his efforts, love that he's always thinking about pleasing me.

"Not that you need it."

"A woman always needs money, don't forget that. You never have to ask her, just hand it to her and she'll suck your dick forever."

"Well, why didn't you suck mine?"

"Coworker and I needed to take care of some business. I was sorry you had to bounce, but hey, business is business."

"Yeah, yeah, yeah."

"Awww, Darren baby, don't be mad," I coo sweetly. "Quiet as it's kept I miss you already. When can we see each other again?"

"I don't know; I'm busy."

"Too busy to kick it with me?"

"Listen, I'll make sure and see your fine ass sometime this weekend, okay?"

"Me and my putty tat will be waiting."

I say more sweet words to him, and we finally hang up. I gotta give it to ole Darren. At least he's trying. I kinda feel for him. He's got problems with his home chick. Since I wasn't gonna be exclusive, I guess he went on and got with whoever was next in line. Weird to say, but I think he deserves better than that woman. But as long as I can still get a significant piece of his loving and know that in his heart he really does treasure me, then who am I to say anything?

Now, with Darren taken care of, I text the same message to someone else. "Call me."

He also calls me within seconds.

"Hey there," Seaphes says, dullness saturating his voice.

"What's up?" I sound three times more excited than him.

"Not much," he says. He sounds bad.

"I called to talk to you about Veron," I say.

He immediately sounds perkier. "Yeah? Why? Thought you said she was over it."

"No, I talked to her again last night, and she was just mad. Ferris is old news, to tell you the truth."

"Why'd you tell me he was her man?" Seaphes asks. He sounds mad.

"Listen, I said that so you'd quit hassling her, 'cause I thought that's what she wanted. Don't be upset, I was just trying to be a good friend to her. But she still likes you for whatever reason. But listen, you need to step up your game with her. She's getting restless."

"What do you mean?"

"You need to be more attentive and stop tripping, running out the door every time she says something you don't like. She still thinks you're prime beef, but you acting like three-week-old hamburger."

"Awww, that hurts."

"I'm just saying; take care of your business with my girl. You don't want her to think that you like me, do you?"

"Why would I like you?"

Shit, I didn't mean to get flirty. Got to keep straight here. "Uh, that's what I'm talkin' 'bout," I say, frowning. "Keep focused on the right thing, even though you might be doing the wrong thing."

"I'll see what I can do."

"Call her, go see her, something, okay? In like a few hours or so. Pretty please?"

"For you," he teases, "I'll do almost anything."

"Almost?" I say, insulted.

And he hangs up.

I remind myself that I have to be careful not to confuse the people who are around me. But when you're trying to be strong and not succumb to temptation, you're always going to give out mixed signals.

Later, I meet Veron at an out-of-the-way, full-service hair salon located off Highway 288 near Pearland. She was going to get a relaxer, so I decided to get my nails and toes done and hang with her. The smell of water, shampoo, and conditioner saturates the entire business. She's sitting at a booth, and I come sit down next to her.

"You doing better now?" I ask.

"A little." She doesn't give me eye contact.

"Don't worry about anything."

"That's easy for you to say. Shhh," she says as her stylist returns to the booth holding a jar full of relaxer.

"We'll talk later," I tell her and get up so I can go place my feet in a bucket of hot water. I sit in the comfortable chair and enjoy the seat massage that pokes and prods at my upper and lower back muscles as the water washes the grittiness off my skin. I'm thinking about Veron and what I can do to make her more like me . . . and whether I really want her to be.

By the time my nails are done, Veron is sitting under the dryer getting a wrap.

"You feeling alright?" I ask.

She smiles and nods.

"It's about time. What's happened?"

"Seaphes called and asked to take me out."

"Good for you," I tell her, trying to exhibit genuine happiness.

"I told him no."

Confused, I ask, "What you do that for?"

"He asked to take me out tonight. I told him I don't do last-minute dates."

Inside I'm thinking, what's that about? But I tell her, "Oh, smart move, you must be following the book's advice. Make the man think you have other things going."

"I wanted to say yes so bad. But I need this man to respect me."

"You're sounding like me."

"I need to do more than sound like you." She hesitates but then looks me squarely in my eyes. "I sense that you two are getting along better."

I shrug. "He's an ass, but I get along with him for your sake."

"Well, whatever's happening now, he'll eventually like you. Guys do that all the time. I should be used to it by now, I guess."

"Nooo, Vee. Nope. I think he's more into you."

"*More* into me? More than he's into you?" She has a hurt sound in her voice.

"No, he does not like me. We fight a lot. More than you and him put together. Why would a guy want to deal with my attitude?"

"I dunno. Why do they?"

"I don't know, Vee. Listen, I think you should just concentrate on doing what you need to do. You told him no, but did you give him an alternate date and time?"

"As a matter of fact, I did. I told him that all three of us can go out midweek."

"What? Why the hell you do that? That's weird."

"I want to observe you more and see how you do things, so I can pick up on some of that," she says, eyeing me closely.

"Girl, that was a wrong move if there ever was one. I will give you advice, but why do I wanna be there with you and your man during your date?"

"I thought it would be fun," she says with a fake smile.

I ignore her attitude. "Look, Veron, you oughta go be with him. You don't need me tagging along, me and him getting into a big argument and spoiling everything. Plus, what would you do with me if you decide you're ready to give him some?"

"You could watch. I can teach you a few tricks."

"Ha, in your dreams. But no thanks. I am not into voyeurism."

She laughs, this time with much more sincerity, but I feel too conflicted to join in.

— 24 —

VERON

When Seaphes calls me hours after I get home from the hair salon, I don't pick up. And when he calls me again a couple of hours after the last time, I give him the busy button. Even though I want to talk to him, and he obviously wants to talk to me.

This is so stupid, I say to myself. Is this what it takes for Demetria to get all her men?

— 2 5 —

DEMETRIA

"You want me to get him on the phone?" I ask Veron. We're hanging out at her crib a week after the beauty salon, finishing up lunch.

"No, that's okay. I just don't understand why he hasn't gotten back to me. I finally accepted his call, we talked and worked things out, and we were all set to go on this date, and now I haven't heard from him."

"See, girl, I told you, you gotta watch out for him. He does things that are ignorant as hell."

"It makes him look bad," Vee admits, "and all these nice things that he did don't seem to mean anything now."

"You still got food on your plate," I tell her. I grab a fork and stick it into a wide piece of lettuce, onions, and fat chunks of feta cheese. "Mmm, this is some good stuff." I chew a little. "Listen, Vee, you have to nip this kind of behavior. Like the book says, the things you start out doing is what's going to keep happening. So everything your boy does now, he's gonna keep doing it unless you tell him to make changes."

Vee laughs even though I hardly cracked a joke.

"I feel like this is my fault," I tell her, trying to shift the blame to myself. I know I need to chill out, but these strong urges to be closely involved overtake me.

"What do you mean?" she asks.

"I just feel like if I hadn't been so hard on him for continually fucking up he might have called already."

"Huh. Come to think of it, yeah. Maybe that's it."

"Hold up." I grab my phone, dial Seaphes, and place the call on speaker.

"Hey, Seaphes, this is Demetria. Why haven't you called Vee? We were all supposed to go out this week."

"Listen, Demetria. I overheard your conversation with Veron on Monday at work and didn't appreciate you telling her that—" I push the speakerphone button so that only I can hear him. I know what he's talking about. On Monday I let something slip about Seaphes kissing me. I covered it up by saying I meant that he kissed me on the cheek, but he must not have heard that part.

"Well, she needs to know that you can be friendly at times, and that it shouldn't be misinterpreted," I tell him.

"Whatever, Demetria. That pissed me off."

"Then you should have hung around and defended yourself," I say, walking into the other room so Vee can't hear.

"I shouldn't have to defend myself from you! Listen, what happens between me and Veron should stay that way."

"Okay," I pout, feeling like he's socked me in the jaw. "I will try to do better."

"Are you sure? 'Cause I'm not trying to get messed up with *two* women here. I like her, but it's just been too much."

I promise, and before we hang up, I tell him about the mix-up that he overheard and how I fixed it.

"Vee, I'm about to leave. He's coming over. He told me to stay outta y'all's business."

"Oh, girl. I know you've been talking to both of us, but I guess he just means that we gotta work things out on our own. But I need you."

"Girl, I'm not going anywhere. I've invested a lot into this so I gotta know what's going on." I feel bad. I really didn't mean to fuck all this up for my friend. I love Vee, and I can't let temptation get the better of me. I say, "You know, I just need to learn how to shut my big-ass mouth sometimes."

"You know what?" she says. "I think you're right."

After I finally get out of Vee's house, after she's made me eat another helping and talked my ear off, I text Seaphes, and ask him to call ASAP. Ten minutes later he's on the phone.

"Okay, go over there and make that girl feel better."

"Listen, Demetria, I just told you to stay out of my business, and I mean it. I already told her I'm coming over; I don't need your help here. And anyway, I can't tell whether you trying to help your friend out or whether you want to get with me."

Pouting, I tell him, "I do wanna help her out, but I . . ."

"You like me, too?"

"It's not that I *like* you like you. I just want to know what kind of man you'd be in a relationship."

"Do you want to know for yourself, or for your friend?"

"It's all about Veron. You just have to go over there. And remember, you need to step things up." I envision him putting his hands all over her body, caressing her like he caressed me. I instantly get horny.

"Seaphes, wait," I plead. "Don't go. Tell her something came up."

"What?"

"I wanna see you. Can you meet me back at my place? But park in my garage."

"Woman, you're tripping big-time."

"Whatev. I just want to share some info with you before you hook up with her."

"Why can't you tell me over the phone?"

"Because."

When he doesn't say anything, I command him, "Just tell Veron you have to pick up a part for my computer. And be back at my crib within an hour." And I hang up.

— 2 6 —

SEAPHES

As soon as Demetria ends the call, I turn to Veron, who's sitting at the breakfast table. "Your friend is something else."

"Isn't she greasy-acting? What was she yakking about this time?"

Right after Demetria sent me a text, I called Veron and told her I was coming to see her. She met me outside while I was talking to Demetria and heard the end of our conversation.

"I haven't finished repairing her computer, so she wants me to pick up a part and get it done today." I don't know why I'm defending this girl. I guess it's because, underneath all the bullshit, I can see she's wounded.

"So you're going to go and help her out?"

I'm surprised. "You think I should?"

"Yeah, I guess," she says. But then she stops herself and I can see wheels turning in her head. "Actually, on second thought, no. I don't want you to go fix her computer. I don't have to be number two here. And anyway," she says, her soft voice bursting with an overpowering huskiness that I've never heard before, "there're some things that need fixing over here."

I swallow hard. "What do you need me to fix?"

"Follow me," she commands. I leave my BlackBerry on the counter and am right on her heels.

She stands at the door of her bedroom. The covers are partially falling off her bed, some magazines strewn on the floor. I know this must be driving her nuts, that I'm seeing this. But when I reach down to pick up the cover, she surprises me again by touching my hand. "Don't worry about that. Have a seat."

I sit down on a chair next to her bed. She grabs a black bandana and says, "You're going to have to trust me," and she begins wrapping the bandana around my head until it fully covers my eyes.

"Can you see anything?" she asks with a smile in her voice.

"Not a damn thing."

"Good, I'll be back," she says, imitating the Terminator.

I hear a door opening and closing and am tempted to peek and see what's going on, but I behave myself since she wants me to trust her. She returns five minutes later. I hear her fidgeting with what sounds like a radio. A sensual ballad softly plays in the background. I smile, wondering what the heck this mysterious woman is up to.

"Okay," she says, "you're in for a big surprise. I want you to keep quiet and just do as I tell you."

I gulp. "Yes, ma'am."

Veron gently removes the bandana. When I see her first thing I want to do is laugh. She's wearing some black reading glasses that are sitting on the bridge of her nose. Her hair is tied up in a tight bun. She looks like someone who works behind the desk of a library. I lick my lips and watch her every move. She's wearing a gray business skirt suit and some high heels. As the music plays she tries to look serious, slowly gyrating her hips back and forth to the rhythm and rocking her head from side to side and rubbing her fingers all over lips, and cheeks and chin. She bites her bottom lip, then sticks her middle finger in her mouth and licks it like it's a Popsicle.

I lick my lips again. Boy, it's getting hot in here. She comes closer to me and thrusts her chest at my face. She begins to slowly unbutton the suit jacket, watching me and locking her eyes with mine. Soon the jacket is crumpled on the floor, and her Wonderbra bulges with her cleavage.

"Ahhh," I murmur.

"Shhh," she scolds and continues slowly wiggling her hips, pumping her torso, and leaving her mouth partially open. She unzips and removes the skirt, showing nothing but some white bikini panties and matching lace bra. She squeezes her breasts together and licks her lips again. My dick is throbbing.

"You like what you see, Seaphes?" she whispers.

"You know I—"

"Shhh," she scolds again and turns around, then wiggles her ass in my face.

"Veron," I gasp wanting to reach out and touch her.

Veron removes her glasses, then unfastens the ponytail and lets her hair down. She slowly starts lowering her bikini panties just below her belly button, then pulls them back up.

"Why you stop?" I pant. "Keep going."

"Can't."

"Why not?" I gasp.

"I gotta first read what this magazine says to do next."

"You gotta be joking."

"Nope, I learned this from a magazine."

I groan and want to shake this woman, but I can't.

"Well, Veron, you've done a great job so far at making me feel good."

She finally smiles widely at me and moves her face near mine. "I was hoping you'd say that. Because you're an expert at making a woman feel good, too."

I smile and lean over to kiss her pouty lips. She beams at me. "See, that's what I'm talking about, Seaphes. I love so many things about you. You're smart, handsome, caring. And you really know how to make me feel so good." Her smile abruptly fades and her facial expression is solemn. "And," she continues, "I realize that I'm not the only woman who's attracted to you." She says this like it's a fact, not something that can be questioned.

I don't say anything. She pauses, then blurts, "Ursula."

I cringe, feeling sick. "What about her?"

"Don't give me that look as if you don't care about her or aren't attracted to her. I saw how you've looked at her in meetings. I've seen you two flirting at work, seen you staring at her walk past. And while I think I look pretty good, I am nothing like her."

"But who says you have to be? See, that's where females make mistakes. They think men only like one type of woman. It's not true. You're the one who I think is gorgeous."

"Really?" she says, looking up at me with her big brown eyes for a moment before she shrugs her shoulders as if she doesn't believe me. I wonder what I can do with this woman-child. Because I know for sure I can hurt her. It seems like her faith in me is undeserved, like at times she's describing a man I don't recognize. Yet the beauty of her innocence inspires and soothes my soul. And I'm starting to feel as though that's the type of connection I need to focus on at this point in my life. I'm going to take Demetria's advice and take this up a notch.

"May I?" I ask and get up to grab the bandana. I gesture

at the chair so she may sit down and I tie the bandana tightly around her eyes.

"What are you doing, young man?" she asks, giggling.

"You're going to have to trust me!" I say.

I finish up. "Veron?"

"Yep." I remove the bandana.

"You may open your eyes now."

She slowly opens her eyes, and then screams.

"Sorry! Sorry!"

"Why aren't you wearing any clothes? Seaphes, you're scaring me."

Face red, I slide on my trousers and zip them up. She's now covering her eyes and repeatedly whispering, "Oh my God."

When I clumsily pull my shirt over my head, I say, "Okay, I'm decent now."

She looks up and stares at me. "What was that all about? What are you doing?"

"I-I just thought I'd . . . I mean . . ." I trail off. I feel so uncomfortable. We look at each other for a minute, and finally I just leave the bedroom and head toward the living room. My hand is on the front door before she catches me, shaking her head and pointing to the couch. I go take a seat while she stands in front of me.

"I don't get it, Seaphes. Sure, I did the sensual dance for you, but when we make that move I still want things to happen naturally. Plus I heard something recently that said that if a man is forced to wait before he sleeps with a woman, he'll think of her as more beautiful, more desirable, and it will make him appreciate who she is."

She sounds like she's quoting words verbatim. It's so strange. I thought she was feeling me.

"I didn't mean to offend you. I don't know why I did

that. No, wait. I do know why. I feel very attracted to you, Veron. But you give me this feeling of uncertainty. I can't believe I'm telling you this," I say with an embarrassing laugh.

"No, go on. Please explain."

"You are like a tender flower and parts of you make me want to protect you and teach you things that'll help you. But then there are other parts of you, and I don't know what those parts are, how they fit in with the rest of you."

"I'm sorry, Seaphes. I try to do what other people say . . . follow rules, yet I'm so afraid. So scared," she says, biting her bottom lip. "I want to make sure to always do the right thing, because, point-blank, I don't want to be hurt."

"None of us do. And I'm glad you told me. Even if you're afraid, I need you to—"

"Listen," she says, that hard look back on her face. "I'm not going to open up just because you want me to. You'll just end up taking my feelings for granted. There is a way this all needs to play out, and—"

"You sound too much like a magazine article. I just want you to be real with me, Veron. Listen, I have to go, I'm sorry." I start to walk toward the door, but she catches my arm.

"Wait," she says, biting her lip again. "I'll try, okay? I'll try to be real."

There's that girl I know. I give her a kiss, a long sweet one, before I leave.

— 27 —

Demetria

I keep myself busy in the house and wait for Seaphes for more than an hour, which is unheard of for me. So when the man doesn't have the decency to call, text, e-mail, or send me a same-day multicolored rose delivery, I decide it's time for me to take some action, even if it's just to make myself feel better. I make an appointment for later that day at the salon that did my pedicure. It's time to take things to a new level. It takes five hours for me to get the type of services I want. And by the time I leave, the price tag added up to four hundred bucks, but this hairdo makes me look completely different, as does the beauty products I get. It's an entirely new look, and it's worth five Gs.

When Sunday rolls around without a phone call from either Seaphes or Veron, I send Darren a text.

"Hi D.F."

He shoots me one right back.

"Hey baby."

I giggle and let my fingers fly across my BlackBerry.

"Hey, what u doing?"

"Thinking about u. U wanna c me? Right now?"

I think about how sweet it would be to have Darren come visit me after thinking all weekend about the disrespectful rejection I got from Seaphes.

"Maybe. What u have in mind?" I text back.

"I got $$$. Let's go eat."

I laugh, surprised. "Where u get $$$."

"Rob a bank 4u baby."

"That's my man," I write back, laughing my ass off. I'm glad Darren is trying so hard to please me.

Darren arrives at my crib twenty minutes later in his seven-year-old black Lexus. His brother gave him the car, but whatev, it still looks good.

He meets me at my front door, grabs me in a tight hug, and takes me by the arm to escort me to his ride.

"Hmmm, this is different," I tell him and smile. I feel less distracted than I've felt all day.

"Yeah, I know, baby girl. We need to connect outside the bedroom, you know what I'm saying?"

"I hear what you're saying. I love what you're saying, too."

He opens my door and makes sure I've settled in before jumping in to the driver side. "I mean, I love eating you out, but I love to eat out, too, you know what I'm saying?"

"I feel the same fucking way, Darren." We laugh as if sharing a private joke. And when we pull into the crowded parking lot of the China Bear restaurant on I-45, I don't even pitch a fit. Sure, an eight-dollar Chinese buffet is nowhere near my usual standards, but I surprise myself by remembering that the fact that he even showed up on such short notice means he values me. After we are seated in the restaurant, Darren piles my plate high with whatever food he thinks I should try. Some of it is nasty-looking stuff that I swear will never touch my mouth. But when he sits next to me and looks me in the eye, feeding me a forkful, I silently obey him. I'm feeling good, enjoying our relaxing time together. And the fact that he can't stop telling me how fly I look with the new 'do . . . well, he might as well have given me ten Gs, that's how rich he's making me feel.

On the way back home I sigh contentedly and relax in the passenger seat.

"You gonna stop in for a hot minute?"

"No, baby girl. I got some things I gotta do, so if you don't mind, I'll make sure you get settled inside, then I gotta roll."

"Oh, honey," I say feeling sad and lonely already. "But what if I insist that you hang around?" I pout.

"You're just spoiled, huh? Guess you ain't used to a man like me . . ."

I laugh, but Darren's words make me think . . . make me think long and hard about just how accurate he is.

The next day when I get to work, I'm still feeling good about the brief but significant quality time I got to spend with Darren and feeling even happier about my new makeover. I sit in my ride, looking at myself in the mirror, fiddling with my hair, touching up my foundation and blush, reapplying a twinge of lipstick, and curling my eyelashes. I notice that my face has a radiant glow. I sashay in the door.

"Good morning, miss, is there anything I can help you with?"

"Hey, sexy boy. Don't you recognize me? It's your girl, Demetria."

"Oh, yeah?" says Percy. I just leave him standing in the middle of the hallway with his mouth open so wide you can see his two gold teeth.

Then I notice Ursula swishing down the hall toting a Shipley Do-Nuts bag. When she looks at me and rolls her eyes, I ignore her and think, You go ahead and double up on eating those donuts this morning, Ursula.

By the time I get to my office, I've counted up four compliments ("That mole near your lips looks sexy," "You rocking the hell outta that baby-doll dress, girl," "Hey sugar, can I step up to you for a minute?," and "Your ass looking so bootylicious I want to eat it up").

Good start, I think. Now all I gotta do is arrange to see Mr. Hill. His ignoring me this weekend made me feel like ten cents. I hated feeling like that, not when I know that I deserve so much more. So in a way this whole makeover is for his benefit.

When I get on the elevator to go to his floor, I am excited to see that Seaphes is standing alone inside it. He must've ridden up from the ground floor. That was so easy! He tries not to stare and doesn't get a good look at my face.

When the elevator door closes he asks me, "Which floor are you going to?"

"Third," I mumble.

"Excuse me, but you're stop-and-stare beautiful. Have we met?"

I laugh quietly but ignore him.

When the elevator reaches the third floor, he gestures with his hand so I can step off first.

"Thank you," I tell him and set off down the hall. I feel his eyes burning through my back, his mind turning. I laugh and pass by his office.

"Hey, excuse me," he says, but I continue down the hallway,

head held up, high heels clicking against the floor. When I pass two other men, they stare and give me that I-love-what-I-see smile. I nod and keep going until I reach the kitchen/lounge and stand in front of the coffee maker.

"May I pour a cup for you?" Seaphes followed me!

Without turning around, I shrug an okay.

His phone rings. He picks up and says, "Let me call you right back." Focusing his attention back on me, he grabs a plastic cup and asks if I want sugar and cream.

"I want it all," I tell him in a light whispery voice.

"You know, you look so familiar. I'm Seaphes Hill."

I finally turn to stare at him, shaking my head. "Is it the new makeup, or my honey blonde highlights? Or is it something or someone else that's causing you to have a brain fart?"

A flicker of recognition illuminates his eyes, and he takes the cup of coffee from my hand and takes a wild sip.

I can't help but laugh. But then I get serious. "Why didn't you show up at my place?"

"Something came up."

"Seaphes, you know, I'm not one for raggedy excuses. I don't like to be disrespected and that's exactly what you did."

His mouth opens but nothing comes out except a loud sigh.

"Are y'all fucking now?" I ask.

"What kind of question is that?"

"A valid one, Seaphes, a simple one."

When he doesn't say anything I place my hands on my hips and look squarely at him. "Look, Seaphes, do me a favor, be a man, and realize that when I'm involved in something, you've gotten yourself into some stuff."

"What are you talking about?"

I don't say anything.

"Look, Demetria, we need to talk. You're getting things a bit twisted."

"Tell you what," I say to him. "I think we ought to talk as well. I've got a thing or two to tell you."

"Such as?"

"This isn't exactly the place . . . so why don't you meet me at your car. No, meet me at my car; I'm parked at the end of the parking lot. Right now." He frowns, then glances at his watch. "C'mon, Seaphes. Spare some time and let's go do this."

"Alright." He gives in, starting to leave the lounge. "By the way, you do look nice, Demetria. I just wanted to tell you that."

"Where are we going?" he asks.

"Um, you're still planning on fixing my computer, right?"

"I can do that, why?"

"I need to purchase some things at the computer parts store. Some memory and a new mouse. We can chitchat on the way there."

"Demetria, we're not on our own time."

"Do you have any meetings?"

"Nooo, but . . ."

"We can just make up the lost time later. Let's get this conversation out of the way. I know you don't want to be around our coworkers while we talk, do you?"

He shakes his head in exasperation and gets in. We take off and whip through the employee parking lot. When I get up to the entrance ramp of the Southwest Freeway, a sea of red brake lights causes all the vehicles to slow to a crawl.

"Awww, what's wrong now?" I ask. "It's only eight-thirty in the morning."

"Probably an overturned truck," he tells me. "It's cool. We can wait."

Suddenly I start thinking about one time when I went to the gynecologist, and the nurse wanted me to get a mammogram because she felt an unusual lump underneath my right breast. She set me up to come back in, but I was so filled with fear that I actually canceled the appointment. But I prayed, and made another appointment, and I went. I had to face my fears no matter how afraid I felt, to endure the physical and mental pain of the test. It came back negative, but it helped me to see what kind of woman I am. Now, talking to Seaphes doesn't actually compare to waiting on medical test results, but I'm still nervous. Can I endure what I may not want to hear?

"So you think I look good, huh?"

"Come on, Demetria. You always look good."

"I do?" I ask.

"Of course you do. It's just that I think . . . your expectations . . ."

I wince and wait for him to finish.

"It's not any of your business if Veron and I are sleeping together. I know you're friends, and normally it's fine to talk, but you've got to mind your own business."

"How come it's usually okay but not with me?"

"Because you are causing problems, Demetria. I don't think you have Veron's best interests in mind. I believe you when you say that you honestly thought that she was pissed at me the other night, and that's why you felt like it was okay to get with me. But you also caused Veron to get pissed at me for way longer than she should have been. I can't have that."

"You really like her, huh?"

He just keeps quiet and looks out the window. But then his phone rings, and when he picks it up I can tell who it is from the way his voice changes, gets softer.

"Uh, away from the office," I hear him explain. "You know, I am actually stuck on the freeway, but the accident is about to be removed, then I gotta take care of some business, and I'll be back as soon as I can get there." A pause. "Just something I really need to take care of. How are you doing this morning?" A pause. "Awww, that's sweet," he says in this sugary voice. But he glances at me and suddenly sounds more authoritative. "Nothing to worry about, Veron. I'll get back with you later. You stay sweet, okay?" Another pause. "Back at ya," he whispers.

Soon as he hangs up I tell him, "Thanks for answering my question."

— 28 —

VERON

I think Seaphes is up to something. He comes to work, gets distracted, ends up going home but still hasn't returned to work, and it's almost three o'clock. What is that? I decided to stop trying to get him on the phone, though. Gotta act like I don't care. Gotta learn not to check on a man every five minutes. I refuse to smother him. But playing by these rules sure affects my ability to concentrate for the rest of the day.

And I've got to step it up. I think I know what Seaphes was trying to say the other night. He wants me to be real, but the book is working! So I have to keep on with the book but polish up my acting skills. He can't think that I don't mean what I say. I have to be strong.

It's hard, though, when Seaphes is missing, and Demetria is, too.

It's past four when Ursula Phillips walks in my office, with her big ole booty tagging along.

"Can I talk to you for a minute?" she asks.

"I guess."

She sits down on my guest chair with this annoyed expression on her face.

"Dang, what's wrong with you?" I ask.

"You know that Seaphes is gone, right?"

I nod as if to say, Yeah, so what.

"I saw him leaving the facility early this morning, with Demetria."

"You're spying on the guy?"

"I wasn't spying. I happened to be in the security room and saw them on surveillance."

"So why do you feel the need to tell me this? And why so late in the day?"

"Only because I've been calling him all day, and he hasn't returned my calls. To be frank, he's pissing me the hell off."

"And so you want to get him back by divulging his personal business to me. As if I am his mother, and you're the tattletale?"

"Hey, Veron. I'm just trying to help you out. You've looked out of it all day. It's easy to figure out your mood has to do with him."

"Well, you figured wrong. I already knew he was with her," I say, hoping I sound like I'm secure enough not to care "They have some business to take care of. So whatever you saw on my face has nothing to do with him."

"Look trick, you're talking to a real woman here. And I can see it on another woman's face when she's hurt and upset by a man."

"You don't know what you're talking about," I say, anxious for her to leave . . . and yet wanting to hear more.

"When's the last time you talked to Seaphes?"

"What difference does it make?"

"Because if he really cared about you, he'd be in constant contact. He'd give you a sense of security, he'd do things to let you know he can be trusted."

I reflect on her words, squirming in my seat and yanking forcefully on my ponytail.

"Let me tell you something about Mr. Hill," she continues. "In my observation, he is the perfect man on paper, but you gotta go beyond what's on the paper. It's like you gotta squeeze him as if he's an orange. Put tremendous pressure on him so what's really inside of him comes out. That way you'll know for sure if he's a solid keeper or if he's just a temporary waste of time."

I eye her curiously. "Is that what you did with him? Put pressure on him?"

"That's what I should have done with him, but I was too afraid. But maybe your faith can take you where mine didn't."

"Huh?"

She notices my discomfort and sits down in the seat next to mine, releasing a thoughtful, deep breath.

"Veron, sometimes we think we women love a man so much that we can ignore his weaknesses, we can become blind to the red flags. We hope so hard that this man is everything that he claims he is, everything we wish he can be, and that we believe it. But if our gut whispers to us to check things out, we oughta listen. It would save us lots of pain and heartache." Her stony face softens. "Reason why I know is because I'm sure you've heard I reconciled with my spouse. In the beginning, when we first married, every one of his flaws was front and center, but I was so in love with him it didn't bother me that his credit was severely jacked up. I didn't care if he wanted to have a men's night out even if his 'night' wouldn't end until three a.m., and I was sitting home crying. Hello? I should have known from the start it was a problem. So why reconcile? Because his four-year-old namesake would ask for his daddy every single day, and I didn't want to deprive our son of that relationship. So now Junior is happy, his hero is back home. But I'm miserable, still looking out windows. And Mr. Husband still gets to do his thing. Why does a man always get to do *his* thing?"

Her strong voice spirals down to a painful moan, and she fiercely grabs and caresses my hand as if her strength is about to give way. "So please, little sista, *please* don't be me, repeating my mistakes. Never fall in love with a man who doesn't treat you like a queen. If you aren't number one, then he shouldn't be either."

I want to touch her, ease her pain through soft words or physical compassion, but all I can do is nod appreciatively at her, unable to formulate an adequate response. Her words remind me of the promise I made to myself: no matter the uncertainties, I was willing to tackle whatever I have to face on this journey of love. Yes, I'm in a terrifying place right now, but that's how love goes. I just have to keep on.

When I get off work, instead of going directly home like I normally do, I stop by JCPenney and buy a pink and white workout shirt and matching shorts for the Walk America event. It's still two weeks away, but I need to concentrate on something besides myself.

Afterward, when I pull up to my apartment and find Seaphes's car parked in the space right next to mine, I don't know what to make of it.

"What are you doing here?" I ask, getting out of the car.

"Waiting on you. Where you been, woman?" he says with a teasing smile.

Even though I am happy to see him, I maintain a blasé attitude. “I was taking care of some business. Why are you dressed so fancy?” He's wearing a crisply ironed white dress shirt, purple and red tie, and some dark pin-striped trousers.

“We're going out. Just me and you.”

“Oh, really,” I remark, thinking how deliciously strange his comments sound.

“Yeah, let me in the crib so you can get ready. I've been burning up gas sitting in my car with the AC on.”

A date! I am tempted to giggle but suppress my giddiness.

I walk inside the apartment, and my mouth pops open. There are roses arranged around my entire living room—I count six dozen. I also notice two stuffed animals (an oversized bunny rabbit and a soft, brown, cuddly teddy bear), and I see a stack of Japanese comic books spread out on the coffee table.

“What the hell is all this?” I cover my face with my hands, trying to cover up the redness that burns underneath my cheeks. “C'mon, you're not telling me something. Is all this for me? How'd you get in the apartment?”

“Yep, I owe you, young lady. I realized how much of an ass I've been.”

“You have?” I ask, confused.

He rushes to say, “Well, I mean, I could be much better than what I am. I haven't given you of myself one hundred percent, and I need to step up my game. And it was all Demetria's idea.”

I scowl. “Say what?”

“I finally got a chance to repair her computer today. And she and I were talking, and she was telling me I've been neglecting you, and everything she said was true. So she suggested I step up my game for you. She knows your landlord, and he let her in your apartment while she filled it with the roses, everything. From me, for you. And now you and I are going out. I just want to make things up to you, give you my best self."

I slump down on the couch, inhale the aroma of all the roses, stroke my fingers across the comic books, and reflect on everything he said. I love that he did all this, but I don't want to be too over the moon. "You know, this is very wonderful, Seaphes, but it bothers me that you couldn't come up with the idea yourself. You only did it because Demetria suggested it. And I'm not sure I appreciate that."

His face drops, but he recovers. "No, babe, don't look at it like that. Sometimes a man can't see himself, he needs nudging, reminders. You gotta look at the positive side. Demetria is looking out for you, hooking you up."

"But why would she do that?"

He stares at me without blinking. "Because she's your best friend. That's what friends do."

"I guess," I tell him as I battle mixed emotions. I do absolutely adore flowers, and the teddy bear makes me feel like a five-year-old again. I pick up the soft, tan-colored bear and squeeze him in my arms. "Okay, this bear's name is Little Seaphes. And the rabbit looks like a female, so her name is Demetria."

"Hmmm, that's kinda odd."

"Then it'll match everything that's happening today," I tell him with a loud sigh. "Okay. I thank you for all your efforts, I do. They're very thoughtful and even though another woman had to steer you in the right direction, I accept that you are sincere. But next time I want more, and I want to know that you came up with it on your own."

He pauses, looking a little taken aback, but then says, "I'm sorry if this was wrong. I just wanna make you happy."

I catch my breath and utter, "You do?"

"You are a sweet person and you deserve to be treated well. And usually a man doesn't realize that about his woman until he sees the back of her head fading off into the distance. That's all I'm trying to say. Maybe I'm not doing a very good job."

I give in—whether he knows it or not, this man has made me so happy. I don't give a rat's ass how it was initiated. He's made me feel so good inside. I stand up and spread out my arms. "Oh, Seaphes, I am sorry. I feel so bad. Thank you, thank you, thank you for all this. I'm flattered, honored, and I would love to go out tonight. I actually love nice surprises, so this is really what I need. I had a hard day."

He takes me in his arms, squeezing me and rubbing my back. "That's what I'm talking about, babe. I need to focus more on you." His eyes are twinkling with relief.

I am happy on the ride to dinner and excited when we reach The Woodlands, a swanky part of town. But when we pull into the parking lot of P.F. Chang's I start to have mixed feelings. This is the joint where Demetria and Thaddeus went for Valentine's Day, and I detect her influence. But I try to relax and enjoy myself with Seaphes, because for the first time in forever I feel like I have him all to myself.

He pulls out my chair for me and I sit down.

"You okay?" he asks, sitting across from me, his eyes searching mine.

"I'm good. I've never been here before. Would you order for me, whatever you think I should have?"

He winks and nods, and we start off the evening with a glass of white zinfandel, wonton soup, and a few vegetarian lettuce wraps, which taste so delicious I want to order some more.

"I must say," he says. "You look stunning tonight. I mean that."

"Thanks, Mr. Hill, so do you. But why are looks always so important to men?"

"I'm sorry?"

"Like today for instance. Not to name names, but I was informed you were all up in some woman's face at work," I say, giving him a sideways glance. "She looked very attractive and was getting a lot of attention, but you apparently followed her around like a puppy. Why y'all gotta overreact?" I say this so sweetly, like a mother gently scolding her four-year-old child.

"Um, uh . . . well, you know how we do. If we like what we see, we're going to look. I've even seen preachers take a look at a beautiful woman."

"Yeah, well, that kind of thing can be rude."

"Well, let's not concentrate on this. That's all surface stuff. Right now is what counts. Let's try and start our relationship anew. That's what I want."

"Mmm hmmm," I agree and take a tiny sip, enjoying the flavor as it stimulates my tongue.

"So you were able to hook up Demetria today?"

"Is that what she told you?"

"That's what *you* told me. I haven't talked to her today."

"Right. Yeah, she practically cursed me out because I had bailed out on her regarding her PC, but I got her a new motherboard and some other accessories. So now she's able to get her taxes done."

"Well, wonderful. I'm glad you were able to help her."

"You know, let's change the subject again, baby."

"But, Seaphes, you assured me I can talk to you about anything under the sun. Did you really mean that? Or is there a list of preapproved topics I should refer to?"

He laughs and shakes his head. "You're starting to sound like Demetria."

"Why do you mention her so much? Demetria this, Demetria that. Demetria, Demetria, Demetria."

"Hold on here. What's wrong, Veron? I want us to have a nice time, but you're going out of your way to pick a fight. What's up with you?" He peers at me for a moment. "I'm beginning to think that you are incapable of being happy."

"I-I, I'll be right back," I say, feeling grief stricken.

I end up hiding out in the ladies' room, my usual course of action when I am paralyzed to the point of not being able to think rationally. I want to kick myself. Instead, I get on the phone.

"Yo, what's up, Vee?"

"Michael West, you gotta help me." I explain things to him, and once again, he hits it right on the nose.

"You keep reminding the man that other women exist. Why do that? As far as he is concerned, you are number one. You're with him on the date, not anyone else. And you gotta keep things that way. Be selfish as hell. Strike Demetria's name from your mouth. I know that's your girl and all, but I doubt that she's talking about you when she's with any of her men."

"You are so right. Thank you, Mike. You always make so much sense."

"Anytime, love. Let me know how things go."

I hang up and turn on the warm water so I can splash my face. I pat it dry and I stare at myself in the mirror and think, "I am number one. I am number one."

— 29 —

SEAPHES

While Veron is in the bathroom, Demetria sends me a text: "Call me."

"Can't," I text back.

"☹"

I ignore Demetria's last text and turn off my phone.

Veron comes back to our table at the same time as the waiter, who brings plates loaded with shrimp and lobster sauce for Veron and stir-fried eggplant for me.

"*Bon appétit,*" I tell her, and she offers me a sincere smile that manages to make my food taste even more scrumptious.

"Seaphes, I'm sorry about that moment of craziness. I want you to know that I am having a wonderful time. Usually my dates aren't this enjoyable and classy."

"Are you still dating?"

She starts to answer but shifts in her seat. "I don't want to answer that."

"Okay. No problem." I shrug.

"I do want to say, however, that I'd rather be with you than anyone else."

"That's good to know, baby," I reach out toward her. She grabs my hand, and we hold each other's fingers while we attempt to eat. The more we talk, the more I feel she is the one

I should be with. There are some things that weird me out, but I feel like the real her is old faithful. The only problem with that is she has to watch it—she can't take a man's mess over and over again, fuss at him but still take him back. I bet men have taken advantage of that.

"You're too good to me," I gently tell her, my voice sincere.

"Oh, you're just saying that. But thanks," she pipes up, blushing like a teenager.

"I mean it. You have no idea how much. I am so happy you agreed to go out with me. You are so important to me."

Her eyes quickly, sweetly brim up with tears, and when one small drop slides down the curve of her cheek, I gently dab it with my thumb. She looks embarrassed.

"To me," I tell her, "you're most beautiful when you show me your true self. Now, tell me. What more can I do to make you happy?"

"Make love to me tonight."

The evening goes on, and we keep talking.

"You ever live with someone?" she asks me.

"Not in the real sense of the word. But I know how it feels to be with someone so much that we're almost living together. She sees my undershirts with the ripped holes under the armpits. I can either throw out all my torn-up T-shirts or see if she can deal with my faults."

"Is a ripped shirt a fault?"

"Is a toothpaste-stained bathroom counter a fault?" I say in a teasing voice.

She nods. "I get you. Well, in the beginning we're showing the side of us that will garner the most approval. We want to show our best self. It's scary to unveil those layers . . . the ugly parts that we try to keep hidden."

"What are some of your faults?"

She laughs out loud. "You don't want to know. Just believe that I am human like everyone else. I even have that book that tells me about how to improve on my faults."

"Why do you feel you need magazines or books to tell you who you are?"

"Because it doesn't hurt to try something different. Even Demetria tells me . . ." Her voice trails off.

"Why did you stop talking?" I say, concerned. "Why are you so afraid to even speak her name?"

"I want our date to be about me and you."

I take a tiny sip of my zinfandel and try to block Demetria out of my mind. Sure, she's a sexy-ass woman, but it's not like I have to have her or the world will come to an end.

The conversation flows easily for the rest of the night, and I'm so glad to get to know more and more about this girl whom I like so much. Our drive back to her place is peaceful and comfortable. Once we enter her apartment, she runs off to her bedroom while I kick off my shoes and pull off my shirt and tie. She comes back wearing a pair of red shorts and a white T-shirt.

I point to her clothes.

"Shoot," she says, "I want to chill for a minute. I want to just lay my head against your chest while we kiss and hold each other. Is that okay? And if things lead to sex, then we'll see."

Frowning, I ask, "You sound unsure of yourself. Did you change your mind?"

We sit hip-to-hip on her couch. She clutches the furry rabbit against her chest and stares into space. "I'm fickle. Can't you tell?"

"But why? What have I done wrong?"

"Seaphes, the easiest thing to do in the world is have sex with you."

"But you don't want to? Do you not trust me?"

"I just . . . I don't know yet."

"Then why are you with me, huh? What are you really trying to say?"

"I just . . ." But she doesn't finish the sentence. She clamps her mouth shut and starts rocking back and forth, clutching the bunny rabbit so tight I'm afraid its ears are going to pop off.

"Watch how you're holding Demetria," I say, pointing to the rabbit.

"Ha," she laughs. "Yeah. What an interesting choice of words."

— 30 —

Demetria

"Boo, it's been so long," I moan as Thaddeus squeezes me tight around my waist. Seeing him and touching him again makes me feel a thousand times better. I adore his caramel-colored skin, wide expressive green eyes, and his salt-and-pepper hair. I also love his big old wallet. The tighter he hugs me, the more I realize his comforting arms are where I really belong, especially when I notice gift-wrapped boxes sitting a few inches from his feet.

"I've been missing you, too, Your Highness. Have you been a good girl, or a bad girl?"

"I've been a horny girl," I tell him in a firm voice.

"That's what I want to hear."

"Gimme my presents," I wail, impatiently pushing him off me when his hugs last too long.

"Wait, let me stare at you a moment. You look different." He rubs his chin and gives me a skeptical look. "New hair color. Nice. And where'd the mole come from?"

"It's a simple beauty mark that I had someone paint on. I wanted to look more sensual for you. You like it?"

"I do. Mission accomplished." He rakes his fingers through the long strands of my hair. I love when he fusses over me like I'm important. Thaddeus is the type of man who knows exactly the way I want and need to be treated.

Thad takes me by the hand and leads me to the couch. He sits besides me and hands me the first enormous box, which is wrapped in purple and gold metallic paper and topped with a huge violet ribbon trimmed with light purple.

"Where were you this time? New York?"

"India."

"India? Why didn't you tell me instead of acting like it was a big secret? When you called it sounded like you were right next door."

He ignores my question. "The business is taking off, and I needed my team to accompany me to Jaipur so we could do an emergency meeting with investors. I also took some time to enjoy the city. The lakes and the mountains are pure eye candy."

"You should have taken me," I grumble.

"Sweetness, I was over there for two weeks, and I knew you needed to be at your job. Now stop pouting and open up your gifts. If you can't go to India, I'll bring India to you."

"Oh, boo, you're the best," I say in a babyish voice. "Me love you so much."

I open the presents Thaddeus got me. They include two beautiful, colorful brocade dresses obviously worth at least two grand each; several collectible crystal elephants that will look impressive sitting on my mantel; three pairs of multicolored chappals that I can wear in the summer; and a printed textile blanket that bears some of the most vibrant colors I've ever laid eyes on.

I hop up on his lap and offer him a big sloppy kiss. He rubs his soft nose against my warm neck, calling me his "precious little baby doll." I tell him to sit tight, and I go mix him a tall glass of Georgia peach, one of his favorite drinks.

"How have you been holding up since I've been gone?" he casually asks after I hand him his drink.

"It's been boring as hell. I've been hanging out with Vee, going to book club meetings. Nothing as exciting as spending time with you."

"I didn't mean that. I meant sexually," he says, looking serious.

"What? Oh, I got a, uh, whatchamacallit . . ."

"Vibrator?"

"Yeah, silly that."

He just shakes his head as if he can't believe I'd resort to getting a vibrator.

"Why you wanna know all that, boo?" I sweetly ask him, motioning at him so he can let me taste his drink. I wrap one arm around his neck, enjoying the recognizable scent of his Burberry cologne.

"I just wanna make sure my baby's needs are being met."

"Meaning?" I ask and begin to play with the little hairs of his mustache.

"Some women might not be completely satisfied with a vibrator."

"Oh, you know I'm not like anyone else. Demetria Elayne Sparks is an originator, not an emulator or a duplicator."

"You not telling me anything I don't already know. Hey, you need anything?" he asks me. It's the question I've been dying to hear.

"Ummm, how about two Gs?"

"I'll deposit the funds this week."

"Cool, honey bun. How's your drink? You gulping it down."

"It tastes good, girl, but why only one glass? Usually you make a gallon."

"Uh, I'm completely out of vodka."

He frowns. I start tugging on his earlobe, then stick my tongue gently in the ear, hoping he'll close his eyes and start moaning. But he pushes me off him.

"You've been drinking so much that you've run out?" he says, sounding accusing.

"What, Thad? You expect me to drink bottled water every freaking day or something? Nothing wrong with me getting my liquor on."

"As long as it's just you who's drinking the liquor, I'm cool. You know I don't want anyone else touching my stuff."

"I know, boo, that's why I feel guilty."

I feel his body stiffen. "Guilty?"

I whisper conspiratorially, "I let Veron drink some vodka, too. She was depressed and crying about her boyfriend. It's a real mess."

"Who is her boyfriend?" He frowns.

"Uh, she doesn't mention his name, just some loser she met."

"Ah ha," he says, clearing his voice. "Well, I hope everything works out for her. She's a nice girl."

"Not nicer than me though, right, honey bun? Please promise you won't leave me for so long next time, Thad. I can't take it when you're gone away for too long."

"Well, maybe I can get something to keep you company. You want a new puppy?"

"No, that's okay. I hate how they smell, and I ain't gonna be cleaning up anyone else's shit."

"How about a freshwater aquarium?"

"Dang, Thad, fish smell, too. Anyway, baby, no animal, no man, no best friend could ever be equal to you."

"That's not what you've told me in the past," he says darkly. "You told me you could replace me so fast I wouldn't have time to feel the pain. So what's happened the past two weeks that you now feel different?"

"I guess it's the time spent apart. I realize that . . ." I bite my tongue, careful not to sound too mushy. What am I doing? I'm sounding too much like Veron. I want him to know I value him, but he can never think I'm totally strung-out over his ass. "Just don't be gone like you have been."

"When business opportunities arise I'm obligated to follow them. But I'll come up with something to keep you entertained." He thinks for a moment. "How about a webcam so we're able to see each other?"

"Are you crazy? That's like high-tech stalking. There are already too many cameras in society as it is."

He looks hurt. "But I thought you missed me so much."

"Oh, I do, I do, honey bun, but no need to spend beaucoup money for equipment I'd probably never use."

"I can afford it."

That's cute, I think. But outwardly I just smile sweetly at my baby and think about how fortunate I am to have this man. Shoot, I can even picture a wedding in the distant future . . .

Naw, hold up. Why am I getting carried away? How in the hell can I be married to a man who travels two weeks out the month? I got needs. And as much as I love the clothes, jewelry, and cash Thad gives me, none of that stuff can eat me when I get hot.

"Mmmm, honey bun," I say. Jumping off his lap, I peel off my latex shirt, jogging shorts, and undergarments. He responds, rapidly stripping off all his clothes, layering the floor with his business shirt, slacks, and jacket. I drop down on my knees and crawl to my bedroom. "Let's do it on the bed for once," I whisper.

"Huh," he says falling against me and gently kissing my ass and hips. I begin to gyrate, enjoying the feel of his lips.

"Thad, flow with me," I gasp. I stop moving and reach back to spread my vagina apart. He pushes his erect penis deep inside of me. I gasp again and let him stroke me hard, making me dizzy with passion.

"You miss this big dick?"

"Always, baby. Oooh, no one does me like you." My hips keep pumping, but his stop.

"What's that supposed to mean?"

"What? It's just an expression. Stick it back in," I command, wiggling my ass.

"No."

No? Thad never says no to me. I drop to the floor and lie down sideways, totally pissed off. His timing couldn't be worse. My vagina is throbbing so violently I'm surprised he can't hear it clapping.

"Why don't I put on a condom?"

"What? Why?" I say, trying not to sound too emotional.

"I just don't want to take any chances."

"You know, this is all wrong. I thought you loved me."

"I do, sweetness, but I'm always careful. You taught me that."

Think, think, think. "Baby, I'm burning up over here. You gonna finish up the job? All this juiciness is waiting for you," I say, spreading my long legs and fingering myself. "Only for you."

He looks torn—a little bit horny, a little bit tortured—but still doesn't move toward me.

Damn.

I sit up and crawl toward him, then gently grab his dick and shove it deep inside my mouth, licking up and down the shaft, then sucking tenderly on the head. Soon I get a nice little rhythm going. Thad closes his eyes and winces—I think he's back under my control. Feeling confident, I suck on him ferociously.

Eventually he moans, shudders, and comes in my mouth. I lick up every single drop like I always do. Then I plant a kiss on his lips.

"Hey, I told you I don't like that."

"I'm sorry, but if you wanna roll with me, that's what's up," I tell him. Slowly I lie on my back, then spread my legs as wide as I can. He hesitates. "Here, eat up, and dig deep," I command, looking up at him.

He frowns at first, but then crawls over to me and sticks his head between my legs. When I hear slurping sounds and feel his long juicy tongue lick me up and down, I know I'm back exactly where I belong.

— 3 1 —

VERON

I know it's way past any normal person's bedtime, but I don't care. I need help. So I find myself once again driving down the familiar tree-lined street with all the brick ranch homes and oversized, landscaped front yards. To be honest, I'm looking for a particular vehicle, but when I don't see it I sigh in relief and gain the confidence I need to go ring the doorbell. I hop out of my HHR, run up the walkway, and frantically press the doorbell. No one responds . . . hmmm. I glance at my watch, which glows in the dark.

Midnight.

Nervously, I ring two more times. Finally, I decide I'm being as ridiculous as an adult who believes in Santa Claus, so I turn myself around and head for my car.

But then the front porch lights of the house flash on, and I hear the squeaky front door swing open. "Vee?" says Demetria into the night.

I turn back around and walk hurriedly toward her. "I know it's late, but I needed someone to talk to. I need you to talk to."

"It's cool." She smiles with encouragement and turns to go back in the house. "We can hang out in the guest room," she whispers. "I have company."

"Oh, shoot," I say, cringing. "I–I don't want to interrupt."

"No, it's cool. Thad just fell asleep, and I was looking at some clothes he bought me. Girl, they are beautiful," she says and grins contentedly. "Come on in. I'll show them to you."

We quietly enter her guest room, where the walls are painted a rich shade of purple. There's a fairly new marble platform bed with a leather headboard. It looks inviting.

"It's so late you might as well spend the night. I can set the alarm for five a.m. so you can rush home and get dressed before going to work, if you want. Dang, this feels like old times," she exclaims. Demetria's countenance is radiant, and I'm certain it's due to her sexual afterglow. Seeing her so happy makes me wonder if I could be smiling that big, if I would've just given in to Seaphes.

"When did Thad get back?" I whisper.

"We don't have to whisper. He can't hear us in here; the walls are thick. He got back tonight, and he couldn't wait to see his baby. I'm *so* happy. I missed his old ass so much that I practically attacked him. Plus he hooked a sista up with some serious cash. And that'll work, because I spent a grip getting myself fixed up last weekend, and then I had to pay your boyfriend to fix my computer. Well, I probably didn't have to pay him, but I volunteered to pay since he was cool about it. He did a good job, fixed me up and everything," she says joyously.

"So you're getting a tax refund?"

"Yeah, chump change. Probably enough to buy me some clothes for the cruise."

"Oh, you're still going?"

"Yep, Thad told me that we'll spend a week visiting San Juan, Saint Thomas, and Aruba. I need to remember to fill out a leave request for a vacation. God knows I need a break. I'm so excited."

"I can tell. I'm happy for you," I say, hoping she thinks my smile is genuine.

Why her, Lord? Why does she get every single thing she desires and the little things I want are always such a struggle? It's unfair. I know she's prettier and more sophisticated than I am, but that shouldn't mean that I get left out of the blessing department. Are you prejudiced? I'm getting so angry that tears threaten to flow. But I bury my pain deep inside.

I try to relax, sprawling on Demetria's guest bed as I wait for her to bring me a pair of pj's. I'm exhausted. Shoot, I may even call in sick tomorrow and take a mental health day, because as of now, my mind is definitely not sharp enough to handle work.

"Here ya go, boo," Demetria says sweetly, handing me a maroon spaghetti-strap gown that still has price tags.

"Thad got this for me one time when he went to Quebec. You can actually have it."

"Oh, no, he's probably expecting you to model it for him one day."

"Baby, all the lingerie he gets me never stays on this sexy body for long. Did I tell you we fucked like newlyweds tonight? This girl still got it. I mean, my boy D. hooks me up big-time, but Thad is giving him a run for his money."

I stare at her and shake my head, amazed that she has at least two men to have fantastic sex with on the regular.

And that's when I realize that something is terribly imbalanced. This girl definitely can't be the poster child for the way women ought to act, but she has men coming out her ears, plus a big bag of extra to spread around. Maybe it's simpler than I'm making it. Maybe if I stop keeping myself from being happy, like Seaphes said, I can be here bragging to her about my own good times.

"Girl, I don't know," she continues. "Sex is just the only thing that truly relaxes me. And if don't get it, I don't know, I can go kinda crazy." She stops abruptly, and then casually stares at me. "You know what I mean? I'm sure when Seaphes does you, you feel the tension lower, too."

"Why would you say that?"

"C'mon, don't be shy. What's he like in bed?"

Laughing, I snatch the gown from her hands. "I don't kiss and tell."

"Why not? You think I'll get jealous and try to hop on his lame ass?"

I pause. "I wouldn't put it past you." I turn my back toward her and start taking off my clothes.

"What did you say?" she asks in a sharp tone.

My head is now covered by the gown that I'm trying to pull on, so I don't respond.

"Why are you acting so funny? Why can't you just spit it out instead of insulting me? Be a woman and say what 'cha want to say."

I finally pull the gown over my head and adjust it until I am comfy, and I crawl back on the bed. I'm still not talking.

"You want me to be your mouthpiece?" she asks. "Are you trying to imply that I will have sex with anybody, anytime? Well, I don't exactly roll like that," she spits out and starts pacing. "I get far too much dick to need to jump on anyone you chasing after."

Finally I find my tongue. "Demetria, stop tripping. I didn't mean to get you riled up."

"Then tell me what's going on," she says, looking concerned. "What the hell happened?"

I begin to describe Seaphes's and my last encounter. And the more I talk the worse I feel.

"So that's probably why I'm acting like this. I'm just frustrated."

"And you're taking it out on me. See, I'm the last thing you need to be tripping about. You need to do everything you can to make that man know that you want his ass before someone else tries to take him. I mean, I'll bet Ursula Phillips would jump back in his bed in a second."

"No, that part of their relationship is over."

"How you know that? You in Seaphes's bed every night? Huh?"

"Well, of course I'm not."

"Then never put it past another woman to be trying to dip back in the pool. Especially if he set her off right."

"Are you saying that from experience?"

"Well, now, I feel like Seaphes—what the hell, girl? Sounds like you don't fucking trust me. What is your problem? I'm trying to help your ass out."

"I know, Demetria. I'm sorry."

"Well, in spite of all your insults, I'm going to figure out a way to get you back in good graces with your man. And let me tell you that it may entail spending time with your boy so I can develop the best strategy for you. For *you*! As much as Demetria flirts, that's just her, girl. She knows your name is written on his dick."

"All right. I believe you. But I don't know how much good you're going to do. Seaphes thinks I don't trust him. He was so mad when he left, and he's not answering my calls."

"Oh, he's just a little bit pissed and probably wasn't quite ready to talk to you. But he'll ease up, especially after I get through with him."

"What do you mean? What you plan to do?"

"Just trust me. I always have a plan. Demetria got your back."

Honestly, she's managed to soften my heart up enough to make me feel better. "So anyway," I ask her. "Now that Thad is back, does that mean you're letting go of Darren, and whoever else you're sleeping with?"

"Girl, please. There aren't *that* many. But, uh, I already have let some of them go. They couldn't hang. But Darren is different; he's a keeper."

We both laugh and end up chitchatting for another hour. It feels like old times—we're not talking about men, only about hair and makeup, the stress of work, our goals and fears. It's like the good old days when we'd be girly-girls and just bond through our similar hobbies, interests, and pasts. It feels nice bonding with her.

Early the next morning she knocks on the door of the guest room and lets herself in.

"Wake up, princess," she coos, trying to balance a large metal tray on the dresser. I sit up in bed, sluggishly rubbing my eyes.

"Oh, wow, what's all this?"

"I know you love some Morning Star sausage and scrambled eggs. And there's a chilled cup of chocolate yogurt and two ripe bananas, too."

"You're too much, Demetria. It's been a long time since I had breakfast in bed."

"Well, hurry it up. Unless you want to wear one of my outfits I figured you'd want to scoot home early and get to work. I need to shower myself," she says and sniffs under the arms. "I gave Thad some before he left, and wooo, I'm surprised I had energy to cook."

Laughing, I tell her, "You know, I think I'll take you up

on wearing one of your outfits. I want to sit here and enjoy this. And I'll drive us to work, since you left your car there yesterday."

"Sounds good."

"How were you planning to get to work today, anyway?"

"Uh, what? I, uh . . . I just figured I could get some guy to come get me."

"Must be nice."

— 32 —
SEAPHES

When I arrive at work, Ursula Phillips is standing outside my office.

"Can I help you?" I ask, sounding unfriendly.

"Yes, you can. You can start off by not being such an asshole."

I shrug and just insert my key in my office door. But Ursula follows me inside and closes the door behind her.

"What you do that for? I don't want to be with you in my office behind closed doors."

"Oh, Seaphes, do you really have to act like this? I just want to talk to you in private. Why so cold?"

"We have no business together anymore."

Suddenly I realize that Ursula is crying. I grab a box of tissue and thrust it onto her lap.

"I am so sorry," she whimpers. "I messed up. I should've tried to make things work between us. I never should have taken him back."

"What are you talking about?"

She reopens her eyes and stares straight at me. "My asshole of a husband is cheating on me. And it makes me want revenge."

"Is that the reason you were trying to get with me? As a pawn between you and dude?"

"I'm not saying that I was trying to use you, Seaphes," she says, her voice catching. "You were there for me when I needed someone to be there. And when I felt you were sincere, I let you know that I wanted to be with you," she insists.

"But it was too late. I had moved on."

"To Ms. Whore?" she spits, her eyes flashing.

"Who're you talking about?"

"Everybody knows you're fucking Demetria Sparks."

"*What?* Everybody is wrong."

"Oh, please. We aren't blind. Folks on the job can tell when people are messing around with coworkers. You can lie and deny, but body language reveals what your mouth won't. Admit it, Seaphes. You two have been intimate."

"First of all, it's none of your business who gets in my bed. And second, just because she's a big-time flirt don't mean that I want her."

"Save your lies for someone that's stupid, Seaphes. I'm telling you that whore is nothing but trouble."

"That's fine, you keep talking. I don't have to listen," I say, not wanting to go there with her. I'm hoping she'll leave, but she stands there like I owe her something.

"Screw you, Seaphes," she finally says. "I hope you get what you deserve. You and Demetria are meant to be with each other. You're both selfish people who are only out to get what you want, and don't care how much you hurt others."

"We have nothing else to talk about. So please leave now."

She continues to sit with a stony look on her face. I roll my eyes and proceed to read e-mails to distract myself.

But ten of the e-mails in my in box are from her. Ignorant forwards about Microsoft giving away money . . . fake-ass "You are my friend" messages . . . even a couple of e-mails with just one line of writing, like, "Hey, what's up?" Probably sent to me just so I would show her some attention. Jesus. If she wants me, she is going about this the wrong way. I wonder what it is about me that attracts these kinds of women. The only nice, sweet woman I know apparently still doesn't trust me. Probably never will.

After ten minutes Ursula finally gets the hint and pulls herself up out of my office, loudly slamming the door as she goes. I vow to myself to never get caught up with an undeserving woman again.

I've got to make amends. Maybe I overreacted. I pick up the phone.

"Hello, this is Veron Darcey."

"Good morning, babe."

She coughs and clears her throat. "Hi. Is this Seaphes?"

Feeling crushed but not wanting her to know it, I playfully ask, "Who do you want it to be?"

"Sorry. But it *is* you, isn't it? I didn't recognize the number."

"Oh, touché. Did you delete me from your address book?"

"Whoever said you were in my address book?" she says, laughing. "Listen, Seaphes . . . I just want to apologize. I know it looked like I don't trust you."

"No, I know I overreacted. I'm sorry, too. Hey," I say thinking fast. "Can a brotha come by and pick you up for breakfast?"

"Um, that's fine. Let me go primp real quickly."

"You do that. Look cute for me. I'll be right down."

We head to an IHOP that's a few miles from the office. Once we're inside, I ask to see the menu.

"We can get breakfast to go," I tell Veron. "Whatever you

want, it's on me. I want to make things up to you. I don't want you to think I'm an asshole. I apologize for leaving. And I should have returned your calls."

She blushes and laughs. "Have you been talking with Demetria or something?"

"No, babe, I haven't seen nor heard from her today."

"So this is all Seaphes Hill this time around?"

"One hundred percent. Let me order for you. Can you trust me to do that?"

"Of course!" Veron beams at me, and I'm grateful because especially compared to Ursula, Veron's such a good catch. I place the order, and we sit down in the lobby and wait.

"If I never told you this I am telling you now. I feel you, Veron. It's taken some tough moments to realize it, but I do. I think I haven't given you a fair chance at all. I know I haven't. It's a wonder you still talk to me."

"Whoa, I can't believe you're saying all this. Are you sure you haven't talked to Demetria?"

I pause. "Why are you bringing her up again?"

"Well, she told me . . . oh, never mind. It's just that you're pouring out your heart like this. I like it, I do. I just . . ."

"You can't believe it's really me? You think I'm feeding you lines of BS? Well, I'm not. As a matter of fact, I'd like to know if you want to spend some time together. Whatever you want to do."

"Well, I've never been to your house before. I'd like to visit. See how you're living."

"That's doable."

We make plans to head over after work. Our breakfast order finally arrives, and we load it into the car, where it smells so good it drives us nuts on the way back to work.

We're holding hands on our way from the parking lot, but then I see Ursula out of the corner of my eye. She's just standing there watching us, staring at us with big crazy eyes. I drop Veron's hand immediately, not sure Ursula could see it from her angle but wanting to play it safe. I start casually walking further apart from Veron, and then I make one of those cheesy phone gestures at her, meaning "I'll call you," and start walking the other way. She looks confused, but I keep going.

I call her when I get to my office, and she answers. "What's that all about?"

"Ursula's nosy ass was staring right at us. I didn't like it and wanted to look strictly professional with you."

"Seaphes, I will not have you disrespect me."

"I respect you, babe, I just don't like how she's been acting lately. She's trouble."

"Why? What has she been doing?"

"She's just . . . I mean, I guess Ursula is still carrying a torch for a brotha, but she can't seem to let go. I feel like she's a drama queen. Just trust me on this one. Stay as far away from her as possible."

— 3 3 —

DEMETRIA

Today work had me so busy that I only talked to Vee on her cell. Sounds like she's doing her thing. She's got herself a little nighttime hookup, and I don't even have to provide my play-by-play input on the deal. Which is great 'cause it gives me an opportunity to spend time with my own boo. But first I gotta take care of some other little business.

"So, it's been a minute since we've seen each other," I say into the phone as I'm driving home from work. "You miss me?"

"You know I do. When can I come see you?"

"Uh," I say, glancing at myself in the vanity mirror. "You can roll by my crib in a few. Meet me there around six. I gotta be somewhere by seven."

"Alrighty then."

I make a quick stop at the Kroger liquor aisle and pick up two bottles of Grey Goose. As soon as I get home, I light candles and slip on a sexy little satin nightgown that hugs my hips in all the right places. I love the way I look in the mirror, and I stand back to admire myself from various angles.

"I still got it going on big time, don't I? Can't anybody tell me anything, right?" I ask, winking at myself. I look for some perfume, but all I can find is a nearly empty bottle of sandalwood, which I dab on my wrists and the skin behind my ears.

When the doorbell rings I wait thirty seconds, then go answer it.

"What's up, playa?" I say, opening the door wide for Mike to come in.

"D–d–dayum, you look hot, baby. Woo, if I would've known how sizzling you are I could've come paid you a visit sooner."

"Aw, you don't love me anymore, do you?" I ask, pouting and swishing my hips back and forth as I walk toward the living room. "I poured you a drink, even though I'm not sure you deserve it. Hey, take off that shirt, you look too stuffy for my tastes," I say, winking. He nods and obeys me, pulling off his colorful Enyce polo shirt.

"Ooo, baby, you been working out for mommy?"

"You know how I do." He can't resist me anymore and finally grabs me squarely around the shoulders and plants a wet kiss on my lips. We tongue kiss for what feels like forever, and I have to squirm and tug at my thong. I enjoy the feel of his heated chest melting against my silk nightgown. He strokes the outline of one of my breasts, and I gasp and tilt my neck so he can kiss and lick it. I grow even wetter.

"That's enough," I tell him.

"No, it's not," he whines.

"What's wrong, babe?" I ask, laughing. Mike is staring at me glassy-eyed and rubbing his pants. I love sexually torturing men.

"Demetria, you are so damn fine it's unreal. Can I hit that?"

I lie on the floor and stare up at Mike. "I wonder what's on the news tonight," I say.

"Demetria," he whispers in urgent agony. I laugh inside.

"What, Mike? You ready for me to turn on CNN?"

"Forget turning on CNN. If I'm hot then you must be, too, 'cause when the sun shines it's not just blazing down on me."

I laugh. "I see I've taught you well about seduction. Okay, c'mere," I tell him sympathetically. I gesture with my finger.

Mike removes his pants and boxers. His dick is average, but experience has taught me that no matter what size a man is, I can pretty much still get what I want. I unsnap the single button of my gown so that he can get a full view of my nipples, which are so erect that I am tempted to rub them myself. Mike kneels and starts kissing my ankles and thighs, and I grab his head between my hands.

"Ooo, right there, right there."

" 'Bout time you got with the program," he mutters like he's still miffed at me. I laugh and kiss his hair, which tickles. Mike caresses my inner thighs and kisses them with loud smacks, a sound that totally arouses me. He presses the tip of his nose gently against my thong, inhaling deeply, and then starts poking the outside of the fabric with his tongue.

"Fuck, oooh," I moan, squirming and pushing his head against me. "That feels sooo good, Mike, keep going. Do what you did last time." I sigh, anticipating the master at work.

When my phone rings I barely blink an eye. No fucking way anyone's call is more important than what's happening to me.

Mike opens his mouth and grabs my thong between his teeth, pulling it off my hips ever so slowly. I move my butt, humping up and down, enjoying his teasing ways.

"You can't get enough, can you?" he asks.

"Not of you, Mike. That's what you get for putting it on me like you did. If it could be hot like this 24/7," I say, gasping when his tongue flicks and sucks me, "I wouldn't have any need for any other man. Just you."

"Mmm, damn, let me know if this feels good," he says. He gently places my legs on top of his shoulders, than inserts his scorching hot dick inside of me. I twist my body till I'm sitting on top of Mike, then pump and thrust, hopping up and down like I'm riding one of those huge inflatable beach balls. And after several minutes I scream so loud that Mike covers my mouth, making me want to laugh.

"What you doing that for?" I ask.

"You're scaring me, Demetria."

"Never be scared of loving me, Mike."

Mike rolls off me and lies back, breathing hard and groaning.

"Okay," I tell him, hopping up and going to grab my clothes. "Gotta go, gotta go. That was great. See you later, okay?"

He gives me a strange look, and I stop to give him a hug and sexy kiss before heading to the shower.

"Where're you going?" he says, trying not to pout.

"I told you I have an appointment."

"As in a date?"

"Michael, c'mon now. Don't start. I'm sorry, I just gotta take care of some business, and I'll call you later."

"You always do this."

"What do you mean 'always'? We've only hooked up twice."

"This is the third time!"

"Hello? The first time didn't count. It was just phone sex."

"But you still got off . . . got off the phone real quick."

"Ha ha, cute. I'm sorry if I have to be somewhere. It's not anything personal, I swear."

"Demetria, you are something else."

"Oh, honey, don't be upset. I'll make it up to you. I promise."

He sighs but lets me walk him to the door.

"You're a sweetheart, and I really mean that. I promise I'll call you, okay? Thanks for everything, Mike. 'Bye."

After drying off, I decide to wear an apple green shirt and matching leggings with some strappy sandals. I grab my BlackBerry and get in the car, very aware that it's now ten minutes to seven. Thad's split-level home is fifteen minutes away from my neighborhood, and looking down I see that I've missed a call from him. I don't bother listening to the voice mail; I just race.

Thad lives in a gated community near Lake Woodlands right behind a golf course. I drive up to the security gate and press in the code, but the gate doesn't open like it normally does. I punch in the code again. Nada.

"Hmmm." I maneuver my car so I can make a U-turn and get out of the way of the other cars that have now pulled in behind me.

When the last vehicle drives through the gate, I follow close behind it, knowing that's against the rules but not caring.

Thad's home sits on a small hill on a corner with manicured lawns, several mature oak trees, and a koi pond. When I pull up on his driveway I notice a black Mercedes SUV with the vanity plate #1 CHICK. My heart sinks, and my vision gets blurry. I swallow so hard it feels like my tongue has disappeared.

Thad? I say to myself in a trembling voice. I dial his cell, but he doesn't pick up. I dial again, praying that he was just temporarily preoccupied, but it hits voice mail again.

When I finally decide to back down his driveway, I delete his voice mail message without ever listening to it.

Sniffing, I give Vee a call, the only person I know I can talk to during a crisis like this.

"Hi there, girl, what's up?"

"Hi," I say, pretending to sound peppy and unconcerned. "You busy?"

She pauses but says, "Kinda. What's going on?"

"Just wanted to see how you're doing."

"I'm just pulling up to Seaphes's."

"Oh, snap," I say. "Sorry, I forgot." I bite my bottom lip and am glad she can't see my frown. "What do you guys have planned?"

"I don't know. I think he's cooking for me," she says. I can tell she's proud that he'd do something so special for her.

I roll my eyes, then mutter, "That sounds good. Well, eat at least some of everything on your plate. And make sure and request a glass of wine, like some cabernet sauvignon. Show him you have some class."

"Jeez, mommy, you'd think I don't know how to tie my shoes every day. But thanks for the reminder."

"Girl, please," I say, ignoring her silly sarcasm. "You know I'm here for you, only a phone call away."

"Demetria, I was just kidding. It's cool. Seaphes seems to be so much more attentive, and I am happy we're starting over on a good note."

"O-okay! Good for you. I guess I'll let you go. Call me later. I wanna hear all the details."

"Okay, how late will you be up?"

"Ain't no telling," I say in a gloomy voice, then hang up the phone.

— 3 4 —

Veron

For the life of me I cannot stop grinning. I feel like an idiot, but a happy, pinch-me-I-can't-believe-how-great-I-feel idiot. Seaphes is finally showing me the side of him I've always been curious to know. I wish I could bottle up my emotions right now and keep them forever.

But then again, I don't know why he's now acting so differently. Why the sudden change? Should I trust it? Be skeptical? Or wait for the next change? Is he being real?

When I get to his house, Seaphes opens the door wearing an apron over his blue jeans and T-shirt. I inhale and notice the aroma of cheese, tomato, and seasonings wafting through the doorway.

"What's that smell?"

"I'm a pro at throwing together a mean tray of turkey lasagna, and there's a side of fresh broccoli. And the cornbread is almost done. Homemade," he says, clearing his throat.

"Oooh, I'm scared of you," I say, impressed.

"Don't be scared. Come in and make yourself at home."

Seaphes's family room has high ceilings, black leather furniture, and built-in shelves completely lined with family photos: colorful, candid moments shared with his nephew, his sister and brother-in-law, his folks. I can tell he is proud of his family, because he's been chattering on and on about how well Tupac is doing and how his sister seems to be adjusting to motherhood, tough as it's been on her.

He continues filling up my ear with his voice after I follow him to the kitchen.

"I am happy that you're with me tonight, Veron. And you look good, as usual. Let me see your outfit."

I spread out my arms so he can get a good look at my new Egyptian dress.

"I know it's too fancy just to wear over here, but I didn't think you'd mind."

"Not at all. I like it when you dress up for me. Makes me think—er, hope—that you care."

"Kinda sorta," I tease, feeling a little bit self conscious "Is there anything I can help you with?"

"I don't want you doing a thing, woman. Sit down at the table. We can start out with some caviar dip and crackers while the lasagna finishes baking. What you wanna drink?"

"I want whatever you've been drinking today. Tons of it," I say, teasingly.

"What do you mean?"

"You seem like a changed man. It's . . . appealing. But I do have a question."

"What?"

"Well, I mean . . . you promise you'll stay this way? Happy, accommodating, sensitive, and caring?"

"I'll do my best. I-I'm just glad you're giving me second and third chances."

I look at him and say with a serious voice, "I'm glad, too."

He sets out a tray of crackers and caviar with cream cheese dip. Then he takes a fork and lifts up a bit of dip, spreading it on a cracker, and shoves it toward my mouth.

"Open up."

I obey him and enjoy the fact that he wants to feed me. The dip has a salty, creamy taste, and I nod my head. "Great job," I cheer. "More, more, more."

Seaphes obliges and prepares more crackers topped with dip. "You need anything else? You alright?" he asks.

"I am perfectly content, Mr. Hill. Oh, how about some music?"

"Argh," he says. "Forgot." He picks up the remote and aims it at his sound system. Brian McKnight's silky smooth vocals instantly fill the room with the thumping jam, "Used to Be My Girl."

"I don't wanna eat too much of this. I can't wait to taste your pasta. It smells so yummy."

"Just as long as I'm making you happy, that's what I'm concerned about."

"Seaphes, what took you so long? I mean, were you holding back on me?"

"No, everything you see is what I am. It's just that today you're seeing the better parts of me."

"Awww," I say, my heart softening with his every word.

"Let's eat."

We sit down at his dining room table, two candles lit, music softly playing, and chow down on some thick, cheesy, perfectly seasoned lasagna. I even have an ice-cold beer—I wasn't going to, but I remember what Demetria told me and say yes.

So now I'm so relaxed. Everything is going perfect tonight.

Seaphes is in the kitchen getting me a glass of lemon-water when the doorbell rings. I squirm in my seat, suddenly troubled.

"Hey, is that the door? Can you get that? Probably someone trying to sell newspaper subscriptions. Tell 'em I can't read. I'm illiterate." I laugh and walk toward the front door.

Demetria is standing on the front porch. Startled, I ask, "You here to sell something?"

"Oh, Veron," she says, looking sad and glancing at the ground. A wide multicolored scarf is wrapped around her head; I notice the soft curls of her hair softly peeking out from underneath it and resting on her shoulders. I slip outside to stand on the porch with her.

"Okay, first I need to know how you know where Seaphes lives. Then I need to know why you would come over here when you know we had a date."

"I know, girl, I know," she says, twisting her hands together. "I got his address from work and did a MapQuest on him. That's how I found the place. Vee, I needed to talk to you really bad and thought he'd be a good person to talk to as well."

"What? I'm sorry, I just—"

"Vee, don't let me just stand out here on the porch. You hear the thunder, see the storm clouds? I won't stay long, I promise."

"Come in. But your timing couldn't be worse."

"Well, I don't have control over when I experience a crisis," she says, actually sounding remorseful. "If I didn't desperately need you, you know I wouldn't just pop over to your man's place. And as I recall you showed up over at my crib at midnight not too long ago, and I was there for you."

I sigh. "Wait right here," I tell her. I want to cut my eyes real hard at her, but I don't. I just walk back into the house, joining Seaphes in the kitchen.

"Hey, who was that at the door?"

"You will not believe this," I say and mute the volume to the stereo. "Who is the worst person who could show up right now?"

"Ursula's here?" he asks confusedly. Just then she walks in. "Demetria, I haven't seen you in a minute," Seaphes remarks in a high-sounding, unnatural voice. I guess he's as bummed out as I am.

"Well, this won't take long. It's about me and my boyfriend," she says, giving me a warning glance. We all go in and sit in the living room. She continues, "He and I were supposed to hook up tonight, but when I stopped by his place, I recognized another woman's vehicle."

"Whose vehicle?" I ask, genuinely surprised.

"Uh, Marilyn," she says matter-of-factly. She stares straight at me, and her look says I should be careful not to ask the wrong questions.

"Ah, her," I say surprised. "Well, did you ask 'your boyfriend' what's up?" I ask.

"I can't get him on the phone! And that's not like him at all. I have a sinking feeling something fishy is going on. I hope they're not fighting. That she's not upping the ante," she says. Her voice drifts off when she realizes she's giving out too much information.

"Who is this boyfriend? I didn't know about him," Seaphes says.

"I don't want to get into all that. I just want a man's perspective."

"Demetria, any man that shuts you out has to be tripping. And maybe you're reading too hard into his not answering the phone. I don't always have my phone on me; doesn't mean I'm doing anything wrong."

"Okay, maybe you're right, Seaphes. At least I hope you are."

Looking at my watch, I say, "You feeling better now?"

Seaphes walks over to me and puts his arm around my shoulders. I want to enjoy his touch but can't help but feel uncomfortable with the way Demetria is leering at him, her face stony.

Seaphes ignores Demetria's stare and pulls me against his chest. "We were going to pop in some DVDs when you showed up. You're welcome to sit and watch movies with us for a minute. You still look very troubled."

"Oh, thank you, Seaphes," she says with a grateful look piercing her eyes. "Hey, I gotta get something out of the car."

The second that she leaves, Seaphes rushes to the kitchen before I get a chance to talk to him. I hear cabinets slamming open and shut and dishes rattling. "Hey, why don't you pull out some good movies while I clean up, okay, babe?" he yells out.

"I, uh, shoot, alright." I drop down to my knees and scour the case that holds his vast collection of films. *Déjà Vu, Fantastic Four, Antwone Fisher*, several Gabrielle Union movies . . .

"What did you find?"

"Lots of stuff. What you wanna look at?"

He sees what I'm holding. "How about something with Gabrielle? I love how she acts, and besides, she's an immensely beautiful woman."

"Well, thanks for the compliment," Demetria says, walking back into the living room with a bottle of Grey Goose swinging in her hand. I notice she left the jacket she was wearing in the car.

I clear my throat and glance at Seaphes. "Let Demetria get her plate of lasagna so we can settle in and watch our movie."

"Oh, that sounds good. I love lasagna. You got a bottle of

hot sauce, too? I like it hot." She makes her way to the kitchen and calls out, "Seaphes, can you fix my plate? And get us some glasses so I can pour our drinks. I'll fix up your Goose just the way you like it."

My shoulders cave in, and I can feel Seaphes staring at me. I turn around and look up at him and see his eyes pleading as if to say, Just don't make a fuss over nothing.

"Remember, I invited *you* over here, not her," he whispers to me before heading to the kitchen. And I try to reason with myself. He's right; I'm the one who got the invite.

I figure out how to turn on the DVD player and reluctantly slide in *Two Can Play That Game*. The movie is nothing to jump up over, but there are several funny moments in it, and I can use a good laugh.

"Hey, babe, come join us," Seaphes yells out.

When I return to the kitchen, Demetria is complimenting him on his cooking. "Seaphes, this is delicious. I didn't know you had these kinds of skills."

"Yeah, Miss Lady, I am very skilled in all kinds of things."

"Tell me more," she says, giggling.

"Demetria," I cut in, a little too sharply. "Have you tried calling Thaddeus again?"

Looking baffled, she sputters, "Hey, if he wanted to talk to me he'd call. Besides, after the way he's acting I might fire his ass and be single for real," she says in a distraught voice, taking a huge gulp of her vodka.

"Ha." I laugh out loud. "We don't have to worry about anything like that."

"What do you mean, Vee? You don't think I can get another man? Do you think another man would want me, Seaphes?"

I cast Seaphes a look so sharp he has no other choice than to close his mouth.

"What I meant to say, Demetria, is that you are the queen of playing the dating game. I'm sure you'll have another guy like Thaddeus Wakely in no time at all. I mean, whoever fits his profile would be perfect for you. Wealthy, older, sophisticated, sexy . . . and taken," I say, unable to help myself.

"Damn, what's gotten into you, Vee, huh? I'm the victim here. Why you putting me on blast?"

She casts Seaphes a distraught look, and he pipes up. "Hey, you two ladies. You look so sexy when you argue, but you don't have to argue to look sexy. Let's play nice, okay? Y'all need anything else? Veron, you okay? Want some more broccoli?"

"No, I want Demetria to tell us more about what happened. I mean, this is a first, Seaphes, you just don't know. Demetria is used to men skipping funerals to be with her. She ain't ever been on the dumpee side of things."

"What you say? He hasn't dumped me, girl."

"Not yet," I snap.

"Hey," Demetria whines. "I know you think that I don't have a heart, but, Vee, I can get hurt. I do get down in the dumps. You just don't know. Sometimes I lay alone in my bed at night crying my eyes out."

"Why?" I ask incredulously.

"Because . . . you don't know everything I've gone through, everything I still go through. I work hard for everything I have, and it's not always a hundred percent perfect, as if I'm some fairy tale princess, like, like I'm, uh, some damned Jada Pinkett Smith or something."

I giggle, unable to help myself. "You read magazines, Demetria. I'm sure you've heard her say that her relationship with Will Smith is not perfect. They're just normal people. I think I read that they're even into swinging."

"Hmmm, that's interesting, but I'm still not her," she says, her voice slurry. She places her hand on her stomach and rubs it. "This here is some good-ass spaghetti."

"That's lasagna, my dear," Seaphes jumps in.

"No, it's not," she says in a whiny childlike voice.

Seaphes and I exchange baffled looks.

"Demetria, maybe you need to drink some water," I say, sliding my untouched glass of water toward her. "I can't believe how horribly you hold your liquor. And, Seaphes, you need to not drink so much, either," I warn him.

"Ugh," she sniffs. "I don't want that. You know what I want?" she asks. "White chocolate martinis. Seaphes, will you be a sweetheart and go to the grocery store real quick? I am desperately thirsty for something . . . something sweet and rich," she says, her voice husky. She opens her purse and talks out loud while scribbling down the items she needs to make the drinks.

"Hey, it's raining out there, right?" Seaphes asks.

"You gonna let some rain stop you? Please, Seaphes, I really want this, okay?" Without waiting for him to reply she says, "Here's a fifty," and places the single bill in his hand.

Finally he shakes his head. "Okay, I'll go, but you don't have to buy anything." He hands her the fifty. "I'll be right back. That okay, Veron?" he asks. He doesn't make another move until I reluctantly nod my head.

I look through the window to watch him drive off, then slowly turn around to face Demetria with my arms folded underneath my breasts.

"What the hell is going on, Demetria?"

"Damn, Vee, don't take that tone with me. Thad is tripping big-time, and I'll confess, I don't know how to deal with it. It's never happened like this before."

"Break it down, Demetria. I'm tired of all your vague descriptions. What exactly went on?"

"He and I were supposed to hook up tonight at seven. I had some business to take care of and was running slightly late. And when I got there, like I said before, homegirl's Benz was sitting up in the driveway," she sputters angrily. "And when my man doesn't answer my calls I figure something stank is going down." Her voice catches. "Uh, and then a minute ago I noticed that Thad sent me a text. Here, you wanna read it?"

She finds the message on her BlackBerry and then thrusts the phone at me.

I've had you under surveillance a couple of times. I love you with all I have, but don't trust you. And where there's no trust . . .

"Damn, Demetria," I say.

She stands up and starts pacing. "He's tripping. I mean, what does the man expect? I can't be by myself for months while he flies across the world. And he's still legally attached, so I never had to be with his ass at all, did I?"

"You can be with whoever you choose to be with, Demetria. So I assume you wanted to be with him."

"I sure as hell did. And I still want to be with him. He's my number one boo, he really is. I–I just wish he hadn't reacted so swiftly. I just don't understand," she says. A loud heart-wrenching sob bursts through her lips. I frown but jump up to hug her. "It'll be alright. Thad's just upset right now. If he loves you he'll forgive you."

"You think so, Vee? I hope he realizes the mistake he's making. We're really good together. He's my ultimate type; you know how hard that is to find? He treats me so good. I mean, I gotta get with other guys just to make that comparison, just to know for myself that a man like Thad is so rare."

"Well, don't worry yourself right now. Chill out with us for the night, okay?"

"Oh, Veron, you're too good to me. A pure Mother Teresa. I know why Seaphes is in love with you. I would be too if I was a man."

"Whoa. That's alright. Calm down, Demetria. Everything is going to line up for you."

I hear a key being inserted in the front door, and Seaphes walks in wearing a wide grin. "Hey, ladies, how's it going? You miss me?"

"We never noticed you were gone, playa." Demetria smirks. "But thanks for getting the stuff. Why don't you two lovebirds have a seat and let me mix the drinks? I wanna do that as my token of appreciation for letting me bust up in here nine-one-one." She giggles to herself and snatches the grocery bags from Seaphes, heading out to the bar in the living room.

He and I look at each other and just shake our heads. I start to load the dishwasher, but Seaphes hugs me from behind, kissing me on the side of my neck and getting me roused up. "Oh, mmm, stop it. No, don't stop, keep going," I tease. He presses his body against my behind. My knees feel ready to buckle. It's been so long, and I thought I was ready to be loved tonight. But it doesn't look like I'll be getting any with Demetria here.

Seaphes grabs me by both shoulders and turns me around to face him. He bends down and kisses me, thrusting his tongue in my mouth and using one of his hands to squeeze my butt cheek.

When we come up for air, I gasp. "Aw, man, how much longer does she have to stay here?" He simply laughs and gives me a wink so sexy that I could get lost in his piercing eyes for the rest of the night.

Demetria calls out that the drinks are ready. I grab Seaphes's hand and lead him to the sofa, so we can finally take a much-needed seat. I am so exhausted that it feels good to do nothing. I know I won't be seriously looking at the movie, either. I just want to sit next to my guy and finally enjoy his presence.

— 35 —

Seaphes

It feels good to be sitting next to Veron on the couch. It feels even better to be holding her hand. But she's squeezing my hand really tight, and it makes me wonder. Is she afraid I'm going to run away? Does she think I'm going to run off with Demetria? Not likely. Women like Demetria are complicated but easy—not right for me. I just wish that her attention-seeking wasn't prohibiting all three of us from having a good time.

Demetria struts into the living room juggling tall chocolate martinis in both hands. "Here, Seaphes," she says and hands me my drink. She takes a sip from the other glass. "Vee, I know how you are," she explains. "I didn't think you'd want one, so I just made me and Seaphes some. I know he'll feel this. It is sooo tasty."

"Hmmm," Veron says, with hurt sewn through her voice. "I'm cool. I can finish sipping on that beer."

"You were drinking beer? Since when?"

Veron just ignores her question.

"Anyway," Demetria says, "you can turn on the movie now. Hey, I wanna sit on the other side of Seaphes. We can make a Seaphes sandwich, okay?" She giggles. "I'm so silly. But this feels good. I sure don't want to be somewhere by myself crying and boo-hooing over Thad while he's behind closed doors with Marilyn. Mmm, mmm, no. This here is much better."

Veron presses the play button, and the previews begin showing. I lower my face toward hers and kiss her on the lips. She blushes and shifts uncomfortably in her seat. We're quiet for a minute, dreamily staring into each other's eyes.

Demetria leans across me to get to Veron. "Hey, Vee, you spending the night here? It's still raining and thundering outside like crazy. I'm getting kind of worried, because it usually floods in my neighborhood and sometimes streets are impassable."

"I haven't thought about all that," Veron remarks without looking directly at her friend.

"Okay. Hey, Seaphes, how's your drink? Did I do a good job? I hope you like it."

"Mmm, yes, Demetria, it's delicious." I nod and sip on the drink again.

It's silent for ten seconds before she scoots forward from sitting on the sofa so she has a clearer view of Veron. "Let's toast. Damn, Vee, go get your beer so we can all do this together."

"Okay," Veron says.

She starts to stand up, but I beat her to it. "I'll get your drink for you," I say.

Demetria rolls her eyes and opens her mouth, poking one finger inside like she's gagging.

"Ha," Veron laughs. "Need a bucket?"

"Need three or four. Y'all are quite sickening."

When I return with Veron's can of beer, Demetria raises her glass and clears her throat.

"To love, friendship, happiness, great sex, and getting whatever the hell we want out of life."

"Here, here," I say, tapping their drinks. I take a sip and

notice that Demetria is really sucking her martini down quickly. It is good, though. I press my glass against Veron's lips. She opens wide and swallows a mouthful of the rich chocolate concoction.

"Mmm," she grins, looking up at me. Her grin falls when she notices a sullen look on Demetria's face.

We all settle back in our seats, and I wrap one arm around Veron's shoulder as she scoots closer so that her thigh touches mine. The movie opens up, and we're all quiet for a few minutes. But then I start hearing this irritating sniffing noise every few seconds. When turn my head and look at Demetria, she's holding her head in her hands.

I glance at Veron. She just shrugs, sits back in her seat, picks up the remote, and increases the volume. I wasn't expecting that, and I have to hide a grin.

We attempt to watch the movie for a couple of minutes, but then Demetria leans across me and shouts at Veron, "Can I get that, please?" She leans across me even farther and holds out her hand, nodding at the remote. I move back so that Demetria isn't touching me.

Veron firmly shakes her head no.

Demetria stands up.

Veron pauses the movie. "What now, Demetria?"

"Damn, I just want to turn the TV down! I like talking and discussing the scenes. Hell, it's not like we're at Tinseltown where they want your ass to keep quiet. What the hell, Veron? What the . . . I just . . . what the hell?" She sounds very drunk, and with her scarf wrapped crookedly around her head and her pouty lips poking out, she looks uncharacteristically distressed.

"Oh, God, here we go," Veron says. But then she relents, looking at Demetria with softer eyes. "It's gonna be okay, sweetie," Veron assures her, giving in like a good friend should. And with that, Demetria breaks down completely, crying and wailing. I feel like this is something I probably shouldn't be watching, but I can't tear my eyes away.

"Do you love him?" Veron asks, getting up to stand next to Demetria. She tenderly moves strands of hair away from Demetria's face. Demetria just keeps sobbing and moaning. "Shhh," she whispers. She keeps soothing her but locks eyes with me.

Finally, Demetria yawns. "I'm sleepy," she slurs. "Maybe I can take a little nap. This liquor is really making a sister feel tired, plus all the other mess—"

"Okay, okay, let's go. C'mon, Seaphes, okay?"

I nod, and Veron grabs Demetria by the hand and follows me down the main hallway.

"Why you acting like a stranger?" Demetria asks Veron. "You act like you haven't been back here before."

"I haven't."

"Really?" She's talking real loud. "Don't tell me I'm the first woman to know where his bedroom is."

"What?" Veron squeals, stopping in front of my bedroom. I fold my arms and stare at Demetria, who looks a mess.

"I mean tonight, dummy. When I was trying to find the bathroom, my nosy self looked around. I found his bedroom, and two other rooms. One I think is a study, and the other looks like his nephew's room since there are toys and a crib in there. I guess only his room is available for me to take a nap."

"Demetria, now wait one minute."

"What, Vee?"

"What, Vee nothing. Why on earth would you think I would allow you to sleep in his bed? Why would you think he'd allow it? How do you think that looks?"

"Ga-*iirl,* please," Demetria whines.

"Girl nothing. What exactly are you trying, Demetria?"

I'm looking at Demetria sternly, and I know that beside me, Veron is, too.

"You're just being silly as usual, Vee," she says, laughing nervously. "Just chill, girl. You read into things too much. It's storming out there; about to turn into Hurricane Katrina Part Two and all you can think about is how it looks. Well, screw it. I'm going to try my best to get home then. I don't need this."

"Oh, Demetria," Veron says.

"Oh, Demetria nothing," she snaps. "Why don't you feel sorry for me? After all I've done for you. I'll tell you why. You feel secure now that Seaphes is finally paying attention to you, and once you got your man, you happily kicked my ass to the curb. Some kind of best friend you are."

She moves down the hallway past Veron and me like she's returning to the living room, but then she swings back around and walks into my room. Veron follows her in.

"No, screw this," I hear her say. "Seaphes is my friend, too. You don't own this house. I don't think he'd mind if I lie down for an hour." She's talking as if I'm not just outside the room. "If he has a problem with that, then tell him to come in here and see me."

"Oh, hell no," Veron says and runs back out in the hallway.

"Seaphes, it's time you put her in check. Demetria has lost her mind."

I stand still for a moment. I don't want to react impulsively and make the situation worse.

"Seaphes, did you hear what I said? Tell that girl she cannot sleep in your bed. She doesn't have to go home, but she's gotta get the hell outta there."

"Wait," I say in a quiet voice. "You two ladies need to turn it down a notch. Now."

"But—"

"Both of you are acting like you are kindergarteners. If Demetria is tired, then she can lie down on my chaise, which is in the study. I can bring it out to the living room, we can quietly watch the movie, and she can rest. Is that an acceptable compromise?"

"Hold the fuck up, why are you siding with her, Seaphes? Am I or am I not your number one?"

When I look into Veron's eyes, I can tell that this is something she's passionate over. She looks strangely upset, and I can tell this is big. I have to make a smart decision here. So I wise up.

I grab her by both hands. "You're about to know what you are to me."

I gaze steadily at her for a minute, then go inside my room. Demetria is lying down on the floor next to my bed. Her clothes are still on and so are her shoes, but she's already snoring.

I kneel down and shake her arm. "Game over, Demetria. You gots to go."

"Hmmm, no, don't wanna," she mumbles.

"C'mon now, get up. You can't drive, but we've got to get you home."

"You gonna drive me home?" she asks, perking up.

"No, I'm calling you a taxi. You need to pull yourself together. I'm trying to treat you with some dignity, because this isn't like you. But c'mon, get up."

She reluctantly sits up, her scarf once again lying crooked on her forehead. Not perfectly pulled together. Not as stunning and beautiful as we're accustomed to seeing her. And for the first time I perceive how really fragile Demetria Sparks is. She's like a little girl trying to act like a woman. And that's another category of females that I've forgotten about: the ones who play that tough role outwardly but inside are as delicate as a baby's eardrum.

"Help me!" she cries out.

I lean near Demetria, who is struggling to properly wrap the scarf about her head and peering up at me with wide eyes. I place my hand on her shoulder, but before I can comfort her Veron comes in and quietly kneels next to me.

"I can handle it from here," she says quietly.

"Vee!"

"Don't worry, baby girl. I got you."

"Take it off, please," Demetria begs. "I'm getting a horrible migraine." Veron touches Demetria's face and then gently removes the scarf from around her head. Her curls are now free to fall around her face, which is puffy with red marks. She reaches her arms out to Veron like a child, requesting a comforting hug.

"Oh, I wish I could tell you everything," Demetria cries as Veron embraces her. "I wish I could tell you the sorrows of my heart."

"Don't worry about it, girl. I know things'll get better for you, and for me."

"Thanks, Vee," Demetria sniffs. She finally sits up and then reaches out her hand for Veron to pull her up to her feet. Throwing us grateful looks, she heads down the hall. We both follow her and find her grabbing her purse.

"I don't belong here. I'm going on home. I'll get a cab. Thanks for everything, y'all. I hope you can enjoy the rest of the evening."

"Are you sure you'll be okay, Demetria?" I ask.

"I'm going to be just fine."

— 3 6 —

VERON

After Demetria leaves, I admit, I feel a little awkward for the first few moments. But Seaphes never mentions what just happened. He simply turns off the TV and sits on the couch, quietly sipping his chocolate martini.

And the fact that he respects my silence makes me respect him even more.

"You hungry?" I ask. "Can I make you another plate?"

"Nope, babe, I'm good. Thanks."

"Okay," I say trying to fill the silence. "I guess I oughta be going myself. It's getting late."

"No way."

"But," I say yawning. "I gots to get up early."

"So do I. I get up to go running at five."

I roll my eyes. "Well, I'm not going to be doing all that, but there're things I want to do at home," I say. I head for the door.

"Okay," Seaphes says, waving me away. "But that means you won't be getting the back massage I was thinking about giving you."

Fifteen minutes later we're naked in Seaphes's shower. I'm giggling while he tickles me. I'm covering up my breasts, and he keeps trying to make me laugh so my hands will fall to my sides and he can get a nice little feel.

"Stop it, Seaphes. I'm trying to be mad at you. You promised me a back rub!"

"Don't," he says, kissing me on the back of my neck, "be mad." Kiss on my ear. "Maybe I'll get to it." Kiss on my hair. "Later." I grunt when I feel Seaphes press his body against my back. He wraps his arms around my waist; the combination of water splashing me against my chest and feeling his erection pressing against my backside makes me even more wet.

"You ready?" he moans, wiggling his butt around until his dick begins to press inside of me from behind.

"Mmm hmmm," I groan, closing my eyes, and reach behind to grab him and guide him in.

He pumps lovingly inside me for a long time, and as I climax I think to myself how ironic it is that I have Demetria to thank that I finally got some loving.

— 3 7 —

Demetria

When I see Veron at work the next morning she's walking with a spirited bounce. I stop her in the hallway.

"Hey, Vee, got a moment?"

"Yes, baby girl, how you doing?"

"Let's go in the ladies' room lounge."

She follows me, and we sit on the houndstooth couch just like old times.

"Thank you for being there when I needed you. I know I'm not easy to deal with . . ."

"Please, Demetria, you don't have to explain. We're good. We're very good," she says, and winks.

I stare at her. "You?"

"Yep."

"Damn! Go girl," I say, and we high-five. I'm glad for her, but I can't help but wonder . . . would Seaphes have liked it better if I'd been there to join in on the fun?

"Well, how was it?"

She hesitates but says, "I don't kiss and tell."

"What?" I screech. "Girl, come on. I always tell you when Thad and I do the do." My face falls at mentioning his name, and I begin fiddling with my hands.

"You haven't heard from him, huh?"

I shake my head. "It's killing me, too. Part of me wants to call, but no way. Unless a woman maintains control, her relationship is doomed."

"Oh, Demetria, you can't be serious."

"What you talking about? That's in the book. I know you know that."

"Yeah, but I'm starting to wonder. You have to read that book critically. There's some stuff in there that I don't know if it works. I mean, sure, there are some helpful tips, too, things that have actually worked in my favor."

"Example?"

"I agree with the part that says if we stay feminine, we'll appeal to the part of a man that wants to protect us. I've noticed that Seaphes really responds when I let him be the man."

"Ah ha," I say and give her a thoughtful glance. Maybe that's part of my problem. I try to be so strong most of the time, which I thought was the right way to be. Except last night my weakness helped me learn that my friends do care about me. That even when I'm not on top of the world and I'm down in the dumps, they're there for me. And that lesson is worth learning, even if it's risky to expose my true self.

"I hear ya," I tell Vee. "Well, I hope to hell that book can help me get Thad to talk to me. But I just don't know for sure." I stand up and pace the length of the room.

"Talk to Seaphes. He'll advise you."

"Y-you sure, Vee?"

"I'm positive. Seaphes has a good heart and he won't steer you wrong. You have my blessing."

Shocked, I tell her, "Thanks, girl. I'll give it a try." We hug one more time. And I'm learning you can never hug too much, never be loved too much.

Later on, right after the lunch break, Seaphes walks into my office. "Hey, I heard you wanna see me."

"Yep, it's about . . . Thad," I say and squirm.

"Who is this guy?"

"It's not important."

"Don't give me that."

"Well, there are certain things that I'm not at liberty to discuss."

"You love him?"

"I don't have to answer that. I just need you to help me get him back. That's your role. You tell me what I should do, because right now I can't think clearly for myself."

Seaphes sighs. "Okay, Demetria. What you need to do is get in touch with him—only give it a few days. Don't delay longer than that, because the more time passes between you after a falling out, the less chances you have of getting back together. He'll assume you've moved on, and that will give him the justification to move on, too."

"That makes sense. But meanwhile, what can I do to keep myself from going crazy? I hate not knowing everything. I mean, he sent me this crappy text message that indicates he's been spying on me."

"Oh, yeah? You didn't tell me that part."

"It's embarrassing. And maddening. I don't know whether to be totally angry or flattered in some sick sort of way."

"Well then, I don't know, Demetria. You may want to

close the door on this relationship. That's not healthy behavior."

"Oh great, just what I *don't* want to hear."

"You're a strong woman, Demetria. I'm sure you'll figure out what to do."

Seaphes stands up and gestures at me. I stand up as well, arching my neck to look in his eyes. I am grateful for his attention, something that I desperately need right now. We hug, and he goes back to his office.

For the rest of the work week I lay low. I want to reconnect with Thad, but every time I pick up the phone to dial his number, I hesitate and hang up before I can press the seventh digit. I know we're playing the game right now. Who can hold out the longest? Who's gonna cave in first and say the dreaded words "I'm sorry"? It's times like these when I wonder if the game playing is worth it.

Regardless, I'm pretty relieved when I get through the work week without crawling back to Thad on my knees. And by the time Sunday morning arrives, I am fueled by a burst of energy from preparing for the Walk America event.

A group of us from work have decided to hang together. I've never participated in this event before, but Vee assures me that it'll be something that I'll never forget, this day spent helping babies born with birth defects. Plus, we'll have loads of fun.

We're at Vee's apartment. I decided to swing by her place by seven thirty this morning, so we can ride to the University of Houston together.

"Demetria," she says, "if you really know someone, you can sense when something is wrong. And I know you, girl."

"Ah, hmmm," I say, then concentrate on tying my shoelaces. "Well, at least I still look good. No man is going to take away my self-esteem forever."

"Amen to that."

We grab our iPods, a water cooler, and a couple of towels, and are on our way.

When we arrive at UH I am amazed at the hundreds of people already gathered for the event—in every direction, there's a sea of walkers wearing colorful T-shirts. From toddlers to college students, to senior citizens, to dozens of uniformed policemen . . . it feels as if everyone and their mama are out here on this hot Sunday morning.

Vee and I cart our belongings to the City of Houston tent. The loud sounds of southern rap songs blare from the stereos.

"Hey," Veron says, "I'm going to try and reach Seaphes."

"Alright, girl," I say, smiling, and for a rare moment I don't mind that she gets to talk to him without me being in on the conversation. I bought new gear just for this event, and to me new clothes represent a new attitude, a new me. So I'm not surprised when I break into another wide smile when I see Seaphes and Veron walk toward me. They're looking at each other and sharing a laugh. Good for them, I think. Seaphes turns around and a petite young lady walks up huffing and puffing and pushing a huge stroller.

I step up to her and hold out my hand. "Hey, you must be Greta, Seaphes's sister?" I say, then stoop down until I tower over the stroller. "And this here must be cute little Tupac. Oh, he's so fine. May I hold him?"

"Okay," Greta says, "but only for a minute. You don't

know how much trouble I had to go through just to get him tied up in this thing. He hates being confined," she explained.

"I don't blame him," I coo and wait for Greta to unstrap her son. "Hey, cutie. We're going to be best buddies today. I'm Auntie Demetria." He smiles at me.

"Don't hesitate to put him back if he gets too heavy to hold," Greta says.

"Aw, girl, don't worry. I got this," I assure her.

We assemble in a growing crowd of walkers behind a rope. Soon we're off. People are chatting away, taking swigs of bottled water, listening to iPods, and taking one step at time, as they will be doing for this approximately six-mile walk.

"You feel okay?" Seaphes asks. He's walking next to me with Veron on his other side and his sister tugging along behind. Tupac is still in my arms. Out of the corner of my eye I notice Ursula Phillips walking behind us, Percy Jones tiredly tagging behind her.

"I feel great, Seaphes," I say a little too loud. "The weather is beautiful. It's great to see all these people out here. Shoot, I may catch someone today."

"That would be great," Veron says, looking carefully around at everybody who's walking nearby. No hot men. She shrugs.

Eventually we step onto North MacGregor Drive, a street filled with aging mansions that reflect the rich history of Houston's Third Ward. With its towering trees and horseshoe driveways, the boulevard is bordered by the wide stretch of Brays Bayou, which includes a curved hiking trail lined by an oasis of trees and shrubs.

"Look, Tupac. Isn't the water beautiful?" I say, pointing.

He hops up and down in my arms, and it's so cute I squeeze him against my chest in a loving hug.

Suddenly I look up and see Thaddeus and Marilyn pass by us, only a few feet away. I stop in my tracks.

"Dang, he's getting a little bit heavy," I murmur and look back at Greta.

"Oh, girl, sorry about that. I'll take him now."

I hand him over and click off the volume on my iPod. I run a few steps ahead, leaving my crew behind, until I am just inches away from Thad.

I pull out my BlackBerry, hands sweating so much that I nearly drop the phone. I dial Thad's number. He isn't even talking to Marilyn as they walk. But I see him reach for his phone, glance at the number, and slide the phone back into his belt clip.

Again I stop walking. Seaphes bumps into me seconds later.

"Oh, sorry," I say.

When I don't move, he turns to me. "You alright, Demetria?"

I point ahead of us.

"Who're you pointing at? There are a million peeps out here."

"Him" is all I say. Seaphes looks ahead and gets it.

I feel close to collapsing. But Seaphes pats me on the back and gives me pep talks, filling my soul with the strength I need to stay on course the next hour or so. His soothing voice and reassurance keeps me from feeling worse about Thaddeus, but it does little to combat the harsh stares I keep getting from both Veron and Ursula.

— 3 8 —
VERON

Despite my better judgment, I agree to go to lunch with Ursula the day after Walk America.

We decide that, if you're in the mood for breakfast food, nothing beats eating at The Breakfast Klub, which is known for its waffles and chicken wings, and is probably among the most popular black-owned restaurants in town. We knew we were going to have to take an early lunch; if you don't get there by 11:30 a.m. the line can extend outside the door and spread down the sidewalk.

We place our orders and find a table in the corner of the dimly lit restaurant.

"Well, I'll just be honest," Ursula starts. "I can't stand what's-her-face."

I want to laugh but don't. "Aw, be nice."

"How can you expect someone to be nice to a backstabbing bitch like Demetria? She totally dominated Seaphes for almost all of the event. I can't believe that he was going to get her lunch and sodas after we got back to the tent."

"Girl, Seaphes is like that. He's a good ole southern guy and hardly ever forgets his hospitality."

"I don't care what his mama taught him about manners; she should've added advice about watching out for fake women like your girl. She acted like she was bleeding to death or something. Now, tell me, this man who dumped her, what's he about?"

"Oh, he's someone who catered to her every need, but then I guess he decided to get ghost on her. It is shocking to see her go from one extreme to another." I feel kinda like a snake telling Demetria's business, but when I think about how selfish she can be, my feelings of compassion are largely quieted.

"Well, there's something about her that I just don't trust. Besides," she says, leaning in closer since the restaurant is getting much noisier. "How can you trust a woman who sleeps with your man?"

"You just saying that, or you know it for a fact?"

"All the signs are there, Veron. Watch how Seaphes and Demetria interact with each other. He is very in tune to her even though he pretends like he isn't. He had the nerve to tell me they operate on a strictly professional level. He must think he's talking to a fool."

"I don't know. It's hard to know from just that. She's just flirty."

"Well, I'm convinced," she says. "And girl, I've seen this enough to know what I'm talking about."

Despite myself, I'm starting to have doubts. There have been enough little things that have bothered me . . . as much as I want to trust Seaphes, what Ursula is saying is starting to nag at me. She sees this and continues. "As a matter of fact, when we get back to work I want you to go in on something with me. It'll be harmless fun."

Ursula leans in further and describes what she thinks I should do.

* * *

When we get back to work I am prepared to conduct a test. Although I have to admit I have been silently stewing at Demetria ever since she dominated Seaphes's time for the Walk America event, I know I have to give in and act like we're on good terms. So I roll by her office still holding my purse and wearing the biggest smile I can muster up.

She is sitting at her desk scrutinizing some documents.

"Hey, Demetria, how was lunch?"

"Oh," she says, looking surprised. "I thought you were pissed at me."

"Why would I be pissed at you? May I sit down?"

"Sure, knock yourself out." She continues concentrating on her work and talks to me without looking at me. "I dunno why. But I passed by your office and said good morning, and you turned your head away."

"Oh, it wasn't on purpose. I was busy."

"You weren't on the phone. No one else was in your office. You looked dead in my face and ignored me. Is it because of Seaphes?"

"Girl, you gotta be kidding me," I tell her with wide eyes. "What does he have to do with anything?"

"Nothing, actually, and it's about time you realized that. I don't mean to sound insulting, but you gotta be more secure."

"Oh, like how secure you are with Thaddeus?"

"What did you say? That's an altogether different thing. Thaddeus is intentionally acting foul—he won't talk to me, and keeps sending me these stupid text messages . . ."

"Oh, yeah, what have the messages been saying?"

Demetria grabs her BlackBerry and scrolls through the messages.

"Look at this. I tried to get him to go talk with me, and this is what he writes. 'I am trying to decide if having a one-on-one will be worth it.' It sounds so cold, like he never knew me, Vee." She puts the phone down between us on her desk. "I am this close to cursing his ass out, but I've been chilling. And that's because of your man, okay? He's been keeping me sane. Talking me out of doing things I might regret. He gives me good advice and I need that, you know that, right?"

"Right," I say slowly. "Of course."

Her office phone rings and she picks up and listens for several seconds.

"What?" she says, looking confused. "What the hell are you calling me about that for?" She listens for another few seconds, then turns around a little to yell into the phone. "Damn, I don't care!" she says. Meanwhile, I reach over and grab her cell phone and drop it into my bag. Easy.

She's still yelling. "Call somebody who gives a damn!" She hangs up finally and turns to me. "I can't believe it," she says.

"What happened?"

"Percy Jones had the nerve to call me just to ask if I looked at TV last night, that *I Love New York* crap with her transvestite-looking ass. He wanted to know who I thought would win. What the hell do I care who she ends up sleeping with? See, Percy and I are hardly on the same level; he can barely hold a conversation with me. That's why he's messing around with Ursula."

"Yeah, they both deserve each other."

"Wait a second, weren't you two acting buddy buddy yesterday at Walk America?"

"Girl, I was just being nice. She was gossiping, wouldn't shut up."

"Well, at least you know how to pick your friends. I don't know what any man would see in a woman like her."

I stand up and excuse myself, grateful that she is so busy

running off at the mouth that she doesn't notice I slipped her phone inside my purse.

As planned, Ursula and I meet up on the third floor in the ladies' room.

"You get it?" I ask.

"No, actually. I was in there for a while, but he wasn't about to leave while I was there. Excuse me for saying so, but your boy was acting like a real prick. It seems like every time he sees me he gets on the immediate defensive. I guess I've screwed up royally with him."

"Whatever happened between you two?"

"We were lovers," she says point-blank, and looks like she's going to keep talking.

"Okay, I don't want to hear any more. But . . . you two are through, right?"

"Huh?" she asks distractedly. "Oh, yeah, you don't have to worry about him ever wanting to hook up with me again."

"But you still want to hook up with him?"

She just stares at me with emotionless eyes.

I hand Ursula Demetria's phone, tell her that I'll see her later, and prepare myself to do one of the hardest things I've ever done. It feels weird to say you care about someone but you still don't know if you should trust him. I guess it's the way Hillary Clinton feels about Bill. She totally stood by her man when he publicly humiliated her with his philandering. You have to wonder if, behind closed doors, she pulled off her earrings and pumps and socked him in the eye on a few occasions.

I head up toward his office, and as soon as I lay eyes on Seaphes I can't help but break out into a genuine smile. I can't believe I'm playing games with him. He looks especially fine today, in his three-piece Armani, shoes shined to perfection, hair freshly cut. And he smells so good that at first I don't say anything, just stand there inhaling him for a minute. Why can't I just trust him? But I can't stop thinking about what Ursula said. She sounded so sure. And I don't want to be the last one to know if anything is going down between him and my friend.

"You going somewhere?" I ask, nodding at his fancy clothing.

"Yep, got an important meeting. And now my freaking printer is acting up. I need to print ten copies of a proposal. Can you help me, please?"

Blushing with the foolishness of what I'm about to do, I ask, "You want me to sit here and try to get the copies to print?"

"Yes, thank you so much! That way I can run downstairs for a few minutes and see if the project manager has the drawings I requested."

And just like a man, Seaphes rushes from his office but leaves his keys and his cell phone prominently spread out on his desk. He makes things so easy, I think, and I grab his phone, rotating the track wheel and clicking it until it displays the call log. It shows me every number that has been dialed and received for the past ten days: Greta, Veron, Timothy, Aunt Crystal, Marimon (his boss), Sparkle, Floyd, Bank, Gerald, and quite a few other names. No Demetria.

When he comes back in, I hand him the documents that I got to print out while he was gone. "Here you go, baby. You get to your meeting. Good luck."

"Thanks, Veron," he says, looking me in the eyes and smiling. "You're the best woman I know." He gives me a quick kiss and leaves.

Feeling lower than the bottom of a coal mine, I sit at his desk and pull out drawers. Supplies, books, stationery. Finally I come across a file labeled PERSONAL as Seaphes's office phone rings.

The caller ID says Demetria.

I pull out Seaphes's personal file and tuck it under my arm, walk out of the office, and go to meet Ursula.

"You get his phone?" she asks.

"Girl, I looked at it, but I'm not going to steal the man's phone."

"Are you kidding?" she snaps. "We can copy and paste his address book and print out the info."

"I don't think it's necessary to do all that."

"Yes, it is! 'Cause with a man like Seaphes, it's not just Demetria that you have to worry about. It's the other freaks that he hides in the closet."

"Ursula, you're scaring me."

"I'm not the one you should be scared of," she insists. "It's those other two conniving people that you gotta watch."

"Yeah, but I didn't see any calls to Demetria, so maybe he's not as into her as you think."

"Homeboy may have erased her incoming calls and texts. I *know* she texts him."

"I'm sorry; how would you know all that?"

"Because people are stupid enough to say things to people, and those people come back and tell me. And I don't forget certain information. You never know when you'll need to use it."

"Well, I'm just going to leave it. I looked through the phone." I pause. "What about Demetria's?"

Ursula waves it at me. "This tramp got so many men's phone numbers in her address book that my hands are getting tired from flipping through this info. Shoot, is there anybody in Houston she hasn't screwed?"

"Well, I got his personal file and I want to look through it, but I refuse to do it here. Let's go sit in my car."

"Great idea," she says.

We head down and settle in my car. Ursula makes all kinds of disapproving sounds as she looks through Demetria's phone. "Yep, she texts your boy a lot."

"Let me see," I say, feeling a little scared.

"See this name Sparkle? It's attached to her cell number."

"Hmm, sneaky," I say and read the texts.

CALL ME.

LUNCH 2DAY?

DID U ENJOY UR SELF LAST NITE?

"Wait, what does she mean by that?" I say. I show the message to Ursula.

"Uh huh. See? I bet they hooked up for a nice little fuck session. Bitches are so stupid. One thing you never do, if you're a smart ho, is leave a paper trail. No text messages, e-mails, nothing that mentions the hookup. Nothing is private anymore, it's a damn shame," she says, energetically looking through Demetria's phone.

I give her a funny look and start flipping through Seaphes's personal papers. His time sheet notes that he's been out several times in the last few years for funerals, which is sad. I dig through a lot of papers with his insurance information, that kind of thing. Suddenly, my eyes enlarge when I notice a silver-framed photograph showing Seaphes grinning as he poses cheek to cheek with a woman sitting on his lap. She's smiling too, holding up her hand and flashing a gorgeous ring on her wedding finger. And she's wearing a sterling silver heart-shaped pendant that bears an inscription: SEAPHES LOVES SAPPHIRE.

"Who the heck is she? I never knew he was engaged. . . ." I stop talking, too angry to realize he had more than one fiancée.

"He's a sneaky bastard," she says, awed.

"You know, I can't do this anymore. My head is starting to hurt," I say, feeling the painful lump in my throat. "Maybe this is why they say be careful what you looking for. That's why I've never done a criminal history background on a man or gotten on that site DontDateHimGirl.com. Some things I just don't want to know."

"Veron, when it comes to your man you have to know certain things, even if it hurts," Ursula says. "Shoot, you think I enjoyed waffling through my husband's shirts and pants pockets after he'd been gone all night? You know how it felt when I went through his briefcase and found hundreds of Polaroids of strange, fat white women in various provocative poses?"

"Ursula, why are you still with him?"

"I don't have anybody else. And having somebody is better than having nobody."

"No, no," I say, reaching out to touch her hand. "Ursula, it shouldn't be that way. You deserve better than that, and so do I."

"Well, all that sounds good, but for the life of me I feel stuck like Chuck right now. My man has physically threatened me, can you believe it? I don't listen to him half the time, but other times I wonder if he's serious or if it's just the Courvoisier talking. Most of the time it's the booze. Anyway, I don't want to talk about this anymore."

"Me, either," I say, trying to fight off the guilt that's plaguing my heart. If Seaphes isn't worthy then let him be unworthy. I don't feel right going through his phone, his personal file. I shut the folder and decide to just take it right back inside and put it back in his office while he's at his meeting. And I'm never going to check his phone again.

I need to figure out for myself what I want to do about Seaphes.

— 3 9 —

Demetria

I am driving like a wild woman down I-45 south, returning to the scene of the crime. Bennigan's. The spot where I met a man for lunch today. The food was good, the conversation was better, and the sex was off the chain.

Mario Rodriguez is my Hispanic hottie. With his buff body, beautiful dark brown eyes, and thick eyebrows, he makes me feel woozy whenever he stares into my eyes, even though he's kind of a slacker who drives an old beat-up van with tinted windows. I haven't kicked it with Mario in months, but it was time for a recharge.

I spent fifteen minutes eating in the restaurant with him, and then another twenty minutes on his lap, in the back of his van, with my dress bunched up around my waist, my panties pulled to the side, and his dick stuffed inside of me, casually making love and continuing the conversation that we started while eating. I loved rocking back and forth on his lap, his arms wrapped around my waist, him speaking Spanish with his thin lips and thick mustache pressed against my neck.

"Amo su cuerpa," he says, squeezing his fingernails into my arms.

"What does that mean?"

"I love your body."

"Mmmm," I moan. I furiously hop up and down on him some more until we both get released and relaxed and are ready to return to work.

And now I am parking crooked in Bennigan's parking lot so I can run inside. I realize when I get in that I took off my shoes in the car and left them there.

"I'm sorry I'm barefoot, but I lost something," I explain to the hostess, who's staring at my feet. Yeah, I'm barefoot, but at least my feet don't stink and I just got a nice pedicure. "Anybody turn in a phone?" I ask.

"No, ma'am. But we have tons of umbrellas and sunglasses."

"Thanks for nothing." I leave the restaurant cursing up a storm. I need to get a grip. It's not the first time I've forgotten where I've left my phone. Sometimes I find it under my bed, inside the linen closet, or beneath the couch cushion in my living room.

Later, I'm minutes away from calling Verizon and reporting a lost phone when Veron walks in holding my phone in her hand.

"Phew! Thank you, babe. Where was it?"

"Ladies' room."

"Oh," I say, puzzled. "I don't even remember going there. Oh well—I'm glad I got it back. You're the best, Vee."

"Thanks," she says, her eyes gleaming. "Glad I could help."

"I'm totally losing it, though. I swear, I don't remember visiting the restroom at all today."

"Demetria, I have never seen you so stressed out. You must still be pining over Thaddeus."

"I guess that's it. He has no idea how much he's hurting me. I can't even think straight half the time."

"You need to do something different," Veron says. "Take your mind off him."

"But I can't. I have to see him, give it one last shot. If I can remind him of all the fun we've had and how much he means to me, I know I can get him back."

Veron sits down and gives me a sympathetic look. "Well, let me know if I can do anything to help. I want to see you happy again. You're not yourself."

"Well, in some ways I still am," I say and laugh. "I got me some on the side during lunch," I whisper.

Instead of giggling with me, her face falls. "With who?"

"Shhh, lower your voice. No one you know."

"You sure about that?"

"What, you know everyone I do? Anyway, his name is Mario."

"Mario what?"

"Rodriguez."

"That his real name or . . ."

"Yeah, girl! What the hell? Stop tripping."

She just looks skeptically at me.

"What? You think I'm lying? He drives a white van and works for Home Depot."

She shakes her head, still looking doubtful. "Describe his penis."

"It's pretty big, beautiful brown, smooth, chunky. But unfortunately it tasted like chlorine. He likes to swim every morning before work, but it was still good."

"Okay, fine."

"That mean you believe me? What's gotten into you, Vee, questioning me?"

"I don't know," she murmurs. "I'm sorry."

"Apology accepted. Hey, I didn't tell you that Thad and I are meeting up tonight. He wants to explain his side of the story, and if I have my way I'm going to spend the night with him . . . and every other night from here on out. I'm just ready to settle down, you know what I'm saying? I'm finally ready. Because I've come so close to losing someone that means a lot to me, well, it makes me want to change. And Thad's the right man, the one who can support me."

"Don't get mad at me for asking this, but Demetria, if you really want to be with Thad as much as you say you do, why do you sleep around with other guys?"

I stare down at my hands and search for words that could make her understand. After several moments pass, she just shakes her head at me and walks out of my office.

She doesn't get it; I know . . . it's something I struggle with. I sniff and dab at my eyes with some tissue. And I spend the rest of the day trying to concentrate on work, but preoccupied with beating myself up. I have to change, be better, be right.

Because tonight is so important, I go through a ritual that I've created for whenever I need to have a clear mind. So I get off work an hour early. When I get home I light seven candles throughout my house. I draw the soapiest and hottest bubble bath I possibly can. When I slide into the water I wince; the heat is so high that I start sweating instantly, but I need the water to be hot, so it can cleanse me of my sins. After drying off, I give myself a facial, exfoliating and moisturizing with a cleanser that is supposed to give my skin energy and make it glow. And I wear the multicolored brocade dress that Thad got me in India. I want to look more beautiful than I've ever looked in my life, and by the time I blow out the candles and step out the door, I feel like my mission has been accomplished.

Thad is picking me up, which is good so I can spend the maximum amount of time with him. He opens the door of his silver Aston Martin for me, and I feel like the old Thad is back. This is a show-off ride if there ever was one. The convertible top is down, and the breeze hitting my face feels good. But the rush of the wind is so loud that I don't feel like competing against it in order to talk to Thad. And he's not saying anything to me either, he just gives me occasional glances, and I make sure to smile at him every time he sees me looking at him.

When we end up at Morton's in downtown, I say, "I thought we were going to P.F. Chang's."

"Is this not good enough for you, Demetria?" Thad asks. We get out of the car and head for the restaurant.

"It's perfect, Thad. Anywhere I can be with you is perfect."

Thad requests a booth in a semiprivate area. That leaves me confused, too. Usually he enjoys showing me off and likes to sit front and center, so all the other men in the restaurant can stare at us with envy. But maybe he has something else in mind, something that requires privacy. I know I do.

We sit, and I order a glass of Cabernet Sauvignon. I'm glad when it arrives; I know my nerves will soon be calmed.

"Thad, I have a question for you."

"I have some for you, too."

"Um, have you missed me?" He doesn't say anything. "Because I sure have missed you."

"What exactly have you missed?"

"You, babe, you. I miss hearing your voice. I miss you calling me Sweetness. I miss you spoiling me. I've been so miserable without you."

"Are you positive about that?"

"Yes, baby, why wouldn't I be positive?"

He just stares at me and quietly sips his wine.

"Most of all," I tell him, "I've missed us making love. I miss touching your body, you touching mine. Oh, Thad, I hope we can work things out, because I'm going crazy without you in my life."

"I see," he says.

"Um, is that all you can say? You sound like you don't believe me."

"I am not sure what to believe."

"Why not, baby? You need me to prove it to you?"

"Yep, prove it. Prove to me that I'm the most important man, the *only* man in your life. Prove to me that you've been faithful to me, that while I'm gone taking care of business, you're doing what you're supposed to be doing at home: holding on to your honor and giving me a good reason to rush back home to you."

"I, I, uh." I take a long, deep sip of wine. It impacts my brain immediately, and I feel like holding on to the table even though I'm sitting down. "All I can say is you're all I want, honey bun. In spite of your questions, in spite of what you think, I want to be with you. And that's final."

I wait for him to respond, but he doesn't.

My appetizer is shrimp cocktail, which is one of Thad's favorites. I dip a huge piece of shrimp in the zesty sauce and lift it toward Thad's mouth, but he shakes his head and munches on his jumbo crab cake.

"Well, I'm so happy we're together tonight, babe," I say. "I got three new outfits and two new bikinis with the money you gave me."

"Good for you."

"They're for our cruise," I say.

He continues munching on crab cake.

"Uh . . . you're still going, aren't you?" I ask sweetly.

"Oh, yeah, I'm going."

I wait for him to continue talking. When he doesn't, I can't take it anymore.

"Look, Thad, I'm sorry, okay? I'm sorry for anything I've done that may have hurt you. But I don't like how this meeting is going at all."

"What do you expect, Demetria, for me to bow down to you so you can kick me in the teeth one more time? You're fortunate I'm not spitting in your face right now."

I pause. "What did you say?"

"It's not what I say. It's the things that you've said. Take a listen to this."

Thad pulls a mini tape recorder from his jacket pocket. And I hear the sounds of me and Darren moaning and grunting while we make love.

"Oh, God, I love this, I love this shit," a recording of my voice cries out. *"You the best pussy-eating mofo I've ever had."*

"Cut it off, now!" I say, looking around to see if anyone heard.

"Isn't that your voice, Demetria? Is that how you prove how much you love me? By spreading your legs wide open to anyone who wants to come in?"

I dump my face in my hands, unable to hold back the tears. If it weren't for all the people sitting near us, I'm sure I'd start wailing. I've never felt so much humiliation, so much pain, in my life. And I can't believe he'd set me up like this, taking me to a restaurant to do this. I calm down and wipe my face with the cloth napkin.

"Okay, fine. I'm busted. Was this in the plan all along? How long have you been spying on me, hiding tape recorders in my house, huh, Thad? You got cameras, too, you pervert?"

"Never think you can outsmart a rich and powerful man. Who knows, you might not see this Darren guy in one piece for too much longer. There's a bayou somewhere with his name on it."

"You wouldn't dare."

"Try me, you lying used-up whore."

I grit my teeth. "Why would you do this? Why would you bring me all the way to this restaurant just to treat me like crap?"

"You, for some reason, don't know how to take no for an answer. I figured you would get it if I pulled you up on a stage in front of a lot of people and *showed* you, instead of just telling you, that you are not good enough to be fucked by a lame dog."

Somehow I calmly get up from the table. I remove the Dodge Nitro car keys from my key ring and toss them in Thad's glass of wine. And I walk away from his hate-filled eyes. My legs feel like bricks are attached to them, and I have a long walk ahead of me, but that's okay. Because if it takes me an hour to get away from this sorry son of a bitch, then let it happen. I'm out.

I walk four blocks in the airy Houston night and dial up Seaphes.

"Come get me, please. I know it'll take you a while to get here, but I don't care how long it takes. I need help. Now!"

It takes him half an hour to reach me, but when I get in his car, I know I feel much safer with Seaphes by my side. While waiting for him to arrive, at least ten men whistled or gave me creepy looks, and I'm so glad to be inside his car.

"You're my boy, Seaphes," I say, holding back tears. "When I call you, you don't laugh at me, you don't tell me to fuck off, and you're there like Johnny on the spot. I don't know how I can ever repay you, but I will. You're a good man, yes, you are."

"It's okay, Demetria, damn, I can't believe old boy would just leave you like that."

"I left him, Seaphes. When I took a good, long look at him and listened to the filth coming out of his mouth, I knew I had to get away. He violated my privacy, and violated me. And then he was talking about some crazy shit. This is a side of him that I don't know. And," I say and take a deep breath, "it scared me. I couldn't deal. And now, of course, I don't have a ride anymore."

"Why not?"

"He, uh, he paid the notes for the Nitro. And I gave my other car to my sister, so I'm screwed. I can't believe my life has come to this."

"Well, you can get another car."

"How?"

"I'll drive you to a dealer tomorrow on my lunch break. I'm sure your credit is good, you should qualify for something. You got a nice-paying job. Think positive, Demetria. You'll be alright."

I lean against him while he's driving and cry out all the pain. When we pull up in front of my house, I'm too angry to move or think. But I let him open my door, and he walks me in.

When we're safely inside, he makes me promise to call him if anything strange goes down. "Don't try to talk to him alone, Demetria. You're strong but never be stupid. Call me, call the police, keep your doors locked, and don't ever talk to or meet this Thad guy again, you hear me?"

I nod.

"Don't nod. Answer me, Demetria."

"Yes, Seaphes, yes, I promise I'm through with him for good. I just want this nightmare to be over."

"It's a hard bump in the road, but that's all it is, a bump. You have too much to offer to let this guy bring you down."

"Yeah, I do, don't I?" I sniff. "I just need something to take my mind off all this."

"I have an idea," Seaphes says. "I'm gonna throw a party. It's called a Conversations Party. I'll invite men and women, and we'll play games, drink, eat, and just chill out. Don't worry. We're going to have fun and learn things about the opposite sex. I'll create an Evite and hook this thing up for you."

"Perfect! That's why I love you."

"You love me?"

"In a brotherly way, silly. Wipe that stupid grin off your face. You know, come to think of it, I'm sure Vee is wondering where you are."

"I called her. I-I didn't know what to tell her. I know she worries. I just said a friend was in trouble, and I was helping that person out."

"You called me 'that person'? That sounds so secretive. She'll be suspicious."

Seaphes just sighs.

I won't let him go until he helps me find the little microphone Thad planted in my house. After he leaves, I smash it to bits.

The next morning, I call in sick and am eager to go back to sleep, but before I can settle in Darren calls.

"How you doing?" he asks in his honey-sounding voice.

"Not so good."

"Oh, yeah, baby? What's wrong? Anything I can do?"

I think for a minute. "I doubt it, Darren. But thanks for the offer."

"Why won't you let me help you, girl?"

"Oh, Darren, if only you understood." I explain that I am at home because I'm not feeling well, and I need to be by myself so I can heal.

"You home alone? What you need? Name it. I'll be there in a second."

"Okay." I laugh weakly. "I need a massage, and I'm hungry for some cold, sweet watermelon, like the kind my family would eat when I was a kid."

"I'm on my way."

And sure enough, within an hour, my doorbell rings. I quickly whisk Darren inside, feeling paranoid about Thad's threats. I give him an extra tight hug and am so happy that he spends the next hour with me, rubbing my back and sore neck, feeding me fresh slices of sweet watermelon, and touching up my pedicure before giving me a long, passionate kiss good-bye.

I have time to take a nap before Seaphes comes to get me shortly after twelve. He drives me to a leasing agency on the north side and recommends that I lease a Toyota Prius hybrid. I pick out a red touring car that includes snazzy wheels and a nice little spoiler; we test-drive the car and poke around under the hood as if we know what we're doing, and we close the deal a couple hours later. I follow behind him and drive the new car back home.

"Veron and I set up the Evite for the party," he says. "Next weekend at my place. It'll be fun, and you'll learn some things in the process."

"I sure hope so. I can use all the help I can get."

When the weekend arrives, we're at the party, comfortably gathered in Seaphes's living room.

The movie *Waiting to Exhale* is looping on the DVD with

the sound down. The men are sitting on one side of the room: Seaphes, Percy Jones, Michael West, and a few of Seaphes's other male friends. The ladies include me, Vee, Ursula Phillips, Fonya and Tweetie from the book club, and a church friend of Tweetie's named Riley Dobson.

Vee and Ursula have been commissioned to serve the food. I guess I was voted out on that task. But it's cool, because the thing I get to do is much more exciting than pouring drinks and passing around trays of finger sandwiches. While Veron gets to play official hostess for this party, I get to MC the game and ask some of the initial questions.

When people arrived at the party, they were asked to write down the questions they had thought up before coming on a sheet of paper—it could be whatever topic they chose. I inserted them all inside a cardboard-covered box. And now that we're all settled, I stand in the center of the room and begin.

"Hey, everyone," I say. "Thanks for making it out on such short notice to the Conversations Party. I've never done this before, but when our host explained how it works, I was all in. Okay, someone will pull a question from the box, and we all have to give an answer, no matter what. You guys knew the deal, so you showing up means you need to participate! The object of the game is to stimulate conversation, learn something about each other that we didn't know before, and perhaps find out something new about ourselves, too. Now, I sure enough hope your questions are juicy, because we wanna get down and dirty up in here. Can I get an 'Amen'?"

"Amen," Riley says and claps her hands. Everyone else joins in with the applause as I raise the box to the sky, then reach inside in the rectangle hole and retrieve the first question.

"Question number one. Where were you born? Borrring.

Who wrote this? Just kidding. Let's stick to the rules, go around the room and everyone respond or comment on the question."

Mike says, "H-town! Born and raised in Third Ward."

Percy replies, "What he said."

"You weren't born in Third Ward." Ursula laughs.

"How you know? Did you see me come out my momma? I doubt it, 'cause I'm younger than you, baby," Percy says, pouting.

"Shhh," Ursula says. "Percy, be quiet about my age."

"Sounds personal. Let's keep things moving here," I speak up.

Seaphes raises his hands, "Houston. Northwest side near good old George Bush Airport. But back then it was called just Intercontinental."

We go around the circle, and everyone says where they were born.

"Okay," I say, "can we get to the good part? Let me pull another question. This one better be good. Question number two: Have you ever smoked weed?" I laugh. "Okay, I can answer that. Uh . . . hmmm."

"Go on, host," Percy says, "don't be scared."

"Shut up, Percy," I say jokingly. "Okay, when I was in college visiting my study partner one night, he convinced me to try it. But I never inhaled."

"Thank you, Bill Clinton," Fonya says loudly. "Lemme answer that. I been smoking weed since I was seven years old. My favorite uncle gave me a joint for my birthday, and I been flying high ever since."

"That's so sad," murmurs Riley. "I haven't smoked weed or anything else."

"Tell the truth, girlfriend," Tweetie says and playfully shoves Riley.

"Oh, don't worry. I plan to be truthful; this just isn't a question that's going to trip me up."

"Well," I say, "we shall find one especially for you, Miss Riley."

Everyone answers the weed question. The responses are split fifty-fifty.

"Hey, Vee," I say, "why don't you pull the next one?"

She reaches inside and begins reading. "Which celebrity would you marry and which one would you sleep with?"

Everyone laughs. Mike speaks up, "Easy. Beyoncé and Beyoncé."

All the guys nod their heads, and I put my hands on my hips. "Beyoncé wouldn't want any of y'all, so keep dreaming. Okay, Vee, you wanna answer that one?"

"Hmmm," she says. "I'd want to sleep with Terrence Howard. He is so fine and sensual, and it seems like we'd be under the covers making love all night plus talking about some deep intellectual stuff."

"He does seem like that type, huh?" Fonya says.

"But as far as marriage," Vee continues, "I read on the Internet that he cheats on his wife. So Mr. T. Howard is good enough to sleep with, but he would never be the father of our kids."

"Miss Priss," Percy says, rolling his neck around. "Well, I would sleep with Angelina Jolie, wooo-eee."

"In your dreams, baby," I say, laughing.

"Don't be calling him 'baby'," Ursula suddenly snaps. There's silence for a minute.

"It's cool, Ursula. You and Percy got something going on?" I ask.

"If we did, I wouldn't tell you," she says angrily.

Everybody is still totally silent. "Ursula, are you okay?" I ask.

She doesn't say anything.

"Ursula, I asked if you were okay."

"I heard you the first time."

Seaphes stands up, "Alright now, I think we should take a short break. It's getting hot in here. Uh, you're welcome to go get some more drinks and sandwiches. And I have some caviar dip made up if you have a taste for something salty. Back in five?"

Seaphes walks over to me. "Thanks, Demetria, you're doing a good job."

"Well, that won't last if Ursula keeps copping her funky attitude. I can't believe you invited her. I thought y'all two mixed like Jennifer Aniston and Angelina."

"I thought she'd cooled down. Surprisingly, Ursula's been real cordial to me the past week and a half."

"Hello? It's probably because she heard about your party and wanted an invite. Who told her about the party, anyway? 'Cause I sure didn't."

"Probably Veron."

"Veron?" I ask, puzzled. "She specifically told me that she couldn't stand that woman. Now why is she playing games like that?"

"I have no idea," Seaphes says, and walks away when one of his friends asks him a question.

"Well, I sure plan on finding out," I say, and wait for everyone to come back from the break.

— 4 0 —

VERON

"Damn, girlfriend," Ursula says. We're huddling in the kitchen during the break in the game. "You see the look on that ho's face when I called her to the carpet? She ain't about nothing. Thinks she's running things and always gotta be the center of attention. I'm sick of her phony mess," Ursula says.

"You may be sick of her, but you're going to blow the plan if you confront her so aggressively," I warn her. "Now, I didn't even want to do this tonight, but you were all about it, so play nice. I don't understand why you gotta blow up so often."

"I need to put Ms. Sparks in her place."

Ursula has so much emotion in her voice I'm seriously having second thoughts about inviting her. "You still need to chill. Some things are better off left alone."

"Yep, mainly your man. Demetria thinks we don't know that he bought a car for her, but we do."

"Well, we don't know how that played out—"

"Keep acting naive," Ursula snaps and returns to the living room.

Seaphes stands in the middle of the room and grabs the microphone. "Alright, y'all, I'm going to draw the next few questions. Here's one," he says and begins reading. "How do men feel about ultimatums? Sounds like a question for the guys."

Chayo, one of Seaphes's friends, answers, "Well, regardless of how we feel about them, I think it's a mistake to give a man an ultimatum, because it can backfire. We're men! And we're not going to let just anyone intimidate us, including our women."

All the men nod their heads.

Then Seaphes speaks up. "I think that some women figure if they give the man an ultimatum it will make him commit to them quicker. But you never should force someone to commit or to marry you."

"Sounds like you know that from experience," Riley says. "I agree with the brother, though. Ladies, we shouldn't be pressuring men to marry us."

"But what if y'all been dating five years? How long is she s'posed to wait? Her eggs are drying up and turning into ducks," Fonya says.

"Then let the eggs turn into ducks, whatever that means," Riley laughs. "All I'm saying is true love shouldn't be forced. If he's the right man, and if it's the right time, he'll marry you when he's ready. Same is true for commitment."

"But," I say nervously. "What if he seems afraid of commitment?"

"Maybe he's not the one," Riley replies. "And why would you want to be eternally linked to someone who really doesn't want to be eternally linked to you? That's where we make our mistake."

"Yep," Ursula says. "That's the truth. I saw the warning signs when I got married, they were as tall as the Sears Tower, but I was too blinded by desire and the fantasy of the perfect wedding."

"May I pick the next question now?" Ursula asks. I watch her closely. She slips her hand inside the box and pulls out a folded-up sheet of paper.

"Hmmm, bingo," she says talking loudly. "Have you ever slept with your best friend's girlfriend or boyfriend?"

"Hooo, boy!" Percy exclaims.

"What, Percy? You touched some woman you shouldn't have been touching?" Ursula asks.

"Actually, no. I've peeped out a couple of my boys' honeys, but nothing ever jumped off. I knew I had to defend my honor and his."

"Okay," I say, "that's easy. I have never slept with a girlfriend's man and never will, and I don't understand how anyone who calls themself a friend can do something like that. I mean, how low can you go?" I say, trying not to look at Demetria.

"Seaphes?" Ursula asks. "You wanna answer that?"

"I can swear on my grandmother's grave I have never slept with my best friend's boyfriend."

"Ha ha, funny funny," Ursula says. She's trying to be sar castic, but she tilts her head and smiles dreamily at him.

"Mike?" I ask.

"Nope. Never. Next," he says, shooting a look at Chayo.

"Okay, okay," Chayo says, lifting his hands. "A long time ago, in the nineties, me and my friend's woman got our quickie on. They had broken up, though, that's why. And she seduced me."

"No offense, but just because a woman throws it at you doesn't mean you have to catch it," I tell him. "Men have to learn how to say no. Think with their minds. Are you still friends with this guy?"

"Naw," Chayo admits and makes a sick-looking face.

"See what I'm saying," I tell him.

"But it wasn't because of that. I ain't dumb enough to tell him that."

"But you're dumb enough to tell us," Demetria says, laughing.

"No, I'm not dumb. We're not friends . . . because he died . . . of AIDS."

The room grows silent.

"Well," Riley says, breaking the awkward silence. "It sounds like you learned from this, brotha, so you kept it moving from there, right? I mean true friendships are so hard to find. I'm sure you now realize it wasn't worth betraying your friend just to get five minutes of pleasure."

"It was more like two point five!" Chayo says, giving us all a much-needed laugh. He gets serious. "But yep, you're right. I still regret it to this day."

"Okay, Demetria, what about you?" Fonya asks, and I'm so glad she threw it to her instead of me or Ursula.

"Nope, never. I would never do anything like that."

Ursula walks in a wide circle.

"Okay," she says. "I am about to throw up. You mean to tell me you gonna sit up here and tell a bald-faced lie that you have never slept with your girlfriend's man? Please. You wrong, Demetria."

"Hey, hey, knock it off," Seaphes says, sounding angry.

"Hey, hey, why are you defending her?" Ursula spits back.

"Why are you concerned that he's defending me?" Demetria asks, getting up in Ursula's face.

"It just seems weird, that's all," Ursula mumbles. She gets up to move next to Percy. He's staring at her like she's crazy, but she ignores him and rolls her eyes at Demetria. "It just seems to me that Miss Popular Ass is being a hypocrite, saying we have to tell the truth and she isn't."

"Ursula, are you implying I've slept with my best friend's man?" Demetria asks. She sounds pissed. "Would that involve Seaphes?"

Percy's eyeballs widen. Seaphes looks calm and stares at Ursula, daring her to answer.

"I mean," Demetria says, "since you seem to know everything, why don't you tell us who has slept with whom, especially if they're sitting in this room?"

"Oh, you don't want me to go there. 'Cause I will do it."

"Then if you do, you may as well include your own name," Demetria remarks.

"Fine, screw it. Yeah, I've had sex with someone in this room. But I didn't betray anyone to do it."

"Oh, then I guess your own husband doesn't count?" asks Demetria.

"I hate your rotten guts."

"Good, that means I'm doing my job right. Now if you will excuse me, I'm going to the bathroom. I gotta drain my vein," Demetria says, pronouncing her words with emphasis. I follow her out of the living room into the large master bath.

"Vee, are you using Ursula to talk to me?" she asks me. "Why can't you just talk to me directly? I thought we were girls."

"I thought we were, too, but lately . . ." I trail off. She starts hopping up and down on one foot, so I stand outside the bathroom door until I hear the toilet flush. She slowly opens the door and invites me in and takes a deep breath.

"Listen, Vee. I've taken this quick moment to think, and there's nothing I want to tell you except this. In spite of what you think, I do care about you, us. Your friendship is important to me. We go back a ways, and I don't think you ought to let Ursula influence you to stand against me. Whether you realize or not, she's still hot for Seaphes, and I think she's using us both to take out her frustration over him rejecting her. That's all it is, boo. How come this girl you said you can't stand has that much influence over you? Think about it," she says and leaves me standing alone in the bathroom.

I'm wondering if I'm stuck on stupid, or if I am just a magnet for being played.

Just when I'm about to return to the living room, Seaphes walks into the master bath looking distressed.

"Did you and Demetria talk?"

"Why? What's wrong?"

"I think there's something you need to know."

Then Demetria steps inside the bathroom and closes the door. "Okay, Veron, it's not easy for me to say this, and I've been struggling with whether or not to tell you. But yes, in case you've been wondering, Seaphes and I . . . we *almost* had sex before, but we didn't go through with it. Seaphes didn't want to do it. So don't be mad at him for being tempted, because it wasn't his fault. It's mine—"

My heart has stopped, but I find my voice. "*What?* How can you just tell me something like that? And you actually want me to believe you care about me and want to still be friends?"

"Vee, listen to me. I know you're mad, but please don't lose your head. You have a good man here."

"If he's so good how could he even think about sleeping with you?" I'm almost sobbing. "You're both crazy. I can't believe I ever trusted either of you." I am breathing so hard now that my chest is heaving, a pain slicing through it that makes me want to go lie down.

"Vee, I'm sorry, we both are. It was only one time, I swear to God."

"How did it happen, Seaphes, and where did it happen?

You got her drunk at your place and she quickly dropped her drawers?"

He just stands there looking pathetic and speechless.

I feel so bad I can barely think straight. "I wanna go home. Gotta get outta here."

"No, Vee, please. Let's just get through this party, okay? And try not to make a scene. We'll all talk about this as soon as the party is over."

"Demetria, you are so selfish! Do you even know how stupid you sound? How in the hell am I supposed to be in a partying mood after that bombshell, huh? How could you expect me to simply pick up and move on after my so-called best friend nearly steals my man out from under me!"

"It wasn't how you think, Vee, I swear to God. He loves *you*, not me. He has pushed me away so many times I can't count."

"Oh, so you're saying you've tried to seduce him more than once?"

"I-I—"

"Shut up, Demetria! What on earth would make you try to get with him?"

"I just . . . I have . . . I mean, I was selfish and jealous. And back then I didn't care about your feelings; I wasn't thinking right, I couldn't think right. Yep, I wanted him at one time, but I feel different, now, Vee!"

Ouch, I thought. Does she not care about the code? If you know that your girl likes another guy he's completely off-limits. You don't kiss him, go out to lunch with him, visit him at his crib, nothing. This girl is *not* my friend. "You know what? I can't even think straight. I don't know what I'm going to do."

"Veron, if I could take it all back I would. Be mad at me. Hit me, curse at me. I deserve it. You've been a good friend to me, the best I've ever had. And I, I . . . I make these screwy decisions sometimes." And she sits on the edge of the tub holding her hands in her face looking very distressed.

Seaphes looks like he's sick enough to call 911.

Suddenly Demetria's moans start filling the room creating a piercing and awful sounding echo.

"Oh, shoot, okay, I'm cool. We'll talk about this, girl, but please stop crying," I beg her. "Pull yourself together. Just sit here. You can spend the time asking yourself what on earth would possess you to want to have sex with the man that you know I cared about, especially knowing that you were my best friend." My voice catches. I almost wish she hadn't confessed. I may never be able to look at her the same again.

I put on my sane face and return to the living room. By then everyone is watching *Waiting to Exhale.*

"Oh, this is my favorite part," Fonya exclaims. "When Robin's standing on that balcony cursing out Troy and throws an orange at him. I love this movie. One of the best I've ever seen."

"I don't know about all that," Mike says. "It basically blasts the brothas."

"Truth hurts, doesn't it, Mike," I say, hoping that no one can see my hurt.

A little later, after Demetria has pulled herself together and emerges from the bathroom, Seaphes says, "Okay, this party keeps getting interrupted, but we gonna finish up these questions! Then ya'll can do whatever you want. Now, let me pull a good one out the box." He pulls a card and says, "According to your definition, what is the number one rule of friendship?"

"That was my question," Ursula says. "I want to answer.

Number one rule for me has to be don't cross anyone's lines. Y'all discuss up front what you will put up with and won't, and crossing the line will cause an ass-kicking."

"Okay, so what would be a line someone couldn't cross when it comes to you?" Riley asks Ursula.

"Me? They better show me proper respect in every way imaginable, or it's going to be trouble."

"For me, a friend should always be dependable, don't be flaky, and do not call me only when you need a loan, or a ride, or a babysitter," Fonya adds.

Demetria pipes up, her voice a little soft. "I'd like to know that my friends are there in the trenches. That no matter what we'll be cool 'cause that's how friends oughta be," she says. "I mean everyone makes mistakes," she says raising her voice over Ursula's loud groans. "And friendships have their ups and downs like any relationship, but I would like to think if we value the friendship, we'd . . ." And she stops and looks down and starts toying with her fingers.

Ursula rolls her eyes. "Another rule is: don't be pushing up on your friend's man. If you see she's liking him, back the fuck off. I don't care if he flirts, I don't care if he's super friendly, I don't care if you're both drunk; don't do your girl like that 'cause you wouldn't want anyone to do that to you."

"Look, Ursula," Demetria yells. "You've just about tore your drawers with me. I'm sick you of talking sideways and acting like I don't know who you're talking about. I'm sorry, but you're going to have to leave."

"What you say, ho? This ain't your house. Or is it? You moved in with Seaphes yet? He got you a new car and that's always the first step."

Seaphes stands up. "Ursula, that's enough. I didn't buy Demetria a car, so talk what you know. I drove her to the lot so she could buy a car."

"Yeah, right, that bitch wouldn't surprise me if she sucked your dick to use your credit."

"Okay," Demetria says, "hold up, girl. Uh-uh. You gots to go."

"I ain't going nowhere."

Seaphes speaks up. "No, I'm sorry, Ursula. It's not Demetria's house, but she and the others are my guests, and I will not let them be disrespected. So I'm sorry it has to be this way, but you've gotta get your things and leave."

"You bastard. You can't throw me out. Your girlfriend invited me."

"Veron has nothing to do with this," Seaphes tells her. "This has to do with you and your ignorant, erroneous comments. I don't want you here, and I don't care if Beyoncé invited you. Now go."

Ursula looks like she's about to explode, when all of a sudden, Riley steps in.

"Ting, ting, ting," Riley says, waving her hands until she has everyone's attention. "Okay, y'all. I don't personally know you all, but I've been sitting here listening to people insult one another all night. I sense so much tension and anger between some of you. I don't totally know what's going on, but I guarantee you that whatever it is, it isn't worth ruining a true friendship, believe me it's not. Whatever happened . . . it hurts, but you gotta let it go."

"But you don't know how bad this person hurt me," I say, staring intently at Riley.

"Have you ever hurt someone? Even unintentionally?" Riley asks. "We've all been wronged by someone in our life. Mother. Father. Sister. Boss. Boyfriend. And yes, even our best friends. But don't allow hurt to remain in your heart. Let it go."

"But it's so hard," I remark quietly. "I'm not there yet."

"Shoot, I'm not gonna let nothing go. Any bitch that does

me wrong is gonna get what she's got coming to her," Ursula claims. "Backstabbing bitches. And who invited Miss Perfect?"

"I guess we're both on the buddy plan, sweetie, because Fonya asked me to come," Riley says. "And I'm glad I did. It's been great, but you guys, please listen to what I'm saying. Folks are dying every day—there's war out there, killings, senseless tragedies. Life is too short to be bitter and carrying around a cancerous anger. Think about how you'd feel if something happened to your friend, and the next time you saw her was in the morgue, or lying in a casket? Wouldn't that little fight you had seem like nothing?"

I think about Riley's question and slowly nod my head and stare at Demetria, who is avoiding my eyes.

Just then the TV displays the ending to *Waiting to Exhale*. Whitney Houston, Angela Bassett, Lela Rochon, and Loretta Devine are gathered together in the final scene where they're standing on the beach at night. And that friendship song is playing with the words:

Count on me through thick and thin
A friendship that will never end.

Back in the day I loved that song. Sometimes the lyrics would bring tears to my eyes, because the words seemed to perfectly convey the importance of true friendship. Being there for your friends through their ups and downs. Standing by them when they're right, speaking up when they're wrong. But today the song brings another type of tears. Ms. Riley is able to say all that nice-sounding advice, because she isn't wearing my shoes. Right now I'm just too hurt, and so, so angry.

Unable to take it anymore, I stand up and run back to Seaphes's bedroom. He follows me, and I swing around to face him. I've never been this hurt. "It goes without saying that I am so disappointed in you, Seaphes. I can't believe you played me for such a fool. I trusted you."

"Veron, I'm so sorry. I know there's no real excuse for this."

"Mmm hmmm. There's nothing you can say that'll make me feel different."

He looks stricken. "Please, Veron. I really—"

"Shut up, Seaphes. I don't care. I don't care what you say! Who cares about you? Hell, who even cares about me?"

"Demetria does."

"Oh, please."

"Demetria really does care, Veron. She just doesn't know how to express it properly."

"Why are you always defending her, Seaphes? You know what, I'm wasting my breath with you. I-I can't do this."

Someone knocks on the door, and Demetria and Riley come in. Demetria mumbles, "She asked to come see you two and I thought it would be okay." Demetria silently dismisses herself, and Riley looks at us carefully before speaking.

"I know it's none of my business, but I just hate to see what's going on. You all are adults and can handle your own problems, but please, young sista, don't do anything foolish. I've had a talk with Demetria. She is sorry, and so ashamed she doesn't even know how to tell you. I believe her. If you can believe her, will it make any difference in your relationship?"

"I don't know, Riley. I just don't."

Riley asks Seaphes if the two of us can be alone to talk. He agrees, but before he leaves the room he promises me that he'll explain everything to me and hopes that I will understand. I don't know what kind of explanation he could possibly have for this.

— 4 1 —

SEAPHES

I convince Veron to hang around after everyone else has left. It isn't too hard to do, surprisingly. I think she's just so exhausted, and my bed is closest.

So after I close the door behind the last guest, I brace myself for what is to come. Part of me wants to go out the door with everyone else, but I know I need to face my demons and have a talk with the one I've hurt.

"Hey, there," I say softly, observing her curvy frame, sprawled out on the far corner of my bed. "You awake?"

"I can't sleep."

"I see." I pause. "I just wanted to come see how you're doing. And I wanted you to hear me out."

She sits up in bed, and my eyes can't stare at her for too long. So I pace the floor like a preacher on a stage.

"Go ahead," she says.

"First of all, I care about you . . ."

"You sure?"

I nod. "I wasn't playing you, Veron. You're a sweet, almost innocent girl. I wanted to protect you, be with you. I've been with a lot of different types, but you are the most different of all."

"Oh, great," she says in a sorrowful sounding voice. "You're calling me weird?"

"Not weird, but challenging. You're almost like a flower, or a piece of china, so delicate that I didn't know how to treat you at times."

"You're still not making sense."

"So I'd go back to what I was used to . . . the Demetrias of the world. Easier to figure out, even though she brings the drama, the game-playing."

"She's more interesting, beautiful, challenging than me. Is that what you're saying? Do you think that I'm so different that I lack a heart? Feelings? Why did you do this, Seaphes?"

I fall on my knees on the side of the bed and reach out to her.

"The other thing is . . . listen, you may not believe me, but I didn't think it was ever going to happen with you. You were treating me so coldly all the time, and I couldn't figure out why. And then you saw me hugging on Ursula—and all it was at that point was an innocent hug, but I kept doing it at bad timing . . ." I stop and drop my head in my hands. "I'm sorry, so very sorry I failed you, Veron. But you gotta know our contemplating getting together happened one time with Demetria. It's such a cliché, but it's true. Other than that we've been just close friends. The bottom line is that it's you I care about. I find you amazing, beautiful, the best woman I've ever been with, and I want to be with you."

She just shakes her head as if she's trying to push out all the info I've given her. "I just don't know, Seaphes. I can't process all this, and I'm about to leave this so-called party. Don't call me, okay? I have to figure some things out."

— 4 2 —

Demetria

"Vee, can we talk? I think there are a few things you need to know." It's a few days after the Conversations Party. We're at work, and I've asked her to join me outside at the picnic table in the courtyard. She said yes, which makes me feel a little more optimistic. I wanted to give her a little time to get the anger through her system, but I need to share something that I hope will help to mend our broken relationship.

"What's up?" she asks.

"First of all, there's something I have to tell you. A couple days ago, I revealed something about myself to Seaphes. He made me promise to tell you, because he thought it could fill in the missing pieces of the puzzle."

She sighs. "Okay, what is it?" she asks.

I take a deep sigh. "Vee, um. This is hard for me to talk about . . . but I've had a painful sexual history. You think I'm promiscuous, and yes, I can say that I have slept with a lot of men. But what you don't understand is why. I've tried to block it out, but it got to the point where I can't deny it anymore."

"What happened?" she asks, looking concerned.

"I'm . . . I'm a sexual addict. Actually, that's how I met Thad."

"What?"

I nod. "It's true. He and I were attending a sex addicts meeting, and I was introduced to him. I never really talked to him until I noticed him again that night at the jazz concert."

"I just . . . I never knew this. What made you feel the need to attend those meetings?"

"It's . . . Well, I lost my virginity as a teen. A . . . young teen. He was an older guy . . . an *old* guy, to tell the truth. He courted me, made me feel very special, beautiful, smart. But he pressured me for sex. I guess I looked a lot more mature than I was. I liked him, though, so I gave myself to him. But then, he treated me bad. He stopped accepting my calls, taking me out, gave me the cold shoulder. I guess he was scared I'd report him to authorities. And ever since then, I've felt the need to prove myself. With men. This means I've sometimes hooked up with that very same type of man. Or with guys who seem out of my league."

"And that's why you'd get so upset and jealous when Seaphes showed interest in me and not you?"

"Exactly. It wasn't so much that I wanted him; it was the challenge, the need for control, for feeling like I am a desirable woman who can hold on to a man, all that. I know it sounds stupid. Vee, I can't stand this part of myself. And I can't apologize enough."

"Hmmm. Well, I'm glad you told me," Vee says, but she has this hollow sound in her voice. I'm starting to wonder if I even should have said anything.

"Well . . . I mean, I just wanted you to know," I say. "And there's something else."

"Now what?" she asks skeptically.

I pause, not wanting to overwhelm her. "Well, Seaphes and I agreed not to even talk anymore. No contact, nothing.

I don't ever want you to experience that awful feeling about me and him hanging over your head . . . wondering if you'll ever be able to trust us again. And, Veron, I know I did you wrong. I was blinded by loneliness and jealousy and the need to be the center of attention, but I know for a fact I won't be again."

She looks a little bit warmer now, but all she says is "Okay. Anything else?"

"Uh . . . yeah, actually. I got a phone call late last night."

"From who? Was it Darren?"

"It was actually my baby Thaddeus."

She gives me an odd look.

"I know, I know. But you know how you really love Seaphes in spite of his ways? I feel the same about Thad. He and I share history. We fight, we make up. I know he bugged my house, and I know he has a temper, but in spite of all the drama . . . we're just very drawn to each other. He told me that being away from me and hanging with Marilyn reminded him why he filed for divorce in the first place. So"—I laugh with glee—"he actually filed the papers."

"And now he wants you?"

"Yes, he wants me back, can you believe it? I was thinking about what Riley said at the party, and I mentioned those things to him in my own words. How usually in relationships, when things go wrong, we both carry our share of the blame. Doesn't matter who started it. I shouldn't have stepped out on him; he shouldn't have planted the tape recorders. We both should have done things different to ensure a stronger relationship. So we agreed to let go of the bad parts of our past. I've completely gotten rid of the guys I used to be with. I realize they aren't worth it. I realize I can be happy with the one who loves me and treats me good."

"Yeah, that sounds all wonderful," she says, still sounding

a bit unconvinced. "But Thad travels a lot. What are you going to do when he goes on the road again?"

"He asked if I would consider putting in my two-week notice, actually, and presented me with this." I flash a five-carat diamond ring at her. "That's my baby, always treating me good. He wants me to be his wife and travel with my man wherever he goes."

"Really? Are you sure that marrying Thad is the best thing to do? Have you given it serious thought?"

"Yes, Vee, yes. When love steps up to your door, you gotta open it and not be afraid. I gotta be with the one who I know is man enough to give me everything I need, and strong enough to put me in my place. Thad is it. He is. So I feel peaceful with my decision."

"I just remember you talking about your boy Darren, and how you felt something so strong with him and couldn't ever give him up. So I just want to make sure . . . you're sure that Thad is absolutely the only man in the world for you?"

I look her squarely in the eye. "Who else would have given me a ring like this, girl? Not Darren, sweet as he is. Definitely not Mario. So, Veron, as sure as I'm sitting here, there is no other lover I'd rather be with . . . than Thad."

"Well, Demetria. I never thought I'd say this, but listening to everything you've said, it sounds as though you've come full circle. And in a strange way, I am honestly happy for you, although I envy you, too, girl. Some guy told me that it's nothing if a man wants to have sex with you. He can do that with anybody. But if he wants to make you his wife, that's true honor. So yep," she says and finally smiles. "I *am* elated. Invite me to the wedding."

"Of course you invited, Vee. You are my best friend, and I want you to be my maid of honor. And I love you for finding it in your heart to listen to me today and be so receptive."

"I'm glad, too." She smiles and it's genuine.

"And guess what?" I tell her and pull out two sets of keys: one is my Brian McKnight key ring; the other is my Disney World key ring. "Check this out; I got my keys to Thad's place back, and he also returned my Dodge Nitro, so I actually have two hot rides now. He really does love me." I laugh in amazement. "Ain't that a bitch?"

"It sure is, girl. Somehow you always come out on top, don't you?" Vee asks. I just smile at her, and we stand up for a much-needed hug. Right now I'm so happy she is happy for me. So happy we've made up and found a way to be friends again.

— 4 3 —

Veron

I am so confused, so angry. When I think about everything that's happened—things Demetria has said, things she's done, and what she ended up with anyway—I can't help but be frustrated. I've tried so hard to be like her: sexy, confident, and good with men, and I've still failed. She betrayed me, and still gets everything while I get nothing. So I decide to do something drastic, to take the last step in my metamorphosis.

The time is right after twilight, when the earth's darkness has swallowed up the sun. I end up in the gated subdivision and park just a few houses away from Thaddeus's pad. His home is still as big as I remember from when Demetria invited me over to have dinner with them almost nine months ago. She was so proud that night; her face was shining, and she looked as if she had hit the jackpot. She nailed a rich, soon-to-be-divorced man, and she wanted to show him off. Show me what I was missing, and what she was getting. I remember trying to be happy for her, but that familiar twinge of jealousy wrapped itself around my heart. Why her? What's so great about her? I've watched her closely, tried to emulate her style, memorized *Why Men Love Bitches* . . . and I still don't know if it's done any good. But I'll find out tonight.

I've decided to give her an engagement present she won't forget. And now I am standing in front of Thad's house, opening up the front door with the key that I stole from on top of her desk when she left her office to go to the ladies' room. She left it there in plain view, and she's the one who taught me that I should do what I have to do to get what I want.

Heart thumping wildly, I slip quietly through the front door. As I knew it would be, the house is empty. This afternoon she described to me in great detail what her evening was going to be. She was going to go to his place and soak in his Jacuzzi first, and then head out to go shopping at the Galleria Mall and get her nails and toes done, as a surprise for him. Once he got home from work the two of them were going to have a romantic dinner out. She twirled around in a circle of happiness so many times I got dizzy just watching her. "I'm back, Vee. The bitch is back," she sang. And I laughed and clapped with her, even though I felt dark and miserable inside.

I timed my arrival here so that she would be gone, shopping or getting her manicure, and Thad would be coming home soon.

I go upstairs, all the way up those long, winding stairs, until I come to Thad's bedroom. I get undressed and slip on the nightgown he brought her from Quebec. Once I've slid my body into the gown I slide onto the bed, underneath the covers, and I wait. I wait for my man to arrive.

He'll come home from work and will be happy to see that his wife-to-be has used her key to let herself in. He'll feel happy and confident. Glad to know she's home with him, not out with some other guy. First thing he'll do is come to bed. I know Thad has the goods, because my best friend has never left out any details about his sexual prowess. And I want Thad to do to me everything he's done to her. Lick me, kiss me, suck me, and fuck me. Do me right, treat me like a queen. Because tonight, I am Demetria.

When I hear noise downstairs I hold my breath. I cannot wait until Thad comes upstairs and finds his lover lying on her stomach, with her ass facing him so he can quickly get hard, slide his dick in her, and start calling out Demetria's name.

I hear footsteps storming up the stairs, and I brace myself and get on my hands and knees.

Then the bedroom door opens.

"Demetria?" he whispers. He flicks on the overhead light.

I quickly murmur my disapproval. The lights go back off and complete darkness surrounds us.

"I'm sorry I'm so late. Are you waiting for me?" he whispers again.

I giggle, then stop.

He laughs, too. I hear him unzip his pants.

"I want you," he whispers. I feel his hands grab my butt and begin massaging its roundness. I hump up and down, moaning, savoring the feel of his hot hands.

"Eat me," I whisper.

"Okay," he whispers.

I feel his lips kissing my butt, planting sweet kisses all over my backside. Then he presses his face in me and starts eating me out from behind. I twist and turn and rock and hump against him; he licks me and tears me up like an animal. It feels so good to be Demetria I want to laugh and cry and moan and scream, but I bite my tongue.

He flips me over and starts rubbing his hands all over my breasts. And I let his foreign hands have his way with my body. Water springs in my eyes. Demetria is right; so far sex with Thad is incredible.

I whisper, "You got a condom?"

"Not this time."

I tense up. As good is it feels, I can't let this piece of revenge go this far. So I clamp my legs shut and roll to the side.

"That's enough," I say in a low, breathy voice. "I'm done."

"What?" he whispers loudly. I detect confusion in his voice.

I'm starting to get very nervous. "You can take your shower now so we can get dressed and go to dinner," I tell him.

"What are you talking about?" he asks, still whispering. Then he gets out of bed and turns on the overhead lights. And I squint and look up at him and say, "Mike?"

— 44 —

Seaphes

It's been tough all week. I don't know how much longer I can wait. I've been so stupid, done so many things wrong. I can't mess this up. She told me not to call her, but I can't handle not talking to her, not figuring things out, how to fit me into the rest of her life. She's the one, I know it. So I'm going to find the courage and go see her, and if she tells me that we fucked it up and can't get it back . . . I don't know what I'll do.

— 4 5 —
VERON

"Let's get the hell outta here," Mike says. "What are you doing in this man's bed?"

"What are you doing coming here? How'd you get in?"

"Demetria! She's crazy; you know that. She wanted one last exciting fling before she settles down with this guy. She wanted to fuck me in his Jacuzzi; she said she'd leave the back door open for me."

"She has finally lost her mind."

"Apparently you have, too, Veron. Were you trying to seduce Demetria's man? I didn't think you'd be the type. You gotta get yourself outta here. I won't say a word, and I know you won't, either. Damn, I never should have listened to her."

"I shouldn't have, either. I shouldn't have listened to any of it. None of her advice is right for me. I'm not like this at all. I keep trying to be something I'm not, and thinking I wasn't doing a good job. But Mike, I finally realized something tonight. I don't *want* to be like Demetria."

"I'm glad, baby girl. But let's get the hell outta here before they both come back and catch us."

"Okay," I say, trembling. I'm not thinking quite clearly yet, but I know what I told Mike was true. I can't believe Demetria would even take a chance on messing up her good thing. I thought she'd learned her lesson. But it looks like I'm the one who needs to learn something.

Mike and I get out of there without anyone seeing us. And after I get in my car, I call him on his cell phone so we can talk.

"Mike, I am sorry. I feel crazy, like I'm not myself."

"Well, I feel bad, too."

"Whatever happened to you and Francine?"

"We're history. She got sick of me, found another guy, and left."

"I'm sorry," I say. I can't say I'm surprised, when I think of how different those two were.

"Hey, Veron. I want you to know that I figured something out tonight, too. I'm through with the game playing. When Demetria set this up, something told me no, stay away from it. But sometimes men get caught up. That's probably what happened to your boy, Seaphes, and it's obviously what happened to you tonight. I mean, think about it. If Thad had come home and sexed you, would you really feel any better? Would you have told Demetria? Would you really want your friendship to end over this silly, juvenile payback stuff?"

"Well, Mike, I guess I won't ever know. I'm definitely never doing anything like that again."

We talk until I arrive home, vowing never to speak a word about what happened. But I sob and toss and turn in bed all night. I feel like I need help in the worst way. I don't want to let anyone else define who I am as a person. I hate that I've listened to the bitch book, to Demetria, to Seaphes, to Ursula . . . and the fact was that I was tuned in to everyone except myself. I decide that from now on, I am only going to do what I believe in my heart is best for me.

Now I just have to figure out what that is. One thing I

know for sure. Lying here in the dark, I'm only thinking about one man.

"As odd as it sounds, I am glad for Demetria," I tell Ursula, who has come to my office to gossip and backstab co-workers.

"So the whore is finally getting married to a rich psychotic punk. But let me tell you, girl, an expensive wedding doesn't mean she's going to keep her legs closed. You watch out for that one and get her before she gets you."

"I know what you're trying to say, Ursula. But I have to learn to trust people. She's made mistakes in the past, and I know she's not perfect, but she loves me."

Ursula looks at me with venom. "I'm disappointed in you, Veron," she says. "Oh well, not my problem. But if I were you—"

"Right, Ursula, you aren't me. And maybe you should be paying less attention to my life and more attention to the mess you've created with your own."

"What did you say, trick?"

"My name's not Trick. It's Veron Darcey. And don't you forget it."

"Humph," she spits. "I'm outta here. Your mind is twisting up something bad right now, and I don't want to have any regrets in the event that you say the wrong thing . . . and cross my line."

"For once you've given sound advice. I think you oughta leave, too. Good-bye, Ursula."

* * *

The next morning, I find Seaphes waiting at my office door. He is holding a single white rose.

"Hey there," I say warily, and invite him to join me in my office. As I close the door, he says, "I won't take too much of your time."

He comes in and sits down, and just stares at me for a minute. He hands me the rose. I shift uncomfortably. "Okay," he says. "Thank you for listening to me. All I ask is that you just let me finish, you just hear me out and think about what I have to say, okay?"

I nod. Considering what I've done, I owe him that.

"Okay," he starts. "Veron, I am so sorry for all the stupid mistakes I've made. There were misunderstandings and all kinds of weirdness, but I think that I know who the real you is, and I'm sorry I didn't recognize it sooner. And I want you to know that you're the one for me. I know you are. You possess all the qualities that I admire in a woman. You're supportive and you don't expect me to call every five minutes. You trust me when I do right, and you calmly question me when I mess up. You're not blind to my faults, but you believe in me . . . but won't let me get away with anything that's disrespectful. You are the most truly beautiful woman I think I've ever met, and your whole personality has a sparkle, and an innocence, that I want to protect and love forever."

I'm astounded, feeling a mixture of emotions. "That's how you truly see me?"

"That and much more. Veron, I know that once you release yourself from the bullshit advice from coworkers, books, magazines, and best friends, you're the most wonderful woman around. You don't need all that. You are an angel just as you are, and one who doesn't realize how wonderful she is until someone tells her. And I will tell you every day forever, if only you'd have me. I just want you to know that, Veron. I'll go back—"

I think about what he says, and it confirms everything I feel inside.

"Of course I'd have you. Seaphes . . . you know I want you. I always have."

His eyes are glistening, and mine are, too. We seal our new commitment with a tender kiss.

And I know that this time our shared feelings are lined up, our future together is more certain, more sincere, more solid.

Have you ever taken a first glance at someone and immediately decided you could never have anything in common with that person? That was me and Demetria. The Odd Couple of women, we were. It doesn't make sense that we grew to be friends, but somehow we are complementary. It's always just worked.

I am at home sitting at my desk, clicking through old text messages on my phone. Demetria's texts are so funny and supportive. I'm also looking through some greeting cards she's written me, thoughtful messages she jotted down for Christmas, my birthday, Valentine's Day. For the life of me I can't pretend to fully understand why she acts the way she does. I know I can't change her, and I certainly can't be her. But I can be myself. I can be a forgiving person and a loyal friend.

I pick up the phone and call her on her cell. "Hey there," I say, making sure enthusiasm fills my voice. "How's it going?"

"Oh, girl, I'm so glad you called." she says energetically.

"You won't believe what's happened. Funny how things change."

"You got that right," I say, debating if I should tell her about me and Seaphes. "What's happening with you?"

"I got two proposals, Vee, two. And the man that proposed to me last gave me an ultimatum. Can you believe it?"

"Nooo," I tell her. "Who was that?"

"My baby Darren Foster."

"You're joking."

"No, girl. Darren is a good man, a good lover, and finally he has a good job," she says excitedly and describes the management program he entered with the City of Houston Aviation Department.

"And so it's strange, but when I took the time to think about it and weighed the two, I had no choice but to pick Darren. He's the man who's always been there for me no matter what. There's something deeper with us, and he always makes sure my needs are met . . . not just financially, but emotionally. How can I reject a love like that? Plus, let's face it, any man who threatens physical violence, who places eavesdropping devices in my home . . . that's just not the man for me. So I broke up with Thad, actually gave the dude his ring back, and I haven't heard from him since. Can you believe that?"

"Yep," I reply. I'm smiling to myself and wanting to scream with happiness and relief for both myself and my friend. "When it comes to love and matters of the heart, I can believe just about anything . . . especially when it comes to bitches like you."

My Best Friend and My Man

Reader's Guide

1 What did you think of Demetria and Veron's relationship? Is their's the kind of friendship you would want to have?

2 Do any of the characters remind you of people whom you know in real life?

3 Seaphes believes there are ten different types of women. Do you agree? Did you recognize yourself in any of the descriptions?

4 How could Demetria have been a better friend to Veron?

5 If you were Veron, would you follow the advice of a book, or would you do something different? If so, what would you do to achieve the results that Veron wanted?

6 What did you think of Ursula Phillips? Do you feel she had Veron's best interests at heart?

7 Do you think any man could keep Demetria happy? If so, what kind of man would he be?

8 What is the most memorable scene in the book and why?

9 Who is your favorite character and why? Who is your least favorite character?

10 Which of the characters seems the most believable, and why do you feel that way?

11 Could you personally relate to any of the scenarios in the book?

12 Should women automatically know better than to try to hook up with their best friend's man? Are there any circumstances where it would be forgivable?

13 Do you trust your best girlfriend to be alone with your man?

14 Were you satisfied with the conclusion? Why or why not? What would you have liked to see happen?

15 What, if anything, did you learn from this book?

ALSO BY CYDNEY RAX

Fast-paced, provocative, and sexy, *My Husband's Girlfriend* is an eye-opening novel about morality, monogamy, and the complexity of modern love.

My Husband's Girlfriend

$13.95 paper (Canada: $18.95)

ISBN 978-1-4000-8219-3

My Daughter's Boyfriend is the spicy tale of an impossibly tricky love triangle, full of sharp, lively observations about mothers and daughters, black men and women, and the truth about love and lust.

My Daughter's Boyfriend

$12.95 paper (Canada: $17.95)

ISBN 978-1-4000-8313-8

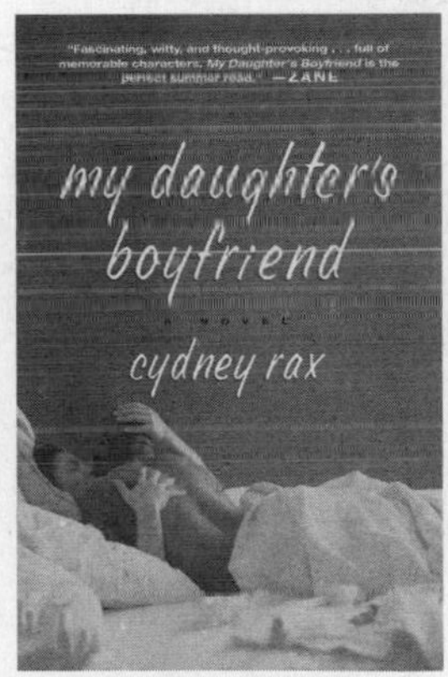

Available from Three Rivers Press
wherever books are sold